THE WEREWOLF PI | BOOK 3

JOHNNY LYCAN & THE LAST WITCHFINDER

WAYNE TURMEL

Black Rose Writing | Texas

This is a work of fiction. Names, characters, businesses, places, events, and incidents are either the products of the author's imagination or used in a fictitious manner. Any resemblance to actual persons, living or dead, or actual events is purely coincidental.

ISBN: 978-1-68513-407-5
PUBLISHED BY BLACK ROSE WRITING
www.blackrosewriting.com

Printed in the United States of America
Suggested Retail Price (SRP) $21.95

Johnny Lycan & The Last Witchfinder is printed in Calluna

*As a planet-friendly publisher, Black Rose Writing does its best to eliminate unnecessary waste to reduce paper usage and energy costs, while never compromising the reading experience. As a result, the final word count vs. page count may not meet common expectations.

Witchfinder is a suspense-filled toboggan ride that will leave readers begging for more."
–Jill Hand, author of the *Trapnell Thrillers*

"A fresh approach to an old favorite. This paranormal feast with a side of savage will leave you craving more."
–Vicki-Ann Bush, author of the *Alex Mckenna Series*

"Adventure, supernatural beings, mystery, and tough choices wrapped up in a PI's fur coat. Johnny is at it again! A threat from someone who should be dead and strange magic, what are they after?

A fast-paced read, Johnny Lycan is faced with another impossible mission when a dead man starts harassing local spiritual gatherings in Chicago.

He's after something, and the boss has it.

Finding out the world's seen his hairy mug by a blogger begging for an interview and planning to rescue the boss and his nurse from a kidnapper, Johnny puts those he cares for in danger as he faces this new enemy.

Can he keep the world from falling into the hands of an evil being from hell and rescue those he cares for, or will he sacrifice himself for nothing?"
–Madilynn Dale, author of *The Chapter Goddess*

"Turmel's latest is full of the punchy, fast paced prose I've come to expect from him. It's delightfully gritty from beginning to end, and Johnny Lycan is that sort of old school of PI Urban Fantasy hero that's grown increasingly rare these days. My only complaint is that this book wraps up the trilogy, meaning I'll just have to reread them to get more Johnny."
–Bob McGough author of the *Jubal County Saga*

"Johnny Lycan is a fantastic gritty story about a werewolf enforcer for various crimes that sometimes solves crimes. Wayne Turmel has created a unique world that is seedy, supernatural, and alive."
–CT Phipps, author of *The Rules of Supervillainy*

"A welcome return for the endearing werewolf PI. Johnny is back on the hunt for another mysterious relic, and that means more feisty full-moon scraps and more dodgy encounters with the diverse cast of Chicago's occult underbelly. After the last book's trip to Vegas, I was glad to be back in Chicago and spending more time with some of the original book's most engaging characters, especially Johnny's makeshift family. Johnny himself remains a winning protagonist – a PI who manages to be at times smart, at times bumbling, and at times a werewolf – and yet still remains entirely believable and a comforting companion through a wild adventure. Newcomers to Johnny Lycan can dive right in and find a polished gem of a fantasy noir novel, while return visitors will be pleased to find all the ingredients that made the first two books such enjoyable rides – a brilliant supporting cast, thrilling action set pieces, and a satisfying seesaw of cynicism and fantasy. A slick, witty, and imaginative romp with the perfect balance of heart and claw."
–Tomas Marcantonio, author *Flamingo Mist*

"Fast, furious and furry, Author Wayne Turmel's reluctant hero, Johnny Lycan, is back in action. Fasten your seatbelt folks, it's gonna be a bumpy ride!"
–Jean M. Roberts, author of *The Heron*

Dedicated to weirdos, loners, and all the former 13-year-old boys
who know that Shaggy is real.

JOHNNY LYCAN
& THE LAST WITCHFINDER

CHAPTER 1

Night of the full moon.

Wendigos are a Native American superstition. They're a myth; cannibalistic shapeshifters designed to scare kids around the fire on long winter nights. This particular figment of the imagination was kicking my ass and laughing about it.

It stood six feet tall with long arms seven feet from fingertip to fingertip. It was all bones and desiccated skin, like a rawhide chew toy with eyes the yellow of dog-pound snow. The damned thing licked my blood off its nasty long fingers and cackled at me.

I'd been in a lot of fights, but never with anything that actually wanted to eat me. That's a Wendigo's deal. They were—are—cannibals but doomed to eternal hunger no matter who they kill or how much they eat. I don't know if this one had ever faced a werewolf, or even knew what I was other than a hairy, annoying appetizer. Yet here we were. Kill or become a taco.

We circled each other in the early April snow, leaving tracks no sane hunter could identify. Standing on hind legs, my Lycan hind claws left prints too large for a wolf. The humanoid monster's feet were mostly skin and bone, leaving marks more like a giant chicken's than anything recognizably human.

It had already killed three people on the Oneida Nation Reservation in two nights. Nothing slaked the damned thing's hunger and thirst or even slowed them down. Shaggy, my werewolf alter ego, was the only thing between this killing machine and a meeting hall full of people, so I needed to figure out something quick.

My breath came out in thick white clouds that crystallized on my snout and around my eyes, while the cold-blooded Wendigo clicked and shuffled through the powdery ground cover. After charging and inflicting damage on each other twice, I backed off. Then I squatted low to the ground, growling and hoping the thing would hold off long enough for me to come up with a plan.

What do I know about this thing that used to be a normal guy named Charlie Powhatan?

Supposedly, Wendigos contain the soul of someone who'd eaten human flesh. *Charming. And so many questions.*

It began stalking the people of the Oneida nation three days ago, starting with the most isolated homes and working its way in. *And nothing has stopped it so far. Good luck, fur boy.*

A Wendigo could be killed by conventional weapons if you messed it up badly enough. Legend has it the surest way to get the job done is to tear out and burn its ice-cold heart. Fortunately, my claws were sharp as scalpels. They'd suffice if I could get close enough. *Without becoming an entrée, that is.*

There was no telling how much of the human host remained inside the ugly sucker. Its actions were becoming more erratic the more I ducked, dived, and dodged. It was rage-filled and starving. I was never at my best when hangry, hopefully the same was true of this guy.

We'd been beating the holy hell out of each other for ten minutes or so. Blood seeped through my thick black pelt. The monster whirled around to face me again. Long dry strips of skin across his chest where I'd gotten my claws on him flapped in the icy wind. The thing's screams bounced off the trees, echoing all the way to my core.

I was scared spitless. Shaggy was pissed about the wounds, but happy to be in a real scrap, so I let him drive. My brain was no longer in charge, only registering scattered, nonsensical images.

I clearly recall tumbling in the snow.

The Wendigo's teeth clicked together with each attempt to get at my throat.

That horrible face leered down at me. Then more tumbling and my werewolf's eyes glared down at its face as my mouth slobbered on it. Thick strands of saliva dripped from my snout onto its howling, agony-riddled face.

The ending came fast. Once I was on top, I felt Shaggy lift his arm high and drive his claws deep into the monster's chest. Ribs cracked. Skin tore. My ears filled with the squishy slurping sound of nails tearing at meat, and then something cold as ice. Victory sent the neurons in my head ping-ponging happily off each other.

Son of a bitch. The legends were true.

The damned thing had a heart. Rock-hard and freeze-dried as it was, it throbbed erratically. As I scrambled to rip it from his chest, it burned like dry ice in my hands. Soon as it was free of the Wendigo's chest, I flung it as far from me as I could. It landed in the snow like a rock. Just a chunk of lifeless, frozen meat.

I regained some control from Shaggy and looked into those yellow eyes. They reflected shock and sadness more than fury now, and I felt a moment of pity. This thing had been a human being once. Charlie. A few of his relatives and others from the village were gathered in the meeting hall. Along with the family of those he'd killed. Awkward.

"Thank you. We'll burn the heart."

I turned, still wolf enough to growl a warning at whoever was stupid enough to come so close. The Tribal Police Chief stood impassively, holding a wool blanket.

I was half-changed. Now-human feet sank shin-deep in snow and the cold was boring through to my bones. I crouched down, growling a warning and hating that he saw me in this condition. If it bothered the large man, it didn't register on his face. The cop spread the blanket open and approached me slowly, like you'd approach a wounded animal.

"You're going to need this."

He wasn't wrong. I stood and tried to speak, but my teeth chattered too much, so I just nodded. Avoiding hypothermia was more important than modesty at this point. With a grateful nod, I wrapped myself in the surprisingly warm wool.

"Thanks."

"No problem. You can warm up in the Hall." He wasn't looking at me as he spoke. In his hand was a thick plastic bag. He strode over to where the Wendigo's dead heart lay like a cinderblock in the snow. Into the bag it went as the Tribal Cop muttered under his breath, "Jesus, Charlie. What did you do?"

Not sure what else to do with myself, I shuffled toward the lights of the meeting hall. A bonfire burned outside, the bright orange flames shooting up into the pitch-black sky. As I reached the bottom step, there came a low mumbling from behind me. A voice in a soft baritone began chanting words I didn't understand. The cop ignored me, looking skyward. He opened his arms to the full moon, singing softly, and then tossed the bag with Charlie Powhatan's frigid heart into the flames.

What the hell was the protocol here? I lowered my head in a polite facsimile of prayer until the stench of something organic burning made it impossible to stay.

"Your clothes are inside. Let's get you dressed and some coffee into you. It's a long drive back to Chicago." He wasn't inclined to have me hang around. That worked, neither was I.

It was at least three hours, assuming the roads were clear. My orange and black Charger was impressive to look at, but it was practically useless in the snow.

Then I remembered why I was there in the first place. "And the thing, for Mister Cromwell?"

My boss had made a simple deal with the Oneidas. In exchange for my doing pest control on their Wendigo, he got something from them in exchange. Because of course he did.

The cop sucked at his bottom lip. "That drum he wants. It's not a toy, and it's not some pretty museum piece. It's got some serious medicine attached to it. We shouldn't let it go. A lot of our people didn't want to give it to him, but this was something we couldn't handle ourselves. Tell him we're grateful and all, but our business is done. This never happened."

I nodded. "You know what else never happened? That coffee you promised me. It's fricking cold out here."

He laughed and slapped me on the back. "You're right. Come on."

The meeting hall was over-packed and overheated. Warm air hit me like a baseball bat as we went inside. Forty or so people stared silently. They'd gathered together for protection, or maybe solace. Most of them averted their eyes. Old people muttered and shook their heads, little kids whispered excitedly to each other. Bodies parted like the Red Sea as we made our way to the little office in the back.

It was just as well that nobody wanted to talk. Shaggy was still front and center in my brain, and the smells of all those sweating people weren't helping. He was still high as hell from both moonbeams and the fight. He still had steam to blow off. I avoided their gazes and set off to put some clothes on.

The police chief watched me as I dressed. "You okay to drive?"

I bled from three places, my head pounded, and my hands shook. I was just ducky. "I will be. Just need to get myself straightened out first." Meaning Shaggy needed to kill something and burn off that remaining anger.

I was in the North Woods of Wisconsin. Odds are I could find an outlet for all my killing and eating needs. "Are there any deer around here this time of year?"

He looked at me for a minute and shook his head. "State says they're out of season. No hunting," he said, stone-faced.

"Dude, seriously?"

His face finally cracked as he laughed and pointed behind me. "Up the ridge to the North. Have fun."

I would enjoy it, but only half as much as Shaggy. Hunting out here would be a ball. None of these civilized city parks department rats with hooves. These were real North Woods deer. Wild game. I salivated on my Lycan's behalf.

There was a knock on the door and a stocky, attractive woman in a Tribal Council jacket came in. She carried something in a wooden box. The cop said, "Thanks, Brenda." She gave him the dirtiest possible look, spared another for me, and dropped the box on the desk with more oomph than necessary. Without a word, she stomped out.

"She's not happy about letting it go. Nobody is, but a deal's a deal." The policeman flipped open the lid. Inside, wrapped in ancient excelsior paper, was an old drum. It was about a foot across the head. They carved the body from a single piece of dark wood. The head of the drum was old leather the color of—

"Is that Wendigo skin?"

He closed the lid and fastened it. "I told you. Serious bad medicine. Do you know what he's planning to do with it?"

I didn't, but it probably wasn't different from any of the other weird crap I picked up for him. "Likely put it in a warehouse and forget about it. He's got a place. It looks like the ending of Indiana Jones."

"That's the best news I've heard all night." He stuck out his hand. "Thanks again. We appreciate you."

"You're welcome. It's what we do."

It was going to be a long drive home, but first we needed venison. And a butt-ton more coffee.

CHAPTER 2

Morning after the full moon- waning gibbous

Oliver Cromwell's voice crackled through the car's speaker. "Just drop it off at the Archives. They're expecting you."

I was a little surprised. Usually, my only client liked to gloat over his prizes in person first. "Are you sure you don't want, uh, I dunno, to inspect it or something?"

"Why? Isn't it the drum they promised me?"

"Yes sir. Yes, it is."

He sounded more miserable than usual, which was saying something. "Then you did your job. What do you want, a damned cookie?"

Maybe not a cookie, but some appreciation would have been nice. I'd risked life, killed a supernatural man-eater, and driven nearly seven hours round-trip. "Thank you," would be lovely. Would it kill him to toss me a bone and a "good job?" And a cookie, dammit. Even oatmeal raisin. After all that deer meat, my stomach still rumbled like a freight train.

"The Archives" was my boss's fancy name for a storage facility up in Arlington Heights, just off the tollway. From the front it looked like a normal, public, You-Store-It operation. The back half of the facility, though, was something else entirely. It was where Cromwell stored his most treasured creepy old stuff. The technical term was "arcana," but if it quacks like a creepy old duck...

Most people wouldn't notice, but a professional could spot where the rented-space-to-store-grammas-furniture ended and Cromwell's personal warehouse began. There were double the external video cameras, for starters. The doors to his special units were a shade darker than the others—the result of being reinforced steel rather than just galvanized metal. There was also a museum-quality air conditioning and dehumidifying unit grumbling away twenty-four/seven.

The chain-link gate rattled open once I remembered the gate code. I drove around to the main door. Then I popped the trunk and pulled out the Wendigo drum and waved at the red dot on the eaves. There was no need to honk or buzz. They damn well knew I was there. I picked at some dried deer-liver stuck to my jacket while waiting to be buzzed in.

It only took a second for a familiar but unexpected face to emerge from inside. This wasn't the usual old, retired, rent-a-cop. This was six feet four of prime ex-Marine beef. "Dude, it's freezing out here. Get your ass inside."

Jarhead Justin. Last name unknown. Usually, he was the main security guy at Cromwell's Gold Coast apartment building. He was also part of Cromwell's muscle squad under the command of Nurse Ball. It had been a minute since I'd seen him, and I couldn't help wondering how badly he messed up to get banished to Siberia.

Once inside, he led me through another electronically locked door into the security office. Justin gestured to a chair. My grateful ass sank into it and exhaustion washed over me. I shook it off. There was still business to be done. "I'm supposed to drop this off."

Justin consulted a computer monitor on his desk. "That would be a... seriously, dude. A drum?"

"Yeah. It's—"

He never looked away from his screen. "Take it back to Golf-Five." Justin still used the Military alphabet. I used to think it was just to sound cool, but he wasn't the sharpest knife in the drawer. I should probably be grateful he knew his ABCs.

"G-Five. You sure?" Cromwell designated the storage units H through A. A storage was ultra-high security, the rarest and most expensive items. The Anubis Disk was double-sealed in B. H was garage-sale quality stuff and personnel records. Obviously, the boss didn't consider a genuine, hand-crafted, Oneida wendigo-hide drum very important. Remembering the Police Chief's warnings about bad medicine and Shaggy's reaction to the thing, it seemed like poor judgment. Such decisions were way above my pay grade, and I was more worried about not falling asleep on my way home than Cromwell's filing system.

Speaking of job descriptions, I had questions. "What are you doing out here? They don't want you lowering property values in his building anymore?"

Whether Justin ignored my sarcasm or didn't get the joke was always a fifty-fifty proposition. We'd been getting along better lately, but today he was all macho bluster and no fun at all. "Mister Cromwell said to beef up security. We've gotten some threats. And suspicious activity."

I was bone weary and wanted my bed, but that got my attention. "Suspicious? Like what?"

Justin wheeled a few inches away from the desk so I could see the security monitor. A guy in a black ski cap, leather jacket and scarf peered through the chain-link gate, shading his eyes, scoping out the parking lot. A pro would have known he was on camera.

I snorted. "Not exactly a master thief, is he?"

Justin shrugged. "Smart enough. He clocked your plate when you drove in. Wrote it down in a notebook. Second night in a row he's hung out. I'd go check him out, but I'm not supposed to leave here."

"Weird. Doesn't look dangerous. He the one making threats?"

"I don't think so. Those are way weirder."

I felt a post-Shaggy headache coming on and had zero tolerance for vagueness. "Weird? You know who we work for, right? Weird like how?"

Justin stiffened. "It's on a need-to-know basis."

"And I don't need to know?" If history served, whatever was going on would involve me eventually. It would be easier to fill me in now. Justin, though, needed to feel like the big-time security guy. Going from Special Forces to a glorified doorman and answering to an old man's nurse can be hard on the testosterone.

I was in no mood to push the matter. Cromwell would tell me when he was good and ready. If he didn't, Francine would. Our pillow talk consisted mostly of work gossip these days. Things between us had cooled down a bit since I got back from Las Vegas. That meant we were only getting together once a week, if that, and being less inventive. Well, she was less inventive. Her imagination always outpaced mine.

It was almost dawn. Along with the weak spring sun, I sensed the onset of a post-Lycan hangover. Jarhead Justin looked exhausted and grumpier than usual. Even the mysterious figure on the security cameras called it a night and vanished. I gestured to the wooden box holding the drum. "Dude, you want to file this or...?"

"Nah, you can put it away. Section Golf—"

"G five. Yeah. Buzz me back. And don't forget to log it into the system. You know how the old man is about paperwork."

"Roger that." He stabbed the console with one of his sausage-sized fingers.

The door buzzed and popped open. The weight of the wooden box shifted in my hands as I navigated the corridor. Whatever magic, medicine whatever, it had was active. My fingers tingled and Shaggy whined at the far end of my brain stem, wanting to be rid of the damned thing. I was getting better at letting him sense trouble and listening when he did. Maybe my Lycan self was being ultra-sensitive at this time of the month, but I doubted it. Even with zero psychic abilities of my own, I couldn't wait to be rid of it. I knew what a Wendigo was capable of, even skinned and beaten on. Anything made from it couldn't be harmless. *G-level threat my hairy ass.*

The storage unit was nothing special inside. Galvanized metal shelving ran along three walls. Two rows of boxes were stacked haphazardly on the floor. I found an empty spot on the shelf and set the box down carefully. The jangly sensation in my hands stopped as soon as I let go. The room was silent, and other than the spooky drum I'd just put there, nothing appeared to be emitting anything more dangerous than dust. Well, there was a low, buzzing hum coming from the far corner. It wasn't worth investigating. What I needed was sleep, not more trouble.

On the way out, I probed one more time to get a sense of the threats Cromwell got. Justin stayed committed to keeping me in the dark, so I dropped it. Whatever crawled up the ex-marine's butt was still there and wasn't worth worrying about.

Once in the cocoon of my Charger, I turned up the music. Ozzie felt appropriate for the ride home and I cranked the tunes. The gate slid open, and I pulled out onto the deadly quiet streets. Habit had me check both ways for the mysterious but inept prowler. Whoever the stranger was had disappeared, and I promptly forgot all about him and headed for my bed.

Even with Ozzie Osbourne numbing my senses, I couldn't help having the heebie-jeebies. *Who even knows this place is here?*

CHAPTER 3

5 days after the full moon. Waning gibbous.

Francine leered at me with a wicked grin and dangled the handcuff key. She raised an eyebrow before asking, "Are you going to be a good boy?" The brunette didn't always refer to our nearly twenty-year age gap, but when she did, it was with evil intent. God love her.

I chuckled, but couldn't wait to get these things off me. Fun was fun, but it still weirded me out. "Yes, I'll be a good boy."

She pretend-pouted, then chuckled. "You need to work on your roleplay game, kid." The remaining fur-lined cuff clicked open. "You okay?"

Smiling and rubbing at the faint red line on my wrist, I said, "Yeah, I'm great." She was right about not using regulation handcuffs for recreation. Having been in police custody a couple of times in my traveling days, I knew there was nothing romantic about fearing for your circulation.

She laid her head on my chest and placed soft kisses on each hairy pec while running fingers through the dark matted curls. I got a Shaggy-assisted whiff of her hair; sweet sweat and industrial-strength oxytocin. I moaned. She gave one of the curly hairs a teasing tug. "Told you it'd be fun, didn't I?"

Indeed, she had. Francine Ball was a woman of her word. While I wasn't completely sold on the whole tie-Johnny-down thing, she'd been hinting around for a while, and it wasn't like I hated it. God knows she'd enjoyed herself. The woman always put body and soul into our carnal efforts, but there was something extra going on with her tonight. Maybe it was finally getting her wish to restrain me, but that wasn't all of it. Something was up.

A faint hint of an emotion I couldn't nail down lingered in the air. Even a few moments ago, while straddling me, she'd ground down hard, like there was something to prove. Just before reaching her peak, Francine grabbed a handful of my hair and her eyes burned into mine. "You will never forget me. Ever." She tightened her fist. "Will you?" She held on, damn near pulling my hair out until I told her what she wanted to hear. It coincided with her going over the top. Her green eyes rolled up in her head and she had a five-point-four quake of an orgasm. Getting to that point was more her doing than mine. She was a woman on a mission. Still, I'd like to think I held up my end of the deal.

Usually, Francine did only the obligatory minimum of post-coital cuddling. Tonight, she laid her leg over mine and settled in. *Okay, this is different. What's up with her?* I stroked her hair, not talking. If she had anything to say, she'd say it. That was how we were.

I was afraid she was going to ask about my trip to Las Vegas. Sure, she'd been the one to insist I get my freak on while I was there, but I'm not sure she actually wanted me to fall for someone. Did she know? Did she really care? The darned woman was harder to read than a Chinese math book.

We lay like that a long time, long enough that when she spoke, it caught me on the verge of falling asleep. "He's going to call you in tomorrow."

Our boss. Cromwell. Okay, we were back in work mode. "What about?"

She hesitated a little too long before pretending not to know.

"Is it about the archive?"

She propped herself up on one elbow. "How did you know? Argh. Justin told you. That idiot."

Justin was a lunkhead, but I didn't want him in trouble with his boss. "No details. Just that there've been some vague threats. There was a guy spying on me when I went by the other day. What's going on?"

"He'll tell you himself. But I think it's serious." Her hand walked like a spider slowly down the line of hair on my stomach. "Did you see who it was? Following you, I mean."

She'd never really wanted to talk shop when we were in bed. This was unusual. "You're really worried, aren't you?"

Her hand stopped its southward journey. Francine traced her fingers back and forth idly. "*He* is, which is what worries me. He's usually unflappable. Even being sick pisses him off more than it scares him. This feels different."

Despite their constant bickering, she really cared for the rich old goat. I'd asked about their history before and she'd always dodged the question. Since she was on the subject, it was worth another shot. "How the hell'd you wind up working for the old man, anyway? You could do so much better."

"No. I really couldn't." The melancholy in her voice surprised me. False modesty wasn't Francine Ball's style, and from what little I knew, she could write her own ticket. Army nurse—I think she was a Major — then a stint in Chicago's busiest and bloodiest Emergency Room. A short, messy marriage in between. Then, poof. She's a private babysitter to a rich old miser. She'd never explained it, and I hadn't pushed.

Her head returned to my chest, taking a moment to adjust as the hairs tickled her face. She stared at the wall, gathering her thoughts. My hand rested on her head, and I left it there. Her voice dropped to a whisper. "You know, when I retired from the Army, I went to work at County."

"That must have been a big change." Despite the press reports and Chicago's reputation, there was a world of difference between a city hospital and a real war zone.

"Not as much as you'd think. Gangs are gangs. Sunni, Shia, Vice Lords, Latin Kings. Fewer bombs and more knives. It was a bit of a shit show, but I pretty much ran the ward."

"I'll bet you ruled that joint with an iron hand." My finger traced little circles on her shoulder blade. Normally she was ticklish, but didn't seem to notice.

"I loved it. I really did." She rolled onto her back, breathing deeply and holding each breath before exhaling, bracing herself.

Damned if she wasn't actually going to tell me. I rolled up on one elbow and watched her face. "What happened?"

Francine pulled herself up and leaned against the headboard, her knees to her chest. Those eyes of hers looked off into space in front of her rather than at me. "Remember? I said I'd met guys like you before?"

I didn't believe her back then. That was before I knew who she really was. Lycans were rare, and surviving the meeting was rarer still. I grunted a response, not wanting to break her train of thought.

"One night three years ago… right around the full moon. Cops bring in a homeless guy, strapped to a gurney. Raving and bouncing off the walls. They said he was all pumped up on PCP, but he didn't look the type. The EMTs dropped him off and left us with him. Me and another nurse. Cute little thing named Rita Moore." It was as if Francine were narrating a movie playing in front of her.

"Somehow, the asshole got loose. Maybe Rita loosened the straps because they were too tight. I don't know. She could never just follow orders. But that's all it took. Next thing I know, he's loose and attacking her. Guy was twice her size. She was screaming so loud. I came running and…"

Not all Lycans go full werewolf. Some just have violent reactions to the top of the lunar cycle. That's what she meant when she said some men couldn't handle the full moon. Whoever this guy was must have been scary as hell, even without fur. I visualized long, straggly hair, a bird's nest of a beard, and a hair-trigger temper. There's one on every Skid Row. Even when they don't completely turn, they're unpredictable and dangerous. The average human's bite can be toxic if it gets deep enough and these guys bite plenty hard.

I waited for the rest, but she would not say any more without prompting. "What happened?"

Francine sucked in a deep breath. Her tone changed. In a clipped monotone, like she was reading from an incident report, she continued. "Suspect Ball fired on the deceased with an illegal concealed handgun. Five rounds caught the victim in the chest, one in the throat. Subject was declared dead on the scene."

"Jesus. But it was self-defense, right?"

She still didn't look my way. "I always snuck a weapon under the Duty Desk at the start of my shift, just in case. Handguns are illegal in Chicago hospitals except for approved personnel. Right or wrong, I pulled a weapon and shot someone in a crowded medical facility. Suspended pending criminal investigation."

I knew she always kept a weapon handy. There were at least two in this room that I knew of. I sat up now, beside her, with my back to the headboard, but kept my hands to myself. I wanted to put an arm around her, but she'd probably snap it off. "Did they charge you?"

She shook her head. "Before they even filed the police report, I got a phone call. Said they could make it all go away like it never happened. All I had to do was—"

"Be Malcolm Cromwell's private nurse." That answered that.

"Among other things." I must have had a funny look on my face, because she laughed. "Oh Christ, not like that. But you know I do more than just manage his dialysis and wipe his ass, right?"

I did. Her team of ex-military was a world-class cleanup crew. And I was grateful for it.

"You like working for him, don't you?"

She chuckled. "More than you do, for sure. He's not so bad. People I work with are usually jerks. His only real demand is that I wear that old-timey uniform instead of my scrubs. Big deal. And, as you know, I like to customize what's underneath. Everybody has their thing. Soldiers, doctors, rich old codgers. Most of them talk a big game but really need a firm hand." As I laughed, her strong, cool fingers found a vulnerable part of my body. The wicked smile had returned. "Some more than others."

That was all the conversation for quite some time.

When we came up for air, I was dressing to leave. Francine lay naked on the bed, looking up at the ceiling with a satisfied grin. She was her old self again. "When you talk to him tomorrow, try to act surprised. He'd be pissed if he thought I'd spoken out of school. Let him tell the story."

I pulled my boot on and winked at her. "What story?"

She winked back. "Good boy."

CHAPTER 4

5 days after full moon. Waning gibbous.

I'd seen Malcolm Cromwell angry. I'd even seen him lose his temper, usually at me. Presently, he was in the middle of what Gramma Mostoy would call a full-blown conniption fit. This time, I had nothing to do with it, so I relaxed.

"Look at this crap." He thrust his gnarled but perfectly manicured hands into the shipping box, and let the fine gray sand sift through them. "Fucking pulverized."

Unsure of the required response, I offered, "That sucks."

He glared at me with a vulture's eyes.

I tried again to say something un-stupid. "What was it?"

"It *was* a quarter of a million dollars' worth of Babylonian antiquities. A pair of small household idols. Museum quality. It's supposed to protect against demons."

I was no expert, but for random destruction, demons had nothing on the average minimum wage delivery person. It was easier to blame lost focus and gravity than supernatural bogey-men. "It wasn't just damaged during shipping?"

My client was three blood pressure points from a stroke. A gob of spit flew from his lips and dripped down the front of his pajamas. "Really, Mister Master Detective? This was no accident."

Cromwell showed me all four sides of the box. I saw nothing unusual, even though he kept turning it as if hoping something would magically explain itself. "The package arrived in perfect condition. They even signed the tape seals when it left my agent in Beirut. And this isn't random damage. Someone kept smashing and sifting and smashing again until it's nothing but sand. This was intentional. And personal."

Malcolm Cromwell was Chicago's most famous collector of odd, haunted and famous old stuff. Moreover, he had a reputation as someone who'd do anything to gain what he wanted. He was part of a tiny circle of equally rich, equally crazy people around the world who had good reason to hate him for it. I'd already run into some of them. This seemed like a lot of work to piss off a sick, eccentric nut job. It wasn't their style at all. People like them craved the items for themselves, not see them destroyed. A broken, useless relic defeated the purpose of their insane games.

Cromwell slapped his hands together until all the grit was off them. "Whoever it is, they're sending a message."

They. Cromwell knew who did this. "They, sir?"

The old man picked up a slick piece of paper from his desk and waved it under my nose. "There was a note. Cocky bastard signed his work."

I stuck my hand out for the note. "Can I read it?"

He thrust the paper at me. As I took it he sat back in his chair, gasping for air. No doubt Nurse Ball loitered next door, hovering like she always did. I considered calling her if he got much worse. Cromwell guessed what I was thinking, because he waved his hands and breathed slowly, until he got himself under control. Once I was sure he'd survive, my attention returned to the note.

It was high-quality textured paper. The writing was fancy calligraphy, like you see in old manuscripts.

Ye shall make you no idols nor graven image, neither rear you up a standing image, neither shall ye set up any image of stone in your land, to bow down unto it: for I am the LORD your God.

It sounded like a bible verse but I was no expert. Written beneath the first message was a clearer, creepier one. In elegant handwriting, it read:

Destroy all such atrocities in your collection immediately.
There will be no second warning.
Yours,
Matthew Hopkins

Cromwell stared at me until I finished. "What do you think?"

Be very careful not to sound like an idiot. "The obvious question is, who's Matthew Hopkins?"

Cromwell slapped the desktop. "That's what I want you to find out. Who did this, and why? After all—"

I groaned but completed the sentence. "That's what you pay me for. Yes, sir."

He nodded. "No cops, if you can help it. I want to know who's responsible. Then make sure it never happens again, if you get my drift."

I don't know, sir. You're so darned subtle.

He steepled his fingers over his thin belly and his tone lightened. "By the way, thank you for that chore in Wisconsin. Was it really a Wendigo?"

Was that actual recognition?. "Yeah. It was."

"I'll be damned. Never figured they were real. Truthfully, I thought it was a good way to get my hands on that drum. Martin and Alecia were after it. Sucks to be them. You're okay?"

I nodded, hoping he couldn't tell how surprised I was that he gave a rat's ass.

He ran a hand through the half dozen hairs he had left. "And the skin on the drum? Is it..."

"I think so. Same color and texture. And the Police Chief said it's got powerful medicine attached to it, whatever that means, and I'd rather not find out. Sir, if I may? I'm not sure you should keep it in section G. Maybe someplace a little more secure? E at least." Despite winning, I never wanted to face anything like that again. Why tempt fate?

Cromwell harrumphed and said, "Justin told me you told him that. Lupul, your job is to fetch and carry. After that, it's my department. By the way, any idea who's been poking around? They might be related."

If the two things weren't connected, it would be a heck of a coincidence. With all the weirdness I've been dealing with, I didn't really believe there was any such thing. "I don't know. Maybe. I'll head out there tonight. See if he's still around."

I got a rush of excitement at the thought of actually investigating instead of muscling someone for trinkets. Maybe I'd get to show off my shiny new PI license.

Cromwell nodded and motioned for me to help him back to bed. His dialysis machine and hospital bed were in the room's far corner. "At least dissuade him from sticking his nose in my business. But this..." He pointed back to the box on the desk. "...is priority one, understand?"

"Yes, sir."

I tucked him into bed, then asked one last time if there was anything I could do. I got a dismissive wave for my trouble, so I made my goodbyes. In my hurry to leave, I ran into Nurse Ball, nearly knocking her over.

Francine stood in the doorway in her starched white uniform, plain white nursing shoes, and hair in the tightest bun ever constructed. Her hand was up, pretending she was about to knock, instead of eavesdropping on everything we said.

"Oh, I'm sorry. I was just coming to check on Mister Cromwell." The sly grin on her face didn't fool me. This wasn't our first dance.

The smile disappeared when I brushed past her without playing along. My mind was already going over the mysterious note, and the guy lurking around the warehouse might give me some answers. Or give me the chance to beat the crap out of someone. Either would be fine. Both would be even better. I hadn't completely shaken off the full moon, even after four or five days.

"Hey. Wait a minute," her voice called out from behind me, but I was already at the front door.

All the way down in the elevator, I thought about Cromwell's mysterious correspondent. In my fog, I almost walked past the new doorman, who wasn't Justin but was definitely ex-military. Silently, he handed over my weapon while I ignored his attempt at conversation. I couldn't shake the image of the joker hanging around the Archives. Maybe it was this Matthew Hopkins guy. Nah, that would be too convenient.

A gust of cold air slapped me in the face as I stepped onto the sidewalk. April in Chicago looks pretty, but the wind off the lake— the Hawk—still cuts right through you if you're not dressed for it. In my flannel jacket, jeans and boots I was a little underdressed, but the chill wasn't too bad. My motor usually ran hotter than most. Maybe it was all my body hair.

The guy standing on the sidewalk was overdressed for the weather. Black parka, black ski cap and scarf. He held his phone up, obviously recording the building and who went in and out. He looked a lot like our warehouse stalker.

I scowled at him and took three strides towards my car. I couldn't shake the nagging feeling, so I turned back for another look.

Any doubt I had vanished when he muttered, "Oh, crap." And took off running.

Yup, definitely him.

I shouted, "Hey, hold on a minute," and took off in hot pursuit.

Only five minutes after getting the assignment, there he was. I kicked it into gear.

Damn, I'm better at this detective stuff than I thought.

CHAPTER 5

Even with a head start, I caught the mystery man before he got to the corner. I reached out, grabbed his puffy jacket, and yanked him hard to the left. Momentum sent him butt-first over a low arbor vitae hedge, into the muck between the building and garden.

The guy huddled down, back to the wall. He covered his face with his hands and panted so hard I was afraid he'd hyperventilate. The plan was to pull him to his feet, but the second I got close, he drew himself into an even tighter ball like a roly-poly.

The chase woke Shaggy up; our combined energy had us both wired and on edge. The Lycan part of me wanted to wail on this guy until I learned what I needed to know. Fortunately, my better nature was in control. I stepped back and gave him space. Whoever the stranger turned out to be, he was no use to me hysterical. I needed answers. As gently as possible I said, "C'mon. Don't freak out, man. Just breathe."

The ragged gasping turned to panting and finally one long breath as he regained self-control. He dropped his hands from his face and looked up. His whole body shook, but eventually, his eyes focused. I knew I'd frightened the bejeezus out of him, but couldn't foresee what came next.

"Dude. Okay. Just don't eat me, alright?" His palms were out to ward me off.

I gawked back with my mouth open, which probably didn't help. "Eat you? Seriously?"

Now that the panic subsided, my mystery man regained a little composure. He scrutinized my face. I studied him right back, neither of us saying anything for a while.

He was about my age. Definitely a couple of inches shorter and a little fleshier than me, but not a small guy. And Asian. Korean, maybe?

"Can I get up?" he asked.

"Oh, jeez. Yeah." I offered my hand. He hesitated just a moment, then took it and rose to his feet. Then he dropped my hand and wiped them on his pants.

After a while, he took a step back, as if getting a better look at me. "You're John Lupul, right?"

It seemed to me I should ask the questions. *Establish dominance while not looking like an asshole.* I was still working on that. Instead of answering his question, I asked one of my own. "That's private property. Why were you spying on Mister Cromwell?"

"Dude! I wasn't creeping on the old man. I was looking for you."

Nobody ever looks for me. Well, not in a very long time. I had a scary reputation as Neal O'Rourke's bagman and then Cromwell's personal collection service. Most folks avoided the pleasure of my company.

I must have stood there with one of my patented moronic looks on my face, because the guy's confidence grew. He held a steady hand out for me to shake. "Casper Pak."

"Casper?"

He rolled his eyes. "Yes, like the friendly ghost." It was clearly not the first time he'd made that speech. "I'm with Horatio Magazine. And the podcast, of course."

If Casper the friendly reporter thought that meant anything to me, he guessed wrong.

With an eye roll, he explained. "Horatio? As in Shakespeare? There are more things in heaven and earth than are dreamt of in your philosophy, Horatio?"

"Never heard of it."

"Damn, bro. We're actually pretty famous. We investigate paranormal activity and cryptozoology."

That set alarm bells ringing. He loved hearing himself talk, and I might learn something if I kept quiet, so continued playing dumb. "Crypto-what now?" I knew damned well what it was, belonging to a whole subcategory as I did.

Casper began speaking faster and waving his hands. His face lit up as he got into his explanation. "Cryptozoology. Mythical creatures. You know, Bigfoot, Loch Ness Monster. Shapeshifters." He looked right at me. "Werewolves."

I maintained a stony expression. "No such thing."

In his passion for the topic, he forgot I was the monster in question. Casper punched me in the arm and had a huge grin on his face. "Dude. I've seen the video."

I didn't know what video he was talking about, but more than a cold Chicago wind sent a chill up my spine. "What video?"

"Oh, come on! The fight with the bear-man. In Nevada. Couple of months ago?"

Fuck me sideways. Torsson. The Icelandic Berserker I had to deal with in Las Vegas a couple of months ago. Clive Bowden, the eccentric rich guy who'd set it up, told me he was streaming our fight on the Dark Web. I'd been too busy surviving to worry about whether we had an audience or what happened to the recording afterwards.

"Wasn't me." I hadn't used that excuse since high school, but the classics never go out of style.

"That's what you're going with? Video, dude. And high resolution." He was going up and down on the balls of his feet. Then he stopped, and the truth lit up his eyes. "Wait, you haven't seen it?"

I shook my head.

He slowly reached into his jacket and pulled out his phone. "Want to?"

Twenty minutes later, we huddled in a snooty Lincoln Park coffee shop, hunched over a table in the farthest corner. Predictably, he'd ordered a chai latte something-or-other. Sitting on the table in front of me was a gigantic black coffee and an apple fritter. My guts were knotted tight. I wasn't starving, but he was paying. Or Horatio magazine was.

Pak seemed like a nice enough guy now that he knew I wouldn't go all Red Riding Hood on him. A little over-eager like most nerds, but smart as hell. He explained how the magazine got word about this video that was circulating. Two shape shifters battling it out. The freaks and nerds who like that kind of thing started sharing and streaming among themselves, and that's how it wound up on Casper Pak's phone.

Sipping my scalding coffee gave me time to get my act together. While I tried looking cool and unconcerned, the squirrels in my head chased each other round and round. *Do I really want to see this? Could I deny it anyway? How many people have seen it and has anyone besides Casper Pak connected it with me?*

The phone sat innocently on the table between us. Casper drummed his fingers on the table. "You ready?"

I set my coffee down so Casper wouldn't see my hands shake. "Who else has seen this?"

The reporter shifted in his seat like a happy five-year-old. "It's got about twenty thousand views just on our site. Probably ten times that on YouTube. You really didn't know it was out there?"

Hell no. I'd always had a mental image of what happened when Shaggy took over, but did I really want photographic evidence?

I faked nonchalance. "Let's do it."

Pak's finger hit the big white arrow on the screen. Immediately, the picture expanded and there it was.

Say this for Clive Bowden. He hadn't skimped on the production values. There I was; naked, hairy, scared, but perfectly lit for the camera. A roar from the off-camera crowd blasted out of the speakers. Heads popped up around the café. Casper scurried to lower the volume, so it didn't freak out any of the other patrons.

"Damn. Sorry, dude." Casper dropped the volume to almost zero. He offered me headphones, which I shook off. Shaggy's hearing picked up everything just fine.

I watched in silence, and Casper watched me watching. It was all on the recording. Every messed-up moment of that fiasco. It was so much clearer—and awful—than my memory.

Torsson turning into a bear-like killer.

The crowd of his personal army; redneck military wannabes screaming their heads off.

And me, morphing from a furry naked guy into an even hairier, scarier rage monster. I'd never seen myself become Shaggy before. For the first time I wondered how Bill, and others like Cree who'd seen the change, stayed sane or even spoke to me again. It shook me to my boots there in the coffee shop, and I knew what was happening.

My table mate's gaze stayed glued on me as I squirmed in my chair. I wanted to run but kept my seat, transfixed, but hating every second of the video. Every scream, bite, and slash. It was all so much uglier and more violent than I remembered. And I was so much closer to dying than I cared to admit. Shaggy whimpered at the back of my brain, demanding that we leave, but I couldn't oblige him. My body betrayed me, and from his grin, Casper knew it.

By the time Shaggy, or me, had gotten over the fence and escaped, I was a sweating, shaking mess. Pak stabbed the phone with his finger and the video, blessedly, disappeared.

"You okay?" His concern seemed genuine, but I wasn't in the mood for sympathy.

"What do you want? Money?" Was it just to expose me? Those damned brain squirrels were leaping everywhere, and I needed to get the little bastards under control before I lost it right there.

There was something in either my tone or my eyes that shook his confidence a little. "I want an interview. With you. About everything."

"Why would anyone want to read about me?"

He leaned across the table, dropping his voice to a whisper. "Seriously? Dude, you're a freaking werewolf. Our readers will lose their collective minds." He realized a couple of our fellow patrons were staring and dropped his voice even lower and leaned across the table. "Interview with a werewolf? That's some Anne Rice shit. It's the ultimate clickbait."

The way he said it made me flinch. "No way."

"Come on. Just an interview. We can do audio only. No faces, no names. We'll keep you anonymous. But the video's out there. Someone's going to out you, eventually. Let me do it."

A dozen options ran through my mind. None of them made me feel better. What would this do in my life? Not to mention everyone around me. Bill? Gramma? Cromwell would probably fire my ass. On the other hand, Pak seemed like a decent enough guy. If I cooperated, he might let me keep some of my secrets. The next jerk wouldn't make the same offer.

I sighed. "Okay. Yeah."

"Really? This is so freaking great. I'm going to interview a real, honest-to-God werewolf." He realized he'd gotten loud again and leaned closer. "Or... what do guys like you call yourselves?"

I kept a poker face. "We prefer Lycan-American."

"Really?"

His seriousness busted me up. "Christ, no. It's a joke. I don't know what I call myself. I've never said the words out loud. But Lycan is a better word. Less cheesy movie baggage. When do we have to do this?"

He sipped his drink as calmly as he could, but it didn't hide his victorious grin. "I'm going out of town for two weeks — there's a big Psychic Con in Philadelphia and then a haunted theater in

Connecticut to check out. When I get back? Oh, and there's a place I know... some people you should meet while we're at it."

Crap. I really didn't want to do this, especially with witnesses, but he had me dead to rights.

"Okay. But you can't use my real name. And absolutely no mention of Mister Cromwell. Keep him out of it. I need the work."

"Deal. You know, you're not at all what I expected."

I finished the last dregs of my coffee and slammed the mug down in resignation. "Yeah, I get that a lot."

CHAPTER 6

Bill, Meaghan, and I sat around the dining room table in Gramma Mostoy's apartment. Bill's grandmother was out playing Euchre with her friends. That was a euphemism for a bunch of old broads getting tipsy and talking smack to each other. The three of us stared at my phone in the center of the yellow tablecloth.

"Did you know about this?" I asked.

My best friend, Bill, shook his head. Meaghan looked away, suddenly fascinated by what was out the window. The bright sun through the glass made her squint and look even paler than usual. Living in that halfway house cleaned up her skin and her eyes, but she was still mostly nocturnal.

"Megs, did you know?"

"Yeah. Saw it a week ago. Maybe more." She turned my way.

"Seriously? And you didn't say anything?"

"I thought you knew, okay? It was all over social media. How could you not?"

Because I don't follow that crap is why. "Why didn't you say anything?"

"I figured you didn't want to talk about it. You must've known it was out there. We saw it and..." Her hand flew to her mouth, but it was too late. The words were already in the air.

Crap. "Gramma knows, too?" I groaned.

Bill slapped his hand on the table. "She didn't say a word to me! Why doesn't anyone tell me anything around here? I only pay the frigging mortgage." That wasn't entirely fair. Bill kept several secrets from his grandmother, including his latest boyfriend. He thought it was a secret, at any rate. It amounted to the same thing. Point was, he hadn't told her. Come to think of it, my rent on the downstairs apartment paid a good chunk of the freight as well.

I pushed myself away from the table. Pacing the dining room and running my hands through my hair, I asked her, "The whole damn world has seen this thing. What am I supposed to do?" I stopped. "What did Gramma say?"

A voice came from the doorway. "She said it's a fricking miracle you've held it together this long without everyone finding out." Gramma Mostoy, all five-feet-and-not-much-else of her, stood with a plastic grocery bag in each hand.

Bill used his crutch to stand. "I thought you were playing cards?" He took the bags from her and clomp-clomped into the kitchen, where he placed them on the counter.

"I was, but then Donna started bragging about her new boyfriend and the wild monkey sex they were having. Again."

Meaghan screwed her face up. "Ewwww. That's disgusting."

Gramma cackled. "Nah. But nobody likes a bragger. Plus, with her bum hip, there's no way she can pull that off anymore." She looked at me and the laugh lines around her eyes disappeared. "What are you going to do about that?" She pointed to the phone.

"I don't know. This guy from *Horatio* magazine wants to interview me and says he'll keep my identity secret. If I don't, he'll publish the story with my name and everything."

Meaghan perked up. "*Horatio*? I love them. They write about all kinds of stuff. Like clairvoyants. And that Skywalker Ranch place."

Bill scoffed from the kitchen. "It's all bullshit."

Meaghan hated it when Bill derided anything supernatural. "Yeah? What about that village of zombies in Central America?"

"Double bullshit," he said. Bill's voice always got whinier when the conversation drifted to anything paranormal. "They don't exist. Jesus Christ." A couple of months after his trip to Vegas, and his own brush with witchcraft, his natural skepticism was returning. It wasn't a great look, but he had to deal with things his own way. Denial had gotten him this far in life.

Meaghan was like a dog with a sock and wouldn't let it go. "What about the Chupacabra they found in Texas?"

I couldn't help myself. "Actually, those are real."

"Really?" Bill and Meagan asked together. One of them was more excited to hear it than the other.

I'd seen a head mounted on a wall back in Vegas. Next to where mine would have been if that fight ended differently. "Yeah, real as hell. Ugly, too. Like a German Shepherd humped a warthog."

Gramma sat down with a grunt. "Charming. Still doesn't answer my question."

The old woman wore three gaudy rings that clicked against the tabletop. Gramma put her hand on top of mine, then looked at Meaghan and nodded to Bill in the kitchen. "Give us the room?"

"What am I supposed to do in there?" Meaghan asked.

Bill piped in from the next room. "You could always go home to your own place for once."

Meaghan yelled through the wall, "Or you could just bite me.' She stuck her pointed tongue way out, making her look even younger.

Gramma winced at the bickering and put her hand to the girl's elbow. "Well, you could practice some more. Are you ready for your big debut?"

"What are we talking about?" Bill asked.

Gramma squeezed her arm with her free hand. "Kid's making her professional debut at the Psychic Fair, in a couple of weeks. Got her own table and everything." From the proud look on her face, you'd think the blonde was graduating from Northwestern with a PhD, not reading Tarot cards for suckers at a folding table in a community center.

It hadn't been too long since I rescued the kid, and she got clean. In half a year, Gramma Mostoy taught her everything she knew about reading the Tarot—and the gullible marks who came for guidance. The women in the Mostoy family made a good, honest-ish, living for years at it, and had no one to pass the grift down to until Meaghan came along. Bill wanted nothing to do with it, and Gramma insisted it was women's work, anyway.

As far as I knew, the young blonde had never read cards for anyone other than us and a few people in her sober house, but it was inevitable she'd start making a buck at it. I hated to admit it, but the kid had saved my ass a couple of times. She was good and only getting better.

"Go home and work on your *drabarni* routine. You're still not setting the hook, so they'll pay for another sitting. That's where the money is. And pick something out that makes you look like you have boobs. Nobody trusts a skinny medium." When doing readings, the swindle- *budjo* in Romani- was everything. But what the fortune teller, the *drabarni,* wore mattered as well. Gramma still dressed in old-country skirts and blouses that worked when her cleavage sat half a foot higher on her chest. Once upon a time it had entranced the marks. At her age, her customers either didn't care about her figure or thought she was eccentric. Meaghan needed to find her own style and couldn't compete with others in the decolletage department. I knew nothing about the card reading hustle, but hoodies and ironic band tee shirts probably wouldn't reel the suckers in.

Meaghan harrumphed but left, while Bill took the hint and went to his room. It was me and the old lady at the dining room table. She leveled her gaze at me. "What are you going to do? Your secret ain't much of a secret anymore."

"I'm getting better at controlling it," I said. It sounded a little petulant.

Gramma tapped my phone with a bright red fingernail. "Yeah. Obviously."

"No really. I am. I can control him way better than I used to."

She bit her lip. "Maybe, but people are finding out. And you can't just wish it away, kiddo." Her cold hand covered mine and gave a gentle squeeze.

That's where she was wrong. I still had two bottles of the potion Cree Jensen gave me in Vegas. There just was no reason to tell Gramma about it. That nasty, icky, brown sludge banished Shaggy for an hour or so at a time. Whether he was completely expelled or just dormant, I didn't know. The exact process was literally witchcraft. I just know it worked.

"Actually, I kind of can." The timing was finally right. For the first time, I told her about Cree, the hedge witch with a chemistry degree. She got the seriously abridged version: Magician's assistant, potions master, trainee Coven leader. I may have mentioned she was a redhead with a killer smile. I told her about the Shaggy expeller potion. I neglected to tell her the last time I used it was so we could have sex in a giant bed at Caesar's.

That level of potion mastery impressed Gramma. The best she'd ever come up with was a half-assed werewolf repellent. If it couldn't be made into tea, it wasn't in her Roma magic potion repertoire.

When I was done, she sat looking at me for a long time. Then Gramma patted my hand. "I'd like to meet that girl someday."

Without thinking, I replied, "I'd like that." *I would, but it ain't gonna happen, so quit mooning about it, Johnny.* "I'm surprised Bill didn't tell you."

The old Roma woman threw her head back and cackled. "Seriously? He blabbed it about five minutes after you guys got home. At least about the girl. He didn't mention the rest of it. I figured you'd tell me when you were ready. You two ain't near as smart as you think you are."

I chuckled. "Figures. He can't even keep his own secrets very well, can he? So, what should I do about this reporter?"

"How much does he know? "

I drummed my chewed fingernails on the tabletop. "Enough. Casper knows that's me on the video. He knows who I work for, and probably where I—we—live."

"Wait. Casper? Like the…"

I chuckled. "Yeah, and he's a little touchy about it. He's an okay guy, I guess. But it's his job to write about this stuff. I can't put him off forever."

"Keep him at arm's length as long as you can, I guess. This used to be easier. In the old country, people… like you…. Would just disappear into the woods and live like hermits. That's not really an option, is it?"

"Do you want it to be?" It wasn't the first time I'd offered to find somewhere else to live. Until now, it was a hollow gesture, but maybe the time had come. Probably wouldn't be as convenient or cheap. I was making decent money. But Chicago being Chicago, and with my credit history, it would be some place with less light and more gunfire.

I closed my hand around her cold, skinny fingers. She and Bill had looked after me since I was a teenager. I couldn't imagine my life without either of them. "I'm not going anywhere until I have to."

She gave a noncommittal grunt. "Yeah. Okay."

I might have to. If word got out, more than my living arrangements would change. Forever. What would happen if everyone knew what I was? Would they come after me with torches and pitchforks and silver bullets? Part of me suspected it would be good for business if I wanted to walk the darker side of the street, which I didn't.

"Make sure you come see the kid work the cards. Your opinion really means a lot to her."

I harrumphed. "Since when?"

She patted my cheek affectionately. "It's a good thing you're pretty, kiddo."

CHAPTER 7

9 days after the full moon, waning gibbous

I'm not a hang-out-at-the-library guy and was way out of my element. The Chicago Public Library has free computers with real keyboards, and I needed a computer. I type like a two-year-old and needed something bigger than my phone to work with.

Not that my computer skills were worth a darn, but I wasn't having much luck with the whole "find Matthew Hopkins" thing any other way.

I checked with my buddy, Darrell. He worked for the delivery service Cromwell used for his more unique deliveries. There was nothing out of the ordinary there. Whatever happened to the little idol doodads happened between Beirut and Chicago. Between signatures and closed-circuit video, they accounted for everything once it arrived on this side of the ocean.

There was no guarantee the mystery man was even in the area. If he spoke like he wrote, he wasn't a local. Nobody learns those fancy words in a Chicago public school. I had to expand my search to the internet.

An hour of hunting and pecking later, it was high school all over again: I wasn't much smarter than when I walked in. I uncovered several clues while searching for Matthew Hopkins:

Four obituary notices in Chicago papers going back thirty years. Not helpful.

LinkedIn had two hundred and fifteen Matthew, Matt or M, Hopkins. None in Chicago. The richest guy seemed to be a real estate magnate in Denver, who also did workshops on Bitcoin. Almost half of the search results worked in HR. Statistically interesting, but useless for my purposes.

There was one promising suspect who checked a lot of the boxes. He was English, which might explain the writing style. A history of religious fanaticism sounded promising.

In the "No," column, he'd been dead four hundred and seventy-five years.

This Matthew Hopkins ran around calling himself the "Witchfinder General." He'd raised all kinds of hell in eastern England in the Sixteen Hundreds. Hobbies included smashing, "monuments of idolatry and superstition," and hanging nineteen people—all women, naturally—for witchcraft. Some of his favorite accusations included consorting with the devil and intercourse with demons. The guy was a Puritan, of course, enormous hat and all. Just another Incel with a hunting license.

Turns out they'd made a movie about him with Vincent Price. The library had a DVD copy. It had been so long since I voluntarily entered a library, I didn't know that free videos were a thing. I wanted to check it out. For research purposes, of course. Plus, nineteen sixties horror films had the hottest girls.

Setting the plastic case on the counter, I said, "I'd like to check this out."

The trans girl behind the counter took it without a smile and ran it over a scanner. "You know, you can check it out with your card at the kiosk."

"Yeah. I guess I need a card."

That brightened her day, like she was working on commission or something. She checked out my still-new driver's license. It felt strange whenever anyone looked at my ID. It was the first legal document with my birth name, Lupul, on it. My adopted name had been McPherson. Here I stood with a legal name change and a library card, like a real person. Hashtag adulting, as Meaghan would say.

From behind me, a female voice butted in. "Excuse me, do you have a bulletin board I can put this on?" The woman was more round than tall, wearing a battered sweater with a photo of a cat on it. Grey, curly hair was piled on top of her head and glasses hung from a drugstore chain beneath her wobbly throat.

The librarian's purple-painted lips twitched into what was supposed to be a friendly smile. "Of course, as long as you're a nonprofit. What is it?"

The woman unrolled a sheet of yellow paper. "We're holding a Psychic Fair in a couple of weeks. At the Community Center."

The librarian nodded and said, "Cool. Yeah, put it on the board over there, but you have to take it down the day after."

Cat Lady obviously printed the poster on her home computer, but she seemed inordinately proud of it.

I played along while waiting for my Library card to finish processing. "A friend of mine is going to be there. She's a tarot reader."

Cat lady "tsk-tsked," and offered a patronizing smile. "Oh, that's adorable. They have an entire section for the card readers. At the back. I'm a clairetangentist. Do you know what that is? It's-"

"Someone who can read items by touching them." I knew what it was. Last time I'd seen my friend Lemuel Collins, he was in Las Vegas University Medical Center from touching something that originated in outer space. I had a hunch she wasn't in his league.

The woman's face almost cracked from smiling so widely. She gave my arm a playful smack. "Very good. People get us confused with clairvoyants. Most of them are terrible frauds. Like Tarot readers.... Although I'm sure your friend is very good. Will you be there?"

All I wanted was to get my DVD and get the heck out, but my new best friend was persistent. Hoping to shake her off, I said, "Probably. I told her I'd stop by for a bit."

"Oh, how fun. Stop by and I'll do a reading for you. We don't get many men at these events. Especially cute ones." She waved her thanks to the librarian. I got a big smile and an extra finger-wiggle as she waddled off to put her poster up.

The girl behind the counter almost snorted her brains out of her zirconium-decorated nose as she handed my card over. In a conspiratorial whisper, she asked, "You're not really going?"

I gave her a what-can-you-do shrug. "Yeah, I have to go. My friend really is going to be there. I think I'll avoid the clairetangentist, though. God knows what she'll want to touch." That earned me another snort and a sympathetic grin.

With my official library card and the DVD under my arm, I was halfway out the door when I heard the sound of ripping paper somewhere off to the right. A loud shriek followed it. "What are you doing?"

The librarian yelled out, "Hey!"

I turned to see the Cat Lady standing in shock. Her mouth hung open in shock while a skinny guy dressed all in black tore her poster into several more pieces. With a melodramatic flourish, he opened his hand and let the pieces fall to the ground. She dropped to her knees and scrambled to pick them up. Her cries of outrage had everyone in the place watching.

I didn't need Shaggy's help to get wound up. I hated bullies, especially when they picked on women. "Yo, what the hell, dude? What'd you do that for?"

The nerd put his chin in the air and straightened his spine, trying to make himself look taller. "This witch was creating a trap for innocents. I put a stop to it."

Even with no idea of who this guy was, I really, really, really wanted to punch him. This low in the lunar cycle I wouldn't have Shaggy's help, but I didn't need it. I had at least six inches and fifty pounds on the guy. Not only was he skinny, it looked like all he'd ever fought was temptation.

He took a step back, then shouted like a town crier with a cracking voice, "Witches and idolaters be on notice. Good people won't be silent anymore. We don't need them in this city, and we're leading the purge."

Between sniffles, the woman on the floor sobbed, "I'm not a witch, I'm a clair... clair..." The rest was incoherent wailing as she clutched the remnants of her poster.

I grabbed him by the shirtfront, lifting him onto his tiptoes. There was fear in his eyes, but also defiance. I knew the look. God botherers all loved being threatened. Potential martyrdom made their dicks hard.

His being a willing martyr sucked all the fun out of kicking his ass. I let go of his shirt with a slight shove. "Who's we? You said *we* won't stand for it."

Now that he had the congregation's attention, the bonehead was surer of himself. He turned in a slow circle, making sure every corner of the library heard him. People stood in a hostile circle around him, giving him just what he craved–an audience. "I am among the Sons of Matthew Hopkins. We're going to rid the earth of witches, demons, and idolaters." He looked down his ferret-y nose at Cat Lady. "Even poor excuses like her." She gathered her scraps and skittered on her hands and knees out of the line of fire.

An angry mutter rose from the crowd. The man in black wasn't making any friends among the patrons, but I suspected making friends wasn't his intent.

He certainly had my attention. "The Sons of Matthew Hopkins? Who the hell are they?"

Now the jerk was in his glory. Louder than necessary, he began, "Matthew Hopkins is–"

I took great pleasure in interrupting his nonsense. "Was. Matthew Hopkins *was* the Witchfinder General, like five hundred years ago. Get to the point." The shock on his face was its own reward. It isn't often that I get to be smart and threatening at the same time.

"He's come back. Returned to help cleanse the world of Satan and his minions." He babbled some other nonsense about end times and the Whore of Babylon, but I was only half paying attention.

There were dots that needed connecting. A week ago, I'd never heard of Matthew Hopkins. Now I find out he's got kids. This wasn't a coincidence.

Crazy guy looked right at me as his rant picked up speed. While I had his undivided attention, the ancient security guard came up on him from behind in his blind spot. The dude didn't know the old guy was there until he spoke.

"Sir, I'm going to need you to leave." The guard was the worst kind of security. Working at a library, he had about ten years of pent-up power trips boiling inside him. A shaky hand hovered over his gun–because you need a big old weapon at a library. His eyes were almost glassy at the thought of doing more than directing old ladies to the romance section.

Seeing the lunatic get shot would be rewarding but counterproductive. I held a hand up to the guard. "That's okay, Uh, officer. I got this." My hand dropped onto the nut job's shoulder and gathered a handful of his shirt.

The Son of Matthew Hopkins was not so far gone he didn't recognize the trouble he was in. If the security guard didn't shoot him, the other patrons would tear him apart. Several older men had moved to the front of the circle. A dozen people stared daggers at him.

I put on what I hoped was a comforting smile. My size and physique scared the crap out of him, but mine was the friendliest face in sight.

"You're just leaving with me. Aren't you?"

"Yes, fine. I'm leaving. We're leaving," he said with little enthusiasm. Security Guy nodded and visibly relaxed. Cat Lady busily clutched the remnants of her poster while explaining to the librarian that she wasn't a witch. She was a clairetangentist, and there was a difference, dammit. The librarian had come over to help pick up the yellow scraps and probably regretted the decision.

Hopkins Junior's feet may or may not have touched the ground as I pulled him to, and then through, the door. It's possible he bumped his head against the glass on the way out, since I used his body to bang the door bar open ahead of me.

"Okay, now who are you?" I said, dropping him on the sidewalk.

"I don't have to tell you." He started fumbling for his phone, obviously prepared to film this whole thing. I'd seen myself on video enough for a lifetime. I backhanded the device, and it flew from his fingers into the azalea bushes.

"Actually, you kinda do," I said. "I'll start. I'm John Lupul."

He ignored my conciliatory gesture. The next move was jaw-jutting defiance and preparing his soul for eternity. His eyes looked skyward. "Do what you want to me. You can't stop us. We're everywhere."

Oh goody. How many of these guys are there?

"Where's Hopkins?" Under the circumstances, asking the location of a four-hundred-year-old corpse seemed a reasonable question.

"Not in Chicago. Not yet, anyway. But he's coming. We're preparing the way for him by clearing out the witches and idolaters and demon worshipers."

"A lot of witches and demons hang out at the library, do they?"

He nodded. "More than you think. And their numbers are growing. Can't you feel it? Something's going on in the world and we have to stop it."

"No, WE don't. Where can I find this Hopkins guy?"

"Why?" I needed to up my intimidation game. I was the investigator. Pretty sure he wasn't supposed to ask questions of his own.

"Let's just say he's made himself a problem for a friend of mine, and I want to know who I'm dealing with."

His beady eyes lit up. "I can help you with that." Shaking hands unzipped the pack at his waist, and he pulled out a small, stapled booklet. "Here's what you need to know: Read it and learn. You might even want to join with us." *And Shaggy might become vegan. Possible but unlikely.*

Snatching it from his hand, I put my hand on his shoulder, squeezed, and got right in his face. "What's your name?"

With his voice stuck in his throat, he said, "Ted. It's Ted."

"Well, Ted. If I ever catch you picking on harmless women again, demons won't be the scariest thing you'll have to deal with. Get it?"

My eyes drilled holes into his skull as I waited for a response. Then I threw in a growl for good measure. He looked for a moment like he wanted to say something smart, but then realized I'd removed my hand and chose that moment to take off like a bat out of hell. Before I could decide whether it was worth chasing him, he'd locked himself in an old white panel van and fired it up.

Rather than chase him, I looked down at the pamphlet. It was the sort of cheap pamphlet Jesus freaks handed out at festivals. "Demons and Witches Walk Among You." Welcome to Twenty-First century America.

One thing stood out. It was the same fancy calligraphy as Cromwell's letter.

CHAPTER 8

10 days before the full moon. Waxing gibbous.

The Logan Square Community Center didn't look like a den of idolaters and evil-doers. The only thing suggesting this was anything other than another Saturday was the handful of protestors gathered at the far end of the parking lot. Most of them were male, middle-aged, or younger. Some held signs with bible verses on them. Most spelled idolatry right. A couple claimed to represent the Sons of Matthew Hopkins. That got my attention. From my vantage point inside the Charger, I checked them out before going inside. My boy from the library wasn't among them. None of these clowns looked any scarier than Ted had been, with one exception. A tall Nordic type. He stood apart from the rest of the Sons. The big oaf was built like he lived at the gym and was quieter than the rest. Arms folded, his eyes constantly scanned the lot, but otherwise stood so still it was surprising a pigeon hadn't pooped on him.

One particularly red-faced lunatic couldn't resist yelling at a pair of young women getting out of the car. Both women turned white and whispered to each other, but continued towards the center, keeping one eye on the crowd.

"Hey. Don't go in there. You're putting your soul at risk. You'll burn." In his righteous indignation, he stepped towards them, moving past the plastic barricades.

A female officer snapped at him. "Get your ass back behind that line. I'm not telling you again." He feared her taser more than he did the minions of Hell, because his mouth snapped shut and he took two meek steps back. The tall blond guy saw it and harrumphed through his nose, but stayed silent.

It was a week, maybe ten days, til the full moon, and Shaggy was more present each day. That was par for the course, and it didn't bother me much, except he definitely didn't want to go into that building. The growling at the back of my head got louder the closer I got to the door.

The young wiccan at the card table near the door smiled and took my five bucks. I got a whiff of her cologne but detected no genuine power there. A harmless wannabe. Still, there was something at work. It was clear from the buzzing in my scalp and fingertips there was real energy somewhere amongst all that cosplay and denial.

It was a typical big city gymnasium turned meeting hall. Row after row of folding tables displayed every imaginable new age book, product, crystal, and fake-Celtic tchotchke. Flat screens on each wall scrolled announcements, urging people to visit the concession stand. That was the only thing that really interested me. To be honest, it looked less like a psychic fair and more like one of those book fairs we had in middle school. The only difference was here the teachers bathed in patchouli and had visible Harry Potter tattoos.

My Lycan side had a serious distaste for magic and paranormal activity. Shaggy was okay around Gramma and Meaghan unless they were doing a deep reading. When that happened, we just kept our distance. As for other phenomena, I was getting better at listening to him. He could detect actual power and had great instincts for differentiating between bad juju and make-believe. My nose hairs twitched. There was a hint of real paranormal electricity in the air, but I pushed on through despite the faint pounding in my temples.

Get in, say hi to Meaghan and Gramma, get home in time to catch the Cubs game. Easy-peasy.

"Hey, what are you doing here?" This would not help my headache. I forced a smile on my face as Casper Pak sidled up to me.

He offered a fist, and with a fake smile, I bumped it. "Hey. Aren't you supposed to be in Philadelphia or something?"

I avoided eye contact by searching for Meaghan's table, but they bunched the Tarot readers at the back of the room. Cat lady wasn't kidding. There was a psychic pecking order and cards were at the bottom of the heap.

Casper couldn't take a hint. "Yeah, about that. The biggest event of the year—largest psychic fair in the country and they canceled because of threats. Got their license pulled, so I came home."

"Threats? From who?"

"Whom. From whom."

I gave him a dirty look. "Okay, from whooooom?"

He shrugged but rattled on like someone had pulled a string in his back. "Sorry, it's the grammar Nazi in me. Writers, am I right? Oh yeah. Philadelphia. A bunch of people complained, mostly church groups. Some outfit called the Children of Matthew Hopkins raised the biggest stink. Got it shut down."

Now it was my turn to be the smartass. "Sons. Sons of Matthew Hopkins." I pointed out the door to the protestors. "The nerds in black. Chicago chapter."

Casper's eyes lit up. "Dude, I should go talk to them."

Excellent plan. Go haunt someone else, Casper. "Yeah, cool. I'm gonna find my friend and then blow this place."

"Okay. Don't forget, we're going to talk this week, right?"

Pak naively took my grunt as a yes and stepped out the door, waving over his shoulder without saying goodbye. The guy couldn't wait to talk to those morons. He could have them. I just wanted to put in my obligatory appearance, keep Meaghan and Gramma off my ass, and chill with a ball game. It was only late April. The Cubs weren't mathematically eliminated yet.

There was no shortcut to the back of the room. To find Meaghan, I'd have to wind my way through the maze of tables. That meant dodging the people arguing over whether the clairvoyants were more reliable than crystal ball gazers. Consciously looking to the left to avoid the attention and tractor-beam gaze of the Cat Lady, I walked past table after table. About every fifth one gave off a small *ping* to Shaggy, but not enough to really upset him, just keep him on edge. That made me grouchy, and I tried hard not to take it out on the people I bumped into on my way to skid row, where they kept the Tarot Readers.

The PA system crackled with the second announcement of a lost child since I'd been there. *You'd think with that many psychics in one place, that wouldn't be a problem.* A dick-ish thought, but despite what I'd seen with my own eyes the past six months, I clung to my skepticism about most psychic nonsense.

Denial. Whatever.

Shaggy's radar started pinging more often the closer I got to the last row. Maybe it was the sheer number of would-be psychics— statistically, some of them had to be more legit than others. Funny, though, most of his concern was coming from elsewhere. His unease, and mine, didn't stem directly from the well-meaning people at the tables. It was something unidentifiable in the air. I rubbed my temples. *I needed to find Meaghan and Gramma and hightail it out of here. Hopefully, before Pak comes back.*

I spotted Gramma first. They plunked her mid-room at a table with her crystal ball. She'd brought the fancy one she used for customers, not her personal version—hoping it would attract suckers. She'd traded her usual sweatpants for a flowing skirt and blouse of bright purples and yellows. dangly earrings brushed her shoulders. She hated the word, but she couldn't have looked more Gypsy if she'd added a gold tooth and pulled up in a caravan. The old girl was engaged in conversation with a Greek woman dressed all in black, who quickly shuffled off, but not before crossing herself and spitting on the ground.

"Hey, how's it going, Gramma?"

"Just effin' dandy. Can't you tell?" She was in a mood. The way my head throbbed, that made the two of us.

"Business slow?"

She pulled the scarf off her head and ruffled her grey hair before replacing it with a sharp tug. "This town is going to hell. Can't get anyone to sit for a crystal ball reading. Nobody appreciates the classics anymore."

I sympathized, but not enough to stick around. "Well, I made it, as you can see. Where's Meaghan so I can get my butt out of here?"

She pointed a bony finger straight ahead. I couldn't see our friend, just the backs of half a dozen young women crowded around a table. There were as many hair colors as there were people, and in between I caught of glimpse of Meaghan.

"Holy cow. Looks like she's doing okay, huh?" I turned to Gramma, who clearly didn't share my enthusiasm.

The old lady crossed her arms and leaned back in her chair. "Sure, lots of traffic, but she's letting them go too early. She's getting the reading fee but not setting the hook to bring 'em back. I taught her better than that. It's a long game."

I couldn't resist. "Jealous much?"

She snarled. "Want my foot up your ass much?" She uncrossed her arms and straightened the tablecloth. "She's doing okay, I guess. I worry about her. She cares too much. Clouds her thinking."

"I'm going to poke my nose in. You okay?"

She waved her hand at me. "Fine. Go. Leave an old woman alone. Maybe you can put me on an iceberg and push me out to sea later."

I grinned and kissed the top of her head. Before leaving, I stood up and looked around. Then I said in a loud voice, to no one in particular, "No way. That's amazing. How'd you know that? That's frickin' freaky."

Several heads turned my way and then to Gramma, who sat there, head bowed humbly. She looked up, eyes gleaming. Louder than necessary, she replied, "I only say what the spirits tell me."

An older guy in a suit shuffled closer, obviously listening in. I gave Gramma a wink, which she returned while shepherding the old man to a seat. Then I left him in her clutches and wandered over to check on Meaghan.

A group of under-thirty women who looked like the front row of a Marilyn Manson concert formed a human fence around Meaghan's table. The girl in the reading seat was a hot brunette in full Goth vampire regalia. Whatever bullshit story the kid was spinning had her full attention.

Meaghan looked great. She was in a black camisole and skirt, which was something I'd never seen. Lest she look too respectable, skater shoes completed the ensemble. Her makeup was dark and spooky, but it set off her white-blond hair and blue eyes. No matter how hard she tried, she still looked barely twenty-one, but completely owned the surrounding space. The audience was seriously fan-girling on her. I'd seen that look only once before, on the faces of Karmen Mystère's acolytes back in Las Vegas. If it wasn't the Meaghan I knew, I'd likely have been more impressed. It was cool to see. I was happy for her, not that I counted for anything. I wondered what her old man would think.

Meaghan lowered her eyes and looked deep in thought. She pointed to a card in the center of the table. "You know he's a dick, right?" Her eyes examined the girl's face. She could work for the CIA with that interrogation technique.

Lestat's girlfriend bit her bright red lip and nodded. "Yeah, I know. But…"

Meaghan leaned forward. "Look, I just tell you what I see. What you do with it is your business. But give it some thought, okay?"

The girl nodded, and the gaggle of young women whispered among themselves. One of them said, "Josh *is* kind of a fuckboi." The others concurred.

Meaghan reached for a piece of paper and slid it across the table. "I know you have a million questions, but we've got a line waiting.

Here's my QR code. Just scan it and put me in your contacts. Any time you want a reading, I'm available. Okay?"

The gullible mark couldn't pull out her phone fast enough. She snapped a picture of the black-and-white pattern, then asked if Meaghan had time next Tuesday. The Tarot card hustler shooed her away and waved the next customer in. She glanced up and saw me. A smile crossed her face and her eyebrows went way up, like she was asking, "Did you see that?" I gave her a thumbs up. Gramma didn't have to worry. Meaghan was fine. Ancient grift, meet modern technology.

Happy for her as I was, my headache was getting worse. Somewhere deep in my limbic system, Shaggy was looking for the exits. My stomach churned and my skin itched. I stood scratching my arms like a junkie, leaving long red marks under all my arm hair. There was serious negative energy at work. I just couldn't determine the source.

The PA system squealed again, and I expected another lost kid announcement. Instead, a deep male voice echoed through the hall.

"Attention please. Will everyone please look at the screens on the walls? Thank you." The voice was commanding, yet a little creepy at the same time. I figured it was some kind of entertainment for the fair-goers.

The screens flickered, and a face appeared on ten surfaces around the room. I knew the face. I'd stared at it while sitting in the library. Sure, he wore a super-expensive modern suit and tie, and wasn't wearing a Thanksgiving Pilgrim hat. But that long hair, pointy goatee, and pale demeanor couldn't belong to anyone else.

Matthew Hopkins looked good for someone who died four and a half centuries ago.

CHAPTER 9

"Who's this asshole?" Gramma piped up from behind me.

"I don't know. Maybe it's some kind of safety announcement." I didn't look at her, but around the room as I spoke. She sniffed, dismissing it as so much bureaucratic bullshit. Probably a city ordinance. Complaining about the City of Chicago was her favorite sport.

I knew in my gut who he was pretending to be. Matthew Hopkins, Witchfinder General. The Scourge of East Anglia, God's Soldier. Blah, blah, blah. But that was ridiculous. Whoever this guy was, he was for real. The figure stared into the camera, blinking occasionally, but otherwise sat like he was waiting for the class to come to attention.

The hubbub died down as people stood or sat where they were and waited for whatever was so important it interrupted their fun. Meaghan came over with WTF written all over her face. I shrugged. Every other eye in the place was glued to a screen.

Which was the whole idea. Hopkins-whoever knew exactly what he was doing. Just as I sensed the crowd's patience at an end, he steepled his fingers in front of him and dropped his head as if in prayer. I couldn't help but notice he had the longest, skinniest fingers I'd ever seen, the nails cut short but coming to a point on each finger like the tip of a spear. Shaggy didn't care for them either and let out a warning growl.

Yeah, buddy. I don't know what this is, but I'm pretty sure it's going to suck.

The elegant figure on the screen lifted his eyes and gave a heavy sigh, as if disappointed with every single person in the room. Then, in a deep, Shakespearean voice, he began. "My name is Matthew Hopkins, and I am appointed by the will of His Majesty King James and the Lord God Almighty to rid the world of idolatry, witchcraft, and demons. It's not a task I take lightly."

He glared straight through the camera lens, as if he knew the ripples of nervous laughter that the statement would cause. Obviously, this mook was an experienced speaker. *Maybe a trained actor? Might be something to look into.* He waited precisely long enough for an uncomfortable silence to fall again over the crowd. His timing was too good. He must have cameras in the crowd. If he did, he hid them perfectly. I couldn't spot any red dots or other clues. *How was he spying on us?*

Every eye was focused on the screen except for mine and one other person. The tall blond from the parking lot leaned against one wall, smirking. He caught me watching him, and his eyes darted away. At least someone was enjoying himself.

Shaggy grew edgier and edgier and the hairs on my arms stood so straight you could put an eye out. The figure on the screen was only part of the creepiness, though. My eyes couldn't stop searching for video cameras or surveillance gear. There was something seriously wrong, but I couldn't get a read on it, only that my Lycan alarm bells were telling me to get out of there.

It was getting easy to tell the real psychics from the wannabes. Most of the crowd stood slack-jawed, confused, and annoyed. A handful of others were becoming visibly agitated. Those with actual abilities were sweating and trembling, picking up on whatever vibes filled the air. Centipedes with army boots marched up and down my spine.

The man claiming to be Hopkins continued. "Gatherings such as this are abhorrent. You treat this as harmless fun, yet mock the Lord God and invite Satan and his demons to walk among you. That will not stand."

Someone shouted from the other side of the room. "What is this bullshit? Shut it off!"

Hopkins raised his eerily long index finger. "My children have control of this building. You'll find my message won't be interrupted. Heed my warning, because I will offer it only once. Disperse. Leave this place and burn all objects of idolatry and witchcraft or face the consequences." Then the smug bastard leaned back as if waiting for everyone to hop to it.

"I didn't think you meant *that* Matthew Hopkins." I didn't need the distraction, but Casper Pak found me. "How'd you know about him before I did?" He had his phone in his hand, recording the figure on screen and the reaction in the room. He was the only person in the place who looked like Christmas came early. The dumbass was enjoying himself.

I didn't have time to indulge him because Matthew Hopkins was pontificating again. The figure on the screen looked genuinely sad as he continued. "I suppose it is no wonder that while other cities have heeded our warnings, Chicago has not. That this cesspool proud of its reputation for gangsters, lawlessness, and encouraging sin would spit in the face of the Lord Almighty."

Casper and I exchanged glances but said nothing. I rubbed my scalp, trying to still Shaggy's increasing panic. He sensed the growing fear in the group as it piled on top of his own Def-Con one level insanity. I sniffed the air, hoping to find the source of the problem with no results.

Meanwhile, the wannabe Witchfinder General continued. "Not only are each of you the Dark One's henchmen and minions too naïve to understand the peril to your souls. Your corrupt city is full of those who would amass objects of deviltry, black magic, and invitations to Demons. I will deal them with them in good time."

I remembered the warning to Cromwell and wondered if that's what he meant. Protecting my boss was my job, but right now it was plain the people in the Community Center were in immediate peril.

The crowd became more and more frightened and confused. The air crackled with negative energy, sparking from person to person. A slow stream of attendees headed for the exits, hoping fresh air would ease their nerves. A few, obviously sensitive as hell, were sniffling, holding back tears. Others were more defiant. Gramma had her hands on her hips, and if Witch-boy had been there in person, I didn't doubt she'd have kicked his ass.

Meaghan and her fangirls were visibly concerned, biting their lips and looking around for more signs of trouble. "Dude, what's going on? Do you know anything about it?"

My temples pounded and thumped like kettle drums. "Gimme a minute to think, Megs."

"You a friend of Johnny's? Me too. I'm Casper. You've got a table here, right? Saw you down with the Tarot readers." Casper was all smiles and Labradoodle friendliness. He stuck his hand out. Meaghan gave him one of the withering looks she usually reserved for Bill.

"Seriously dude? Pay attention." Was the reporter seriously hitting on Meaghan right now? That was only the third creepiest thing happening right then, and it might have been my imagination. I wasn't thinking clearly. Shaggy's concern was becoming aggression and tension constricted my throat. I was sniffing and growling, and it was increasingly hard to keep him under control. The only calm person in the place was on screen.

Hopkins looked into the camera and through the screen, making it look like he was laser-focused on every person in the joint at the same time. His voice rose to a full-throated hellfire and brimstone sermon. "Since you refuse to abide by the word of the Lord Almighty, you've proven yourselves to be vermin. Next time heed the warnings and turn from such sin. For now, let it be known that vermin will always attract vermin."

The screen suddenly went black. All hell broke loose as the hall buzzed with fear, confusion, and the righteous anger of a couple of hundred pissed off new agers. The dank, evil feeling saturated the air now. I ignored all questions from Meaghan, Casper and Gramma and stepped away from them, trying to locate the problem.

Just then, my Shaggy hearing detected a squeaking noise from above.

Is it in the ceiling? What the hell?

I got my answer. A rat the size of a chihuahua fell from between the cheap ceiling tiles. He landed smack in the middle of the Cat Lady's folding table. The ugly thing reared up on its hind legs, squeaking at her as the poor woman emitted a horrified squeak of her own. I was about to run over and help when an identical sound came from the other end of the room. Then a third big black rat squirmed out of a heating grate on the nearest wall.

Shaggy knew what was happening a split second before I did. I shouted, "Everyone get out! Now!"

It was too late. The world exploded in squeaks and screams as a torrent of filthy rodents burst into the room from every direction.

CHAPTER 10

It's widely known Chicago is the most rat-infested city in the country, and every one of those evil bastards was piling into the Community Center. They dropped through ceilings, chewed through walls, and nosed out of vents. Hundreds. Maybe thousands of them.

Time stopped. The attendees froze in place for a moment. Then a lone woman's voice screamed, "Get out!"

I clutched both Gramma and Meaghan by the arm and almost threw them at the reporter. "Casper, get them out of here."

Casper was wide-eyed." Yeah, okay. Wait. What are you going to do?"

No idea. You can bet it will be stupid, sure as hell. Instead of answering, I shoved him towards the door, the women hot on his heels.

Gramma turned around just long enough to yell, "Don't do anything stupid, ya big dummy!"

The voice that rose from my throat was raspy and terrifying. "Go." Shaggy was already trying to burst out of my body. Between the stench of live rats and the thick, oily aura of the nastiness controlling them, he wanted to attack something. Anything. But I couldn't let him just run wild.

Nothing good would happen by shifting in a room full of people in broad daylight, even if their attention was elsewhere. Fortunately, I had a week until the full moon and could hold a full change off—barely. There was no way I was changing right there in front of God and everyone. As much as it felt like I was being torn apart from the inside, I had to maintain control. Even if it boiled my guts to do it.

Something snagged my pant leg and looked down into the beady, hateful eyes of a brown, scab-faced rat and its partner. I kicked wildly. Its little nails just sank deeper into the denim and they held on for a bumpy ride, emitting a noise that sounded like the rat version of "whee!"

The fact they were enjoying it was too much for Shaggy. I felt a twitch, and scalding heat ripped down my arms and in my hand. My nails grew into razor-like claws.

Don't do it. Don't you fucking do it.

I managed to stop him with only my hands morphing, but screamed in frustration, pain, and fury. One of the nasty buggers scampered onto a table, and I swung a claw with my full weight, knocking it flying across the room. Shaggy approved, and I let out a feral chuckle. It felt so good. I reached down for the critter hanging off my pant leg. Blood spattered everywhere as a razor-sharp claw gutted it. Another little bastard got his. Hers. It didn't matter. My hands became deadly weapons. I scythed my arms wildly at anything that moved.

My eyes fogged over with a red mist and rendered me nearly blind. Concentrating so hard on not going full Lycan, I had no time to think. It was all a disjointed nightmare mix of high-pitched screaming, squealing, and shrieking, accompanied by the tearing of rodent flesh and gore flying everywhere. I shuffled forward, looking for more critters, and had no problem finding them. They came looking for me.

Even the vilest deep-dish pizza rat was aggressive, but not stupid. Rodents were brave, but knew when to back off. Not these suckers. No matter how many of their comrades met ugly ends, they kept coming, driven by something I could sense but not define. Something seriously pissed them off. Whether it was Matthew Hopkins driving them or some crazy feeding instinct, nothing slowed them down. And part of me dug it. Guilt-free fighting and blood were like oxygen.

Shaggy screamed at me to let them come while I roared out my response. A couple of hundred vermin to one. We liked those odds. I flailed wildly. My clothes barely contained my rippling, screaming muscles. It went on and on until my arms ached, my head throbbed, and my vision became less blurry.

Then everything went black.

The next thing I remember, I was kneeling on the floor in the far corner of the room. My back leaned against the fire door, covered in blood, fur and rat guts. My hands throbbed . There were bruises and bite marks all over my arms and body. My mouth tasted like garbage stew. Shaggy was doing a victory lap around my cranium.

Blinking and squinting, I looked up to see Casper Pak and his ever-present phone staring down at me.

"Dude," he said.

My stomach churned, barely holding onto its contents. "Is everyone okay?"

He nodded. "Yeah, I think so." The concern on his face said maybe everyone but me.

"How bad do I look?"

He tried saying something, but the words stuck in his throat. Instead, he motioned with his finger to the corner of his mouth. I did the same, feeling something skinny and slick. With a grimace, I caught it with my fingernail and looked at about an inch of rat tail. It had been hanging from my lips. *Christ, I didn't really eat some of those...*

A nuclear blast going off in my guts told me I had. I spun against the fire door, pounded on the bar, and stuck my head outside. It was barely in time to empty my guts down to my toes onto the pavement. My colon spasmed and I let out a weapons-grade fart but avoided the ultimate humiliation. I tried ignoring what looked like little paws and toenails in the bloody mixture in front of me.

Great. On top of everything else, I probably have the bubonic plague.

Gasping for breath, I looked over my shoulder. Pak wasn't alone. Three very unhappy EMTs stood with him. And about a dozen cops with their guns drawn.

"Something wrong, officers?" I asked.

It turns out that wading into a sea of carnivorous vermin and possibly consuming a high percentage of them isn't technically against the law. While I heard several variations of "what the ever-loving fuck did you do?" there wasn't a lot they could do to me.

The paramedics wanted to check me out, but I wanted nothing to do with that. As long as I could get up under my own steam, I just wanted to leave. They couldn't make me go to the hospital. Nurse Ball would give me a thorough inspection later. She'd insist on it, and there was no arguing with her. First, I needed to go home. Or at least some place other than here.

Casper stuck his hand out to help me up, but I shook him off. I was a walking hazmat site. Christ only knows what cooties I'd picked up and didn't want to share them with anyone else if possible.

A barrage of chaos and noise from the main entrance caught my attention. Every TV crew in Chicagoland was trying to push their way in. This was definitely not how I wanted my fifteen minutes of fame to go.

I beckoned Casper close and dug into my pocket for my car keys. "Get my car and bring it around back here. I need to get outa here."

He looked like it was a really awful idea, which made me fear for the Charger, but I was out of options. "Which one's yours?"

"It's the only black and orange Charger in the lot. Swing it around back here, okay?"

He gave me a nervous nod and took off. Then he stopped and looked back at me. "It's not a stick, is it? Because I can't..."

My beautiful muscle car would have been so much cooler with a standard transmission. But they were a pain in the ass to drive and park in the city, and it took every penny I had back then to buy the car. I settled for the wimpy drive train but the badass sound system. Broke, single-guy priorities.

The shake of my head was enough for Pak. He took off like his head was on fire and his ass was catching.

One cop, the African-American woman from the parking lot, bent over me. "You going to be okay?"

I wiped my sleeve across my mouth, which wasn't the most sanitary thing to do, and fought back a gag. "Probably, yeah."

The cop wrinkled her nose. "Uh-huh. What you did here? It saved hundreds of people."

"Yeah thanks."

"It was also seriously messed up. At least get a rabies shot or something. That was just nasty."

She wasn't wrong. I nodded and breathed deeply until the comforting sound of tires screeching on the blacktop told me my ride was here. I rolled onto my knees, then hauled myself to my feet, using the door for a prop. Casper motioned to the passenger side, but I shook my head. *No damn way.*

"Dude, seriously?"

"You. Shotgun. Move." He got out and ran to the passenger side while I staggered to the Charger and flopped my rat-bitten ass into the seat.

I peeled out without buckling my seat belt, which was only the fifth most dangerous thing I'd done in the last hour. As I rounded the building and out onto Rockwell Street, I almost ran over the tall brooding guy dressed in Sons of Matthew Hopkins black. My old friend Ted, the skinny guy from the library, hovered two steps behind him.

The human oak tree didn't move a muscle even when I almost clipped him with my left fender.

As I drove away, I glanced in the rearview mirror. He stood expressionless, watching me leave.

CHAPTER 11

The only thing I wanted was to get as far from the Ratapalooza as possible. My knuckles death-gripped the steering wheel and my head pounded. The pulsing in my temples matched the bass from Ozzy and made it hard to navigate Saturday afternoon Chicago traffic.

Casper was strangely quiet. In my peripheral vision, I saw him bent over his phone, lips moving silently and thumbs just a blur. He sensed me checking him out and looked up with a sheepish grin.

"Bro, my phone is blowing up. Everyone wants to know what happened."

Great. I need this like a third ball. "What are you telling them?"

"Just about the rats. I haven't said anything about you yet. But seriously, that was epic." His slightly chubby face lit up like he'd spent the day at Six Flags instead of knee deep in sewer-dwelling critters. "The whole thing was legendary. I mean that freak on the video, the rats, the whole thing. Wish I'd gotten it on video."

That was my first pleasant surprise of the day. "You didn't record it?"

He turned towards the window. "I started to, but then I dropped my phone, and.... No way was I picking that up. All I got was ten minutes of ceiling tiles and rat asses running across the screen and me screaming like a little girl."

"Geez, that's too bad." I felt like a tool being sarcastic when he was so obviously disappointed. "Think anyone else filmed it?"

"I don't know. Don't think so. Everyone was too busy freaking out. They'd have posted it on socials by now if they had anything. The cops were doing crowd control in the parking lot. Only people who were already there would have seen anything." Casper shook his head. "No, I don't think anyone saw you do... that. We were all running the other way. Meaghan tried coming back for you, but the old woman wouldn't let her. She's a pistol, by the way. Nah, nobody filmed anything. Until it was all over, at least."

I was too relieved to watch where I was going. Suddenly I slammed on the brake and almost put myself through the windshield trying to avoid the food delivery driver in the crosswalk. Casper, of course, was safely buckled in and never stopped talking. "And it wasn't even the full moon. But bro, you were awesome."

My guts disagreed. I was just a freaking idiot with an acute case of vermin breath. Oh, and a butt-ton of questions.

"How did he do it?" Pak was the only other person in the car, so I guess he thought i was talking to him.

Casper turned to me, almost vibrating with excitement.

"Dude, maybe it was telepathy. Like he did it with his mind—"

"Come on, man. There's no such thing." *A dime for every time I've said that.* "But I'm not talking about the rats. I mean the whole thing. The video and tapping into the screens and everything. That was carefully planned."

The pest's energy dropped now that I'd nixed his little mind-control theory. His face showed he was still kicking the question around. I really needed Bill so we could play Sherlock and Watson, but under the circumstances, I'd dance with the partner I had.

I took the first stab at it. "Okay, let's start with, who is this guy?"

"We know who he is. Matthew Hop-"

"Come on. Did that guy look four hundred years old to you? Who is he really?"

"Whoever it was. They had really messed up hands. Did you see how long his fingers were? That was freaky." Casper wiggled his fingers at me in fake creepiness and I cracked a smile.

"Almost as creepy as that accent. Real or fake?"

"Fake?" Pak was no surer than I was. I considered the possibilities as I negotiated traffic down Halstead through Boystown. There was something in that voice I couldn't place. It was probably phony. Maybe Shaggy was overreacting in there. He was pretty wound up.

"Okay, so whoever he is, he's pretending to be the last witch-finder. What's his angle? Why is he doing it?"

Casper gave me the "Duh," face. "He hates witches and demons. I mean, he's pretending to be the mack daddy of demon hunters. There's lots of people who hate the occult. Especially church groups and stuff."

That wasn't it. In my experience, God botherers were annoying but not this imaginative. I thought about Ted, the skinny guy at the library. Then his bigger, quieter. infinitely scarier colleague at the community center. The sons of Matthew Hopkins were growing, but outfits like this usually weren't that organized. Or effective.

None of this made sense. "Where's he finding his Men in Black? Have they shown up anywhere else?"

Casper opened an app on his phone. "Not really. They got Philly shut down, but could have done that from anywhere. "

That made my eyebrow shoot up. He grinned. "What? I've been looking into them." He waved his phone at me. "There isn't a lot. They've never done anything like this. I hear they got blamed for busting up an oddities Museum in Las Vegas a couple of months ago, but there was no proof. My contacts there say someone was scapegoating them."

I flinched, thinking of Karmen Mystère's museum. When the Bowdens and the Berserker busted up the joint, I told Karmen and Cree to lie to the cops. They said it was one of the nut jobs who'd been threatening them. Apparently, Hopkin's boys were already on their radar. My heart sank. Had I sicced these idiots on Karmen and Cree? This was becoming more personal all the time.

Pak thumbed through his messages. "The Sons started popping up a couple of months ago online, but nobody actually claiming to be a witch-finder."

"Nope, he's pretending to be THE witch-finder. That's really fricking specific. And why Chicago? If he's English, it's not like there's no occult crap in London he could chase after. Boston is closer to Salem, which would at least make sense if this was really about witchcraft. Today was a bunch of low-level card readers and new agers. There couldn't have been more than a couple of legit magick users in that room."

I winced when I realized I'd mentally added the k to magick, like Cree and the rest of her coven did.

Dammit Johnny.

Casper studied me with his reporter's eyes now. "I thought you didn't believe in the occult?"

"Mostly, I don't. But I know a few genuine witches. Hopkins knew he was dealing with amateurs. He wanted the attention."

"He's getting it," Casper said. I raised my eyebrows instead of asking the question. "What, you don't think I'm going to write about this? Our readers are going to freak out. This is almost as big a deal as your werewolf video."

Yeah, there was still that petty matter to deal with. More important; why did this Hopkins guy have such a hard-on for Cromwell?

What was that adage about 'speak of the devil and he appears'? Think of him and he calls. My phone buzzed. It was Cromwell. I held a "shut up" finger to Casper and hit the answer button.

"Hello sir. What can I do for you?"

A female voice cooed, "You really want to know? It's a pretty long list, but it'll be fun." Crap, it was Francine using the boss's phone. I turned off the speaker and held the phone to my ear. Casper didn't need to hear this.

"Hey, what's up?" Driving in my condition without being hands-free required more concentration than I could maintain for long.

"He asked me to call. We've gotten another message from Hopkins."

"Seriously? What's it say?"

"Same nonsense. Something about showing proof of his power. Said you'd know what he was talking about. Do you?"

Crap, crap, crap. "Kinda, yeah."

Casper leaned in to hear what we were talking about. I shot him a dirty look, and he pulled back against the door, pouting.

"He wants you here ten minutes ago."

I looked at my passenger and then at my gore-stained shirt. "An hour? I need to drop someone off, then shower and change my clothes first."

She made it clear the old man wouldn't like it, but she'd see me in an hour. Francine had to be stressed because there were no further innuendoes or flirting. Just a terse 'see ya' when she hung up.

I gave Casper my best I'm-sorry face. "I have to go to work. Can I drop you at the El?"

"I thought we were going to find more about Hopkins?" HIs face said I'd told him there was no Santa Claus.

"We will. But I need to do this first."

The reporter grabbed his phone and typed furiously. "I'm seeing if those friends I told you about know anything about this guy. They're pretty tapped into the community. With your investigator skills and my contacts, we'll find this guy for sure. I'll text you tomorrow."

I nodded, but all that rodent meat swirled in my guts.

Wait. We? Since when were we, we?

There had to be a way to shake loose. But for the moment, he was useful. Maybe he'd find something else I needed to know.

Trying to sound happier about the situation than I was, I gave him a weak smile. "Okay, yeah. We'll figure this out. About the other video... I can't have that getting out if we're going to be a team." The very word, Team, stuck in my throat. I knew almost nothing about this weird Korean guy, and I'd always been—as the expression goes—a lone wolf.

"Cool. I'm the only one who knows you're that guy. There's no rush. And this story is way bigger. I mean, this guy actually tried to hurt people. And I was a witness. That gives me a leg up on everyone else. This is great. I've never worked with a partner before."

The reporter geek's eyes shone. He probably ate a lot of lunches alone in high school. I knew that feeling. "We can do your interview later. Let's crack this case first." He drummed on the glove compartment and let out a "whoo."

Crack the case. Good God, what have I gotten myself into? I forced another grin and looked for an El stop to drop him off.

A stay of execution was as good as I was going to get. I'd take it.

CHAPTER 12

I got home before Meaghan and Gramma, so I ran in, changed, and headed for Cromwell's. Halfway there, I realized some pit wipe and mouthwash would have been a good idea. I settled for downing half a tin of breath mints.

Running late, I blew through the doors into the lobby. Jarhead Justin greeted me at the front desk with a scowl plastered on his mug. The sleeves of his polo shirt were close to bursting from those giant, thick-veined biceps. That stone face would have frozen a smarter man in his tracks, but smart isn't my most notable attribute. Last time I'd seen him, he was out in the burbs doing night duty on The Archives. The poor sucker looked like he hadn't slept since.

"They finally let you out of Siberia, huh?"

If he thought it was funny, he didn't tell his face. "She said she wanted me close to the old man."

"She," was Francine Ball. That chiseled granite chin warned me further joshing was a bad idea. Justin had no problem facing insurgents or terrorists in redacted parts of the world, but Cromwell's nurse put the fear of the Almighty in him.

"Serious, dude. She's crazy stressed about something."

That wasn't good news. Nurse Ball usually maintained the ice-queen act in public, particularly with the help. If she was this freaked out, it's because Cromwell was, too. Not great news.

I pulled my Ruger out of my shoulder holster and offered it to Justin, like always. This time, he shook his head. "No, I have a feeling you might need that at some point." Now I was really worried. Justin and I played this stupid macho game where he took delight in taking my gun and I pretended like it bothered me. He had no time for frenemy silliness today.

"For real?" I asked. In reply, Justin scooched his chair aside and opened a desk drawer containing more weaponry than the average Schwarzenegger movie.

"You'd better get up there. They're waiting."

"No shit. Any idea what's going on?"

He looked down and shrugged. "She said it's need-to-know. Apparently, I don't qualify. How am I supposed to protect him if I don't know what I'm looking for?"

Clearly, that insulted him. I didn't have the heart to rub salt in the big lug's emotional wounds, so I let it go.

Justin grabbed my arm as I walked past him toward the elevators. "Lupul, how bad is it?"

"I don't know yet." That was true. Apparently bad enough to have everyone on edge. The situation was likely headed to pure batshit insane, but I couldn't give him an honest status report. Something told me if things got hairy and we needed muscle, firepower, or cannon fodder, he'd get dialed in soon enough. Til then, he could be his usual intimidating meathead self and stop trouble at the front door.

"Whatever it is, you'll know. Hell, I'll tell you if I can. But you might want to set out some rat traps."

"Huh?"

"It's a metaphor, big guy. But keep your head on a swivel. Especially for anyone dressed all in black."

He nodded and wrote it down on a notepad, like he didn't trust himself to remember. I wasn't giving away any secrets. Odds were anyone dressed in black in the middle of a Chicago spring was up to no good. Or a mime. Either way, they had no business hanging around this building.

A few minutes later, I hunkered down in Cromwell's office, looking across a desk the size of Iowa. My number one client looked smaller and frailer than usual, cocooned in an oversized bathrobe. His glasses magnified his eyes, making him look more insectoid than normal.

Francine Ball hovered over him, one hand on his bony shoulder. With her steely gaze, she inspected me head-to-toe and didn't much care for what she found. Something was wrong, she could tell, but since I wore a flannel shirt with the sleeves down and jeans, she couldn't see much. My eyes avoided hers and focused on the boss.

"I got this video message from Hopkins—or whoever—this morning." He slapped a tablet on the table and hit play.

Hopkins' long, bony face appeared, staring into the camera. Once again, he was dressed exactly like on the video at the psychic fair. Those freakishly long fingers were steepled just below his immaculately whiskered chin.

The creep was good at those pregnant pauses. Had to hand it to him. Just when I wondered if the camera had frozen or we'd lost the internet, he let out a heavy sigh, as if disappointed with the world and all in it.

"Malcolm Cromwell, you no doubt have heard about an incident in your city that demonstrates our power. And our seriousness."

His voice resonated with that rich English accent, although Shaggy was picking up something wobbly underneath it. There was a wavering note that itched at the back of my brain, but I couldn't identify it. I focused, shutting out all the other noise.

He went on. "Your collection of abominations and demonic relics is an affront to God, and all that is right. You have two weeks to not only destroy your entire collection of evil, but the building that houses them. They have defiled it."

Cromwell sniffed defiantly, but Hopkins continued. "Not only are graven images a sin before God, but contaminate all they touch.

Scripture says, 'Ye shall defile also the covering of thy graven images of silver, and the ornament of thy molten images of gold. Thou shalt cast them away as a menstruous cloth. Thou shalt say unto it, Get thee hence.'"

Damn. "Did he really just say to toss them away like a used tampon?"

Cromwell held a palm up. "Hush up. It gets better."

Hopkins' voice rose to a crescendo, and I swear actual flames blazed in those dark eyes. It was a hell of a performance, but he wasn't done. "If you doubt our seriousness, ask your dog. He witnessed today's demonstration. You have two weeks to burn that abomination to the ground or God's wrath will surely descend on you and all you hold dear. If you are too chained to the things of this world, you can start with King James's book."

"Did he call me a dog? What a dick." Again, I got the hush-up stare.

The picture froze and then disappeared. I leaned back in my chair. "Damn."

Cromwell asked, "do you know what he's talking about? What demonstration?"

Francine's glacial voice chimed in. "Johnny, what happened?"

I related the story as best I could: the community center, the video takeover, the rats. I left out how I dealt with the nasty buggers, just that they were gone, and nobody was badly hurt.

"Nobody?" Francine stepped from behind our boss and grabbed my arm. She pushed my sleeves up and revealed my arm was a mass of bruises and obvious bite marks she didn't cause. She stretched my arm out for Cromwell to get a good look, then turned on me.

"Are those rat bites? Why didn't you go to the hospital?" The woman was in full Army nurse mode now. It was kind of hot, but this wasn't the time.

I yanked my arm back. "Just a couple. And you know why."

Cromwell let out a loud, hacking cough, then grabbed his back and moaned. Through his pain, he spit out, "Inspect him for fleas later. What are we going to do about this guy?" He backhanded the screen.

I wanted to snap at him for the crack about the fleas, but besides the pain his illness caused, there was a perceptible scent of fear rolling off him. That video shook him deeper than he'd like to admit. Shaggy hated that smell and grrr-ed within me. It took a couple of deep, settling breaths to bring me back to the task at hand.

"We're trying to find out who he is—really is."

Cromwell's eyes narrowed. "Who's we?"

I hadn't intended to tell him anyone else was involved, but it was too late. "I have a friend. More of an associate, really. He's looking into the Sons of Matthew Hopkins for something else and we're, uh, comparing notes."

I flinched, expecting to get an earful about confidentiality. Instead, the old man leaned back in his chair, took a slow breath, and expelled it at the ceiling. "I suppose every boot on the ground helps." He was more worried than I thought if he let that slide. The old man muttered, more to himself than me. "Who the hell worries about witchcraft and demons in the twenty-first century?"

Fair question. On the drive over, I'd developed a list of my own. "And why Chicago?" He and Francine both looked at me. "What? These guys have made threats in Philadelphia and Las Vegas that I know of. But the only place they've taken action is here. Today. Right?"

"How do you know that?" The old coot eyed me suspiciously.

Screw him and his cynicism. I knew stuff. "Because you're paying me to find this kind of thing out. I'm a professional, dammit." Being nearly eaten by rodents made one cranky billionaire less intimidating.

Francine gasped and dug her nails into my shoulder. She figured I'd gone too far. All I got from my patron was a quiet, "I'll be damned." Nurse Ball released her death grip. Okay, I was still employed. Cool. Still, better not play that card too often.

To get things back on track, I asked another question. "What's this book he's asking for? King James—has to be a Bible, right?" I was pretty proud of figuring that one out. Of course, I was wrong.

Cromwell shook his head. "No, it's something else. A book nobody knows I have. At least they're not supposed to." He shot a quick glance over his shoulder at the wall behind him. Behind the paint and artwork was a foot-thick concrete wall and a panic room-slash-safe. I thought I'd convinced him to move everything out of there to the Archive. He still had some secrets stashed back there.

"What's the big deal about a book?"

The old man took his glasses off and wiped them with the sleeve of his robe. His eyes looked tiny and watery and ancient now. Then he sighed. "What do you know about demons?"

CHAPTER 13

Thus began a long dissertation on the specifics of demonology. While Cromwell rambled, I gulped and "umm"-ed and tried to follow along as best I could. It was just him and me in the room. Francine stomped from the room half-way through, muttering that we were giving her a headache. "Call me when you get back to planet Earth," she said.

I didn't blame her, except that left me alone with him. I felt a little abandoned.

It was a disturbing lecture on multiple levels. Of all the things I didn't believe in, demons were near the top of the list. The way I saw it, if there were demons, there had to be a devil who was the boss, which seemed unlikely. Worse, if there's a devil, it stands to reason there's a God. And if there's a God, I'm truly screwed. My working theory of life didn't leave room for an Almighty.

It was hard to tell if Cromwell believed in demons, djins and other uglies, but the old goat certainly knew the stories. From what I understood, there was a whole sliding scale of the damned things, ranging from the big nasty servants of Satan with Middle Eastern names and too many vowels, to little ankle biters who created minor havoc. Some worked for the Big Bad Guy, others were just independent troublemakers. It depended what part of the world they came from and your tolerance for Latin.

When he was done, or at least stopped to breathe, I asked the big question. "You believe all this?"

The old man shrugged. "I believe people believe it, which makes the book so valuable. I know that throughout history, people have tried manipulating demons for their own goals."

I knew Malcolm Cromwell had a deep desire for immortality, or at least to extend the years left to him. "Have you? Dealt with de—them?" I couldn't even say the word.

"Nah. I don't mess with that stuff. It rarely ends well for anyone."

Okay, so my boss wasn't actually summoning satanic beings, but was at least demon-curious. Charming. "The book Hopkins mentioned... what is it?"

Lecture part two began. "In fifteen-whatever-the-hell, there was a huge outbreak of witchcraft. At least hundreds of people were accused of it. All bullshit, of course, but King James the Sixth of Scotland was a genuine believer. He had this book commissioned to warn people about witches and demons. Sent out a crew of witch-finders armed with the book. How to find them, kill them, control them. It's called *Daemonologie*. When he became King of England, he reissued it with some minor changes. It omits the most powerful spells and conjurations so they wouldn't fall into the wrong hands."

The original Matthew Hopkins surely had version one point zero. He likely treated it like a user's manual when he was out hanging milkmaids.

"And you have a copy." He nodded. I winced. "Back there?" He bobbed that bald turtle's head again.

He held a clarifying finger up. "Not just any copy. You can buy editions of the damned thing at any bookstore. Hell, I have a beautiful second version as well. As far as the world knows, there are only two existing original Scottish versions left. The British Museum has one and the Vatican the other. Mine's the third. Nobody knows it exists, let alone that I have it."

Except someone did. And they wanted it.

My phone vibrated in my pocket. I ignored the incoming text while pondering the next move. "Maybe we should take it out to the Archives. It'll be safer there."

"No, it won't. We're on the twelfth floor. There are armed doormen downstairs, plus a panic room that can withstand a hydrogen bomb. It's safer here than anywhere."

It was hard to focus as the buzzing in my pants became more insistent. "Excuse me, sir." I answered, turning away from Cromwell and his disapproval.

"Johnny?" It was Bill. I knew right away something wasn't right, but I was on the clock and didn't have time for social niceties.

"Yeah, what's up? I'm kind of—"

"You need to get home right now. Gramma and Meaghan are freaking out."

After the day they had, it wasn't a big surprise. "Tell them to have some tea and chill. I'll Be home when I'm done here." I gave Cromwell a what-can-you-do shrug, hoping it would appease Bill while letting my employer know I was paying attention. It didn't work on either front.

My buddy wasn't having it. "But dude, I–"

Bill's whining and Cromwell's stare were both stoking my blood pressure. "I'm with Mister Cromwell. Gimme a break."

"Jesus, it's not all about you. Something happened." The hair on the nape of my neck stood at attention. Bill was usually the calm head in a crisis. Sure, when little things freaked him out, he could get bitchy as hell. When it mattered, he was a rock. Usually. Whatever was going on had him on red alert.

I promised to be right there and hung up. Cromwell barely waited for me to pocket my phone before sneering. "Trouble at home?"

"Yes sir. I have to go. If that's alright."

He dismissed me with a backhanded wave and a sniff. "Go deal with your little domestic crisis. But I want to know who—and where this guy is. Use your assets, whatever you call them. But I want answers. Like, yesterday."

"You're positive you don't want to get the book out of here?" If Hopkins-whoever knew there was a first volume, it was a pretty safe bet the location wasn't a secret either. Cromwell's contemptuous glare answered my question. "Okay. I'll check in tomorrow. Maybe we'll... Right. I'll definitely know something by then."

Thirty seconds later, I was waving to Francine as I shot past her and out the door. The elevator took forever. I kept pushed the button every two seconds, as if it would make any difference. At least it made me feel like I was doing something. The brass doors finally opened, and we descended in slow motion to the lobby. I dashed past the desk and was all the way to the door before I turned around.

"Justin?" The big lug looked up in shock. I don't think I'd ever called him by his name before, and he wasn't sure how to process this development.

I took a deep breath, shifting my weight from leg to leg. "Look, man. I told you I'd fill you in when I knew. I can't tell you everything, but the boss has something in his office that's in high demand. Don't let anyone up there you don't know unless Miss Ball approves. Yes?"

He sat more upright and nodded, his eyes already checking out the street over my shoulder. "And seriously, watch out for anyone wearing all black. Punch first and ask questions later."

"Roger that."

It was the best I could do. A few minutes later, the Charger was barreling north from the Gold Coast up Lakeshore Drive. I checked my messages with one eye, while trying not to crash the car. Three texts from Meaghan, two from Bill, and one from Gramma. She'd only texted me once before in her whole life. Her note read, "SOS."

I floored it, wondering what else could go wrong today.

CHAPTER 14

When I got to the apartment building, there wasn't a need to ask what happened. Someone scrawled the answer in red paint on the stairs.

Burn Witches

Splattered next to the words was a sloppily painted cross stretching from the top landing to the sidewalk.

I burst through the door. "Gramma, Meaghan, you guys okay?"

The two women were huddled in the living room. Bill was there as well, shooting daggers at me. Gramma had done what she always did in a crisis; make tea. The three of them clutched giant, steaming mugs of the stuff as they looked up at me. I was out of breath, and barely squeaked out a quick, "when?"

The answer was obvious. It had to be between the time I left for Cromwell's, and they got home. That left only a narrow window.

Someone was watching the building.

Gramma swallowed and glared at me, "While we were gone. Got back from that shitshow and it was there waiting for us. Paint was still wet."

The old lady looked me up and down. "First things first. What happened in there?"

With a shake of my head, I muttered, "you don't want to know."

The old girl accepted that answer for the moment. Meaghan begged to differ. Her blue eyes were bloodshot, and her carefully constructed look was now an unholy mess. Mascara slithered down to her chin like long, grey-black riverbeds. "I do. I don't understand any of this. Where did those rats come from? And we're not witches. I'm barely a card reader."

She looked as freaked out as I'd seen her since she got clean. Gramma's tea—if that's what it was—only worked so far. If she was going to stay straight, we needed to keep her off the ledge.

After carefully measuring my words, I said, "This group- The Sons of Matthew Hopkins- they're a bunch of anti-occult kooks. They've threatened psychic fairs in other cities. It was just our turn. It's nothing personal against you."

Gramma didn't buy it. "Matthew Hopkins, Is that who that freaky asshole was?" She harrumphed. "Feels pretty Goddam personal to me. I've seen this stuff before. In the Old Country, when I was a little girl. Everyone picks on the Roma. I just never expected it here. Fricking *gorgers*," She drained her teacup. "I talked to Emma and Lourdes. Nothing like this happened at their houses."

Maybe it was personal. But why them?

Bill found a coaster and set his cup on an end table. "Okay Sherlock. If it wasn't about them, how did Hopkins or whoever know to come here while they were at that bullshit fair? Or that you or I wouldn't be home."

I grinned and relaxed a tad. Sherlock and Watson was one of our favorite games and always helped focus my thinking.

"Okay, Watson, what do we know?" *What did I really know?* "Fact, whoever did this knows Gramma and Meaghan are psychics."

Bill snorted, but knew what I was doing, so he played along. "Or claim to be. Same difference. Go on."

Meaghan and Gramma didn't bother defending themselves. Our little verbal ping-pong match fascinated them. They watched in silence.

I shut my eyes to focus. "It's Saturday. You always go into the office because you're Mister Anti-Social and you know no one else will be there. They knew the women would be at that event because the programs and booth assignments got published over a week ago."

Bill was doing his "nod and keep Johnny on track" thing. "How did they know you wouldn't be home?"

"Damn, good question. We'll come back to that one." *Wait. I told the Cat Lady and the librarian I was going to the fair. They knew I was there. And I was home for a minute. They came right after I left. Was someone watching me?*

Bill leaned on his crutch and stood. Then he paced noisily behind the sofa. "It doesn't look like anyone else got targeted, right? There were dozens of exhibitors at that fair. So why these two?"

Something gnawed at me like one of those rats. It wasn't exactly true that nobody else got messages. Cromwell got his cryptic video from Hopkins about the time I left the fair.

"Ah, dear Watson. Someone else got a message. Old man Cromwell. A video from Hopkins. Said to get rid of his entire collection, death to demons and idols, all that stuff." The light dawned. "They knew I'd been at the psychic fair because he said so. Bastard even called me the old man's dog."

Meaghan sniffed. "Rude."

"Right?" The fog cleared. When in doubt, follow the money and the old man was the only one of us that had any. This had to be about Cromwell and his collection. But Hopkins knew I was there, so in a way it was about someone else, too.

It was about me. Meaghan, Gramma and all those innocent psychics were collateral damage.

I held a finger up to the others. "Hold that thought." I hauled ass down the stairs, outside and to my basement apartment door. The two women stood on the top landing, staring down at me. Sure enough, there was a pee-yellow scrap of paper sticking out of the doorjamb.

Yanking it out and opening it, I saw it was another Sons of Hopkins pamphlet. This one bore the charming title, "The Witch of Endor and the Whore of Babylon." These guys had serious women issues, but that wasn't the point. Handwritten on the back, just above The Sons of Matthew Hopkins logo and a copyright sign, were these words:

Abomination
You Don't Want This Fight
Stand Aside

In fairness, it was good advice. The name-calling seemed a bit much, but someone had my best interests at heart. Too bad for them. They'd threatened my employer. More to the point, they'd gone after Gramma and Meaghan. That was unforgiveable. If the goal was to get me to withdraw from the fight, their little plan backfired.

It was personal now. They'd messed with the wrong abomination.

CHAPTER 15

8 days before the full moon. Waxing gibbous.

For as much as I didn't want to deal with Casper and his hyperactive-chihuahua stream of chatter, he might have uncovered information I didn't have. I closed my eyes, let out a couple of terrible curse words, and hit "dial."

As usual, he picked up on the first ring. "Bro, good to hear from you." The reporter said it all in one breath, almost one syllable.

I faked a smile and said, "Yeah, hey buddy, did you find anything out about the Sons of Matthew Hopkins?"

"Maybe. I mean, I think so. Meet us at Black Cat Coffee in Andersonville. You know where that is?"

The Black Cat was a hipster coffee house. The walls were Goth black with lots of silver and red, so it looked like a teenage vampire's rec room even at high noon. "Yeah. Gimme twenty minutes," I said and stabbed my thumb at the hangup button. Of course, that's where he'd want to meet.

I was so focused on piecing out what happened at my place that I was halfway up Lawrence when I thought to ask, "who's *us*?"

The answer came when my eyes adjusted to the lack of light in the café. Casper sat in a corner booth under a Nosferatu painting by some local artist. Sitting with him were two women and a guy who just stared and nodded over his mocha-whatever. The reporter gestured wildly. "Johnny. Dude. Over here."

I held up a finger in the universal sign for "wait til I get my coffee, dammit." First, I really needed coffee. Second, it gave me a chance to scope out what I was getting into.

They were an odd bunch. Casper was the only one smiling. The other three frowned and tried to look at me while not appearing to look. Well, two of them did. The other, a pretty woman about my age wearing a purple hijab, looked at Casper and muttered under her breath. A young guy, who might have been twenty-one but maybe not judging from the acne, studied me with disgust. The other woman, a chunky blond about forty, crossed herself for the second time since I walked in. Clearly, they were no happier to see me than I was to meet them, but I needed to get this over with and find Hopkins.

Casper scooched over to make room against the wall. Instead of getting in the booth, I grabbed a chair and spun it around so I could sit on it backwards, facing the rest of the group. Figuring offense was the best defense, I gave them a toothy smile and said, "Hey."

Pimples visibly retreated a few inches. He protested to Casper, "What's he doing here?"

This wasn't going according to whatever master plan the reporter had. He did his best to get the positive mood back. "Dude, I told you he was coming. This is Johnny."

"I know who he is. Why's he here?" Neither Shaggy nor I sensed any real threat from the kid, other than a crappy attitude, so I remained cool. Inside, I seethed. Casper lied to me. At least three other people knew who was in that video. Nobody is that scared of me based on my pretty face alone.

Casper knew he was busted and had the look of a squirrel that got halfway across a busy road before deciding it was a bad idea. "I figured you guys should meet. I mean, you're all..." His words trailed off.

The Muslim woman sipped her tea. "What he means is we're all part of Casper's little freak collection. Abandon hope all ye who enter here." She toasted me sarcastically with her teacup.

My boy nodded enthusiastically, ignoring her obvious disdain. "That's not completely fair. That's Zara by the way, but it's true that all of us have some connection to—okay, I know you hate the word occult—but some kind of, uh, phenomenon. Right?" He looked at the others for support.

The Adam kid let out a *harrumph.* The older woman shifted her eyes from me to the door and back, clearly wondering if she could make a break for it. She settled for subtly crossing herself again. She was a few pounds and a couple of rough years from being pretty. Deep sadness wafted off her like drug store perfume.

I didn't want to be here, and it was clear they didn't want me. "You said you learned something about the Sons of Matthew Hopkins?"

Casper nodded and pulled out his phone, thumbing for a second until he found what he was looking for.

"Right. Seems they popped out of nowhere about a year ago. A few reports in various cities, but it's clear they're focused on Chicago, for some reason."

Because Cromwell's here. And me. I had a hunch I was on their radar only because I worked for the old man, but that was still just a wild ass guess. If Casper's team knew about me, others probably did, too.

Pak continued. "And they're only targeting the traditional spiritual practices."

My eyebrows met somewhere at the top of my head. "What does that mean?"

Zara's voice chipped in. "White. Anglo. Christians. That's who they recruit from and worry about. Apparently, the rest of us aren't any threat to them, so they don't give a shit about us." She explained outsiders like Muslims, Asians, Africans, hadn't heard squat from them. "Like it's not in their bible so our experience isn't real to them. But they've been all up in Magda's world. Her church is ground zero for these dicks."

"Which church?" I asked.

My attention was the last thing Magda wanted. She pulled her legs onto the chair and tried to vanish. I followed her gaze to my chest and felt myself getting hairier by the moment. I quickly closed another button on my shirt and pulled my sleeves down over my wrist, so I looked less werewolf-y.

Casper spoke for her, like he was her lawyer. "St Hyacinth's. Magda spends a lot of time in church. It's her recovery."

Adam moaned. "Dude, you're not supposed to out anyone. That's like a rule, right?"

"I know, but Johnny's one of you. And he's trying to find these guys. They're hurting people and we can help stop it."

This was getting uncomfortable quickly. "I don't want to get up in anyone's business. I'm sorry, Magda," I said.

She finally spoke, her voice soft and wary. "I see them all the time. Handing out their stupid pamphlets about idols and demons. They don't know nothing about that stuff."

The quiet but assertive way she said it led me to the next question. "But you do, right?"

Magda bit her lip and nodded. Casper piped in. "She was totally possessed by a demon for a year. Finally got exorcised a couple of months ago, but you can still detect demonic activity. Right?"

He looked at the woman for confirmation. Magda studied me, her body language passive but her scrutiny more intense. "And other evil things."

Shaggy nudged and let out a little whimper inside my head, picking up some signal he wasn't crazy about. Is that what the woman was picking up as well? Did she know he was there? Of course she did. She saw my video debut. Whatever happened to her, it hadn't been pleasant and maybe I should cut her some slack.

"Dude, she doesn't like you. I don't blame her." Whatever Adam was on was wearing off, leaving him irritated and itchy. This kid was a different matter altogether. I had no time for his BS.

His snotty attitude was contagious, and I snapped at him. "He's... I'm not evil."

"Looked pretty fucking creepy on that video."

He had me there. That didn't mean I had to deal with his crap attitude. "What about you? What's your superpower?" There really wasn't time to get into all this, but I would not learn a damned thing until we put everything on the table.

Casper wasn't finished being everyone's spokesman. "Adam can astral project."

I knew a little about that and flashed back for a moment to scouting Bowden's compound in Nevada by spiritual remote control. "Don't you have to be clear-headed to do that?"

Adam shrugged like junkies always do. "Yeah, well, it's not always voluntary. It just kind of happens sometimes." Okay, two down. That left the woman in the headscarf.

Zara sighed. "I talk to dead people. That's not really a popular trick in my circles."

Casper clapped his hands. "Okay, so here's what I know about the Sons—"

Zara held her palm up. "Wait just a minute. Aren't you going to say anything about yourself?" She turned to me. "You know his deal, right?"

I didn't know Pak had a deal. I'd assumed he was interested in the paranormal and started writing about it. Now that she mentioned it, it stood to reason that he'd have some motivation. I turned to Casper, who clearly didn't want this to become all about him.

"I, um, I see *gwishin*."

That was no help to me. Casper sighed. "Ghosts. I see ghosts, dude."

Adam giggled. "But only of kids. Calls them *Dogjos* or some Oriental crap. He's like a spiritual pedophile."

Casper's eyes and voice dropped. "Shut up, Adam. And it's *dongja.* You can still be an asshole without being racist about it."

It was comforting to know that the occult community had its own diversity problems, but this was awkward and deeply weird.

God knows I had enough of that in my life already. "Well, this has been fun, but I don't have all day. Get to it. That many guys need to meet somewhere, right? Does Hopkins have like a secret clubhouse or something?"

My phone vibrated once in my pocket. I ignored the incoming text as best as I could to stay on task. "What about Hopkins? Have any of you heard anything about him? Who he really is?"

Magda shook her head. "The only people that hang around the church are the weirdos with the pamphlets. They talk about him like he's God, but no one I know has actually seen him in person. Except father Piotr, maybe. I just know Hopkins claims to hate d-demons and whips his fanboys into a frenzy." The word seemed to stick in her mouth, but then if I'd gone what she supposedly went through, I wouldn't have wanted to talk about it either.

I fought the Pavlovian response to answer my phone. Whoever it was could wait. "Well, hey. Nice to meet you all, but I need to get going."

Casper's face fell as his plan deteriorated. "Come on man, stick around. I thought we could, you know. Talk."

"About what? What is this like AA for psychics? Hi, I'm Johnny and I'm a Lycan?"

"Hi, Johnny." Zara said in a monotone, then smiled and chuckled at her own joke. Her, I liked. The rest of them creeped me out.

Casper scrambled to regain control of the situation. "Come on, dude. It helps to hang with people who know what you're going through."

My eyes burned into him, and I enjoyed watching him flinch. This bunch might go through their own crap, but it was their crap. Mine was different. For starters, I didn't see dead people. Or talk to them. I made them, and that meant I was in a league of my own. And who the hell was he to share my business with a bunch of strangers?

Another tingle down my leg gave me the excuse I needed to get out of there. I turned my back on them and studied the screen. The call came from Cromwell. I'd check voicemail when I got to the car.

Both texts were from him. I thumbed the icon and saw two brief messages that made my hair stand on end.

Mr. Cromwell

There's been a break in at the Archives

It was followed two minutes later by

Mr. Cromwell

Get your ass out there. No cops.

"Dude, you okay?" I hated that Casper cared. He was a legit nice guy, he was just a bit much most of the time.

I shoved the phone in my pocket and kicked the chair aside. "I gotta go."

CHAPTER 16

At the Archives

It was nightfall when I pulled the Charger behind the building. Three-quarters of a moon peeked out from behind thick overcast. The wet blacktop reflected circles of amber streetlight. The new LED security system over the rolling door at the rear burned way too bright, overwhelming my Lycan eyes.

I sat in the car, rubbing my eyes and taking a moment to scope out the scene.

Saturday night in a district of warehouses and logistic businesses is usually quiet. The streets are empty and dead as a banker's soul. There was only one vehicle in the lot; a giant dual-exhaust Dodge pickup with a Semper Fi sticker in the window and a plastic ball sack hanging from the trailer hitch. It took up two assigned employee spots. Nothing unusual there, just another over-macho ex-military type pulling guard duty. Francine definitely had a type, at least when it came to hiring security.

A rectangle of dry asphalt, lighter than the rest, told me someone had parked there for a while but was long gone. If anyone was inside, they got dropped off. Unless they were already gone, but that was unlikely. Best guess was the driver was coming back. Maybe not. I didn't for a moment believe I got lucky and the intruders had left.

There was no telling how many of them there were. I stepped out as quietly as I could, wincing at how loud the Charger's door was, and took a good long Shaggy-assisted sniff of evening air.

The chilly breeze carried nothing but damp, cold, and the odor of oil puddling on cracked asphalt. Shaggy's eyes darted from one corner to the next, looking for any sign of the bad guys, but nothing pinged. It was all too quiet, which wasn't encouraging. I thought about pulling my Ruger, but didn't bother. Better to know what I was up against first. That doesn't mean I didn't make sure it was on my belt and loaded.

Cocking my head, I used Shaggy's help to listen. Nothing. I picked up the subtle whoosh of traffic on the throughway a few blocks away. No sound emanated from inside the warehouse, but no news wasn't necessarily good news. Where was the guy on duty?

Looking up at the security camera, there was no comforting red dot. That expensive state-of-the-art camera was a lifeless, useless, blackened shell pointing skywards. Not promising.

I snuck along the side of the building, trying to stay out of sight. I pressed my back to the cinderblock wall and closed my eyes to concentrate. My nose hairs tingled at the faintest odor of rotten eggs, but I couldn't make any sense of what I was that might be, other than rotten eggs. I held my breath and moved my head around the corner.

The chain-link gate twisted in on itself. There was a ragged hole large enough for someone, maybe several someones, to pass through on foot. Shaggy issued a warning growl, and I shivered. Anything big and mean enough to do that wasn't something either of us wanted to run into. For sure, it should have gotten the attention of whoever owned that pickup truck—where was the guard? My guts churned. I'd have given my left ball for the moon to be full so I could draw on its full power. Instead, I had a Walmart pistol and a little more physical extra strength than usual, but probably not enough. Check that. Not enough by a long shot.

Taking a giant step, I passed one leg through the gaping hole in the gate, balanced on that foot, then brought the other through. Of course, my flannel jacket snagged on a sharp piece of the metal mesh, making a lovely "ting" sound that echoed in the quiet parking lot and my paranoid brain.

Frozen in place, multiple sounds drifted in from ahead of me somewhere. It was a chilling combination of gasping breath and terrified whine. And distinctly human. I took several crouching steps, pressed to the wall, and neared the corner. The mystery man gasped and sucked in his breath at my approach.

Someone that scared wouldn't appreciate me coming around the corner without some kind of warning. If it was Semper Fi boy, there was a pretty good chance my hairy ass would get shot before I could explain I was all the cavalry that would show up.

Decision time. If I let him know I was there, there was a good chance whoever was inside would know I was here, too. I voted for not getting killed before I even got inside. "Cromwell sent me. Don't shoot."

There was a scuffling of boots on the pavement, the rustle of clothes, and the disconcerting click of a safety catch disengaging. "Come around the corner, slowly." It was the same voice I'd heard whining and gasping a moment ago, only deeper and more forceful. The good news was, he was well enough to put his war face on. It was also likely he had very little patience for dicking around and would rather shoot me than take chances.

Making a wide circle, I turned the corner, so that I was far enough away it wouldn't spook him. My hands were above my shoulders in as nonthreatening a position as I could manage while keeping an ear out and preparing for trouble.

Faint light passed through an open door, making a bright triangle in the parking lot. The security guard huddled on the ground, hugging his knees in the building's lee. He looked up at me with wide, frightened eyes. His pupils were tiny black dots in huge white circles. "Did you call the cops?"

"It's just me."

He shook his head. "No, we need all the help we can get." I didn't take his lack of faith personally. In fact, I agreed with him whole-heartedly. I just couldn't do anything about it right then.

"Cromwell's decision, I'm afraid. Got the orders direct from her."

He nodded and tried to get to his feet. With a moan, he sank back down, clutched his side and let out a string of curse words.

"You okay?" Again, my razor-sharp powers of observation were on full display. He clearly wasn't.

The guard groaned and lifted his left arm. In the faint light, I made out three dark wet streaks running up and down his ribcage. They weren't deep, but looked plenty painful.

I let out an involuntary, "Jesus," then knelt beside him. The scent of his blood filled my nose and Shaggy required some calming before I continued. "I'm Johnny. Lupul." His eyes widened. There was no need to ask if he knew who I was. It was written on his face.

He thought twice before answering. "Jasper."

"Okay, Jasper. How many of them are there?"

"Three. I think. A big blond guy." *Same guy? Maybe.* I chose to believe it was my boy from the psychic fair. It was easier than thinking there might be more than one of those goons. Plus, there were no coincidences in my life anymore.

"Wait. Was it one guy or three?"

"He had two...things... with him."

That was neither helpful nor encouraging. "Things? What kind of things?"

Instead of an answer, his mouth moved in an imitation of a landed carp, lips forming noiseless circles, unable to even describe what they were. He settled for a shrug that made the scratches bleed again.

I reached down to get a closer look at his wound. "One of them did this?" Another nod. Those weren't bites. I was becoming something of an expert on claw marks. His assailant had three nasty talons and wasn't shy about using them. Mixed in with the blood, I got more of that rotten egg odor, a little stronger this time. Christ, I hoped that wouldn't get infected. I didn't think penicillin was going to be much use against whatever was lodged under those nails and made that putrid stink.

Jasper's breathing came faster and shallower. His training saved him. He's put off going into shock as long as he could, but his defenses were running low. The ex-marine was going to pass out in a moment. Not the worst option, come to think of it. The body knows what it needs. In his current condition, he was more of a distraction than a help.

Before I could say something encouraging but useless, a loud crash emanated from inside the building. After the bang came a high-pitched outburst that might have been a scream or a laugh. The source of that uncategorisable sound was definitely not human. Shaggy rippled under my skin and the hair on my arms stood to attention.

Jasper grabbed for me, but I was already to the door. Turning back, I muttered, "I'll get help *soon as* I can. Hang in there." Like he had a choice.

I, however, did. And like a dumbass, I went in anyway.

CHAPTER 17

The only lights on in the reception area were the blue-grey haze of monitors and the bright white hallway emergency lights. I entered and froze, waiting for an attack that didn't come. Intentionally slowing my breath, I put Shaggy in charge of recon. The sulfur smell was more detectable and clearly drifting from up the hallway. Whatever that stink was, the culprit was down the hall.

The monitors rotated through nearly a dozen cameras, with the two at the back of the building just useless static. The first screen showed the front door. Jasper was still on the ground, slumped over. I nearly went back to help him, but either my misplaced sense of duty or Shaggy looking for a fight nixed that idea. The next screen was useless—probably the messed-up camera from the rear parking lot. After that, it was a constantly changing view of the corridors and each of the storage units that made up Cromwell's Archives.

Another crash from down the grey block-walled hallway said someone was having a grand old time in the archives. But where? The monitors provided part of the answer. Each screen featured one room, A through H. Whoever was in there clearly started with the simple stuff in H and was making their way to room A at the back. H was the stuff nobody cared about, including the intruder. There was a scattering of books, idols and fake Roman statues knocked off the shelves and cluttering the floor but not a lot of damage. It was like someone looked around, threw a tantrum, and moved on to what they were really looking for.

If the book was everything Cromwell claimed it was, they'd probably find it at the end of the rainbow, but they were getting impatient. With each room, the damage got increasingly worse.

There he was. The corridor camera just outside room F showed a familiar tall, blond figure dressed in black. From the way his eyes lifted to the camera and his mouth formed a sneer, he obviously wasn't worried about being seen. In fact, he seemed to enjoy himself. Why not? He'd brought toys with him.

My mystery man carried a black tube with handles on top—a fireman's battering ram. With another glance at the camera and one back and forth warm-up swing, he smashed the tube against the door. The metallic clang echoed through the whole Archives. Given how reinforced those doors were, he was delivering some serious force. It took four good, loud swings before the door cracked open. The monitor in room F blazed to life.

I tried showing good sense. It wasn't wise to go charging in there without knowing what I was up against, despite the rage monster in my chest itching to fight something. The monitor screen showed the guy step boldly through the door, then stand aside. Two black forms brushed past him and separated. Even on a high-res screen, it made no sense. They looked like man-sized shadows, shifting shape and oozing against the wall. Then the fun started.

Each of the shadow-things chose a shelf, started at the bottom, and worked its way up. One by one, items flew to the floor or bounced off walls. Some got casually back-handed onto the floor. Others sailed in high arcs, smashing against the wall. All the way from the monitor room, I could hear high-pitched giggles. Those things were obviously enjoying themselves.

Blondie wasn't having nearly as much fun. He leaned against the wall, arms folded and tapping his foot. Occasionally, he'd peer down the hall and frown. I knew that look. He was expecting someone—probably the cops—to come, and they weren't. He couldn't figure out why the hell not. Plus, his playmates clearly hadn't found what they were looking for, and there were only three rooms left to search. He looked like a babysitter at the end of their rope.

The creatures had already created an impressive swath of destruction through six of the chambers. So far, it had been things Cromwell didn't consider dangerous or particularly valuable. Even so, I couldn't imagine how much it would cost to replace or fix what they'd already demolished. Unless they found what they were looking for, the bill would keep climbing. Clearly, it was time to put a stop to this. *Whatever the hell this is.*

It was too far from the full moon to go full Lycan on them, but I slipped off my flannel, tossing it over the empty security guard's seat. My arms swung back and forth in a last-minute attempt to stretch out my lats and delts before heading down the hall to do battle. Shaggy growled at the base of my skull and my arm hair—all of it— stood at full attention. My Lycan self knew this was very wrong and couldn't wait to find out what it was. Hopefully, he could kick some ass. If those things had asses. Or even kickable body parts. We might have to settle for the big blond guy, which would have suited both of us just fine.

I stepped out into the corridor. It was empty, as expected. There was a sharp right turn after room F, and that's where Blondie and his shadow buddies would be. Getting as close as possible before alerting them to my presence would give me a minor advantage. Better than nothing.

It was the best I was going to get, anyway.

I moved silently as possible, Inch by inch, pressed along the wall. The closer I got, the more my Shaggy hearing picked up the high-pitched squeals of delighted destruction from the shadow figures. The noises confused Shaggy while riling him up simultaneously. But his senses also recognized the sulfurous, nasty reek. It was the same odor he'd detected at the Ratfest, as well as on Jasper's body. I felt him struggle to make sense of it. I didn't bother to try. It's not like I had any choice but to put an end to whatever was going on.

Stopping at the corner, I took long, centering breaths. Not too far away, someone's breathing drew closer. Blondie was bringing the fight my way. Perfect. On a hunch, I crouched as low as I could and leapt to the middle of the corridor.

There was a whoosh of air as a crowbar passed inches over my head and smashed into the corner of the wall. Better to be lucky than good. Growling as loudly as I could just for the effect, I launched and lowered my shoulder and ran, attempting to tackle the other man. Amazingly, he didn't go down, but staggered backwards into the wall hard enough to make him drop the steel bar. A quick kick sent it skittering down the tiled hall. A fist the size of a basketball blew past me, followed by his shoulder slamming me into the far wall.

Every time Shaggy was present in a fight, my nose picked up all kinds of things I'd have never noticed on my own. Blondie reeked of drug store cologne, sweat and that ever-present sulfur smell. None of that mattered. What confused me—us—was what we couldn't detect.

Fear.

Not only was this guy not afraid, he wasn't even breathing hard. Out of the corner of my eye, I saw him reach for that bar. I launched a kick right into his gut. My reward was the clang of metal on tile and the satisfying "oof" of air leaving a body. Love that.

The big dude bent over; the wind knocked out of him for the moment. I'd seen too many movies to stand there and gloat—that never goes well. Not wanting to be a movie cliché, I stepped into him. A good uppercut made his teeth click together and his head smacked into the wall. Blood trickled from his nose, which felt great until I watched him wipe it clean on his black sleeve and show me his perfect pearly white teeth.

Why is this dumb bastard grinning at me?

From my left, I heard an unidentifiable, creepy noise. It sounded like a bizarre mix of birds twittering and babies laughing. From inside storage room F, two shadows drifted like fog into the brightly lit hallway. I watched as the wriggling shapes pressed against the corridor walls, one on each side. For a moment, they seemed to take solid form. What they were, exactly, I couldn't tell.

The creatures looked like monkeys crossed with toddlers. Sort of. They had huge golden eyes, drooling lips and long fingers with nasty cork-screw nails at the tips. After more chirping laughter, they dissolved into shadows that crept along each wall in my direction.

My voice cracked a little as I asked him, "What the hell, dude?"

The big guy chuckled and shrugged. Calmly—way too calmly for my liking—he checked his nose for any more blood. The chittering drew closer, and he finally spoke in a harsh whisper. "Where's the book?" It was the voice from the phone call.

"I don't know."

"They won't like that answer." For the first time, I pinged on just a microscopic trace of, if not fear, at least anxiety. This guy was more scared of them than of me, which didn't bode well at all. Just to make myself feel better, I punched him in the nose again. Then I turned to face whatever those things were.

Cromwell always complained I never listened to him, but that wasn't entirely true. Now, for instance. As I faced the forms that kept shifting from black fog to evil-monkey-children, I remembered his lecture from the other day on the various demons.

These things were small. Childlike. Destructive.

They were imps.

My first reaction was to tense up and brace for impact. Shaggy had other ideas. Before I could stop him, my hands twitched, and a deep growl burst from my throat. Blondie took a couple of steps back, and I was afraid he might make a run for it. If he had, there wasn't a damn thing I could do about it. The evil mini-demons were almost on me.

On hearing Shaggy's ferocity, the shadows slowed and took solid form. They squatted on the floor, bared pointed teeth, and hissed at me, spit flying everywhere. I crouched low, daring the little creeps to come at me and hoping they wouldn't. Frankly, I had no desire to touch them at all.

A guy I knew back in my construction days was a notorious street fighter. He used to tell me, 'never fight a guy uglier than you. He has less to lose.' The imps had way less to lose than I did. Ugly doesn't really do them justice.

The furry, pissed-off little gargoyles emitted high-pitched shrieks that were met by a full-on Shaggy howl. The imp on the left was a split-second ahead of the other one, so took a Lycan-inspired punch right to the head and stopped dead in his tracks. He, or it, looked more confused than hurt. I'd settle for that. There was no time to feel good about myself because the other little bastard flew at me, claws first.

He wasn't heavy but came at me so fast I staggered backwards. Nothing good would happen if I wound up flat on my back, so I groped at the walls, trying to keep my feet. I somehow stayed upright, but it gave Thing Two an opening. He took it and aimed his screwy fingernails right at my eyes. Without thinking, I lashed out back-handed, catching him in mid-air and sent him tumbling down the hall, screaming bloody murder the whole time.

The other mini-monster continued slashing at me and howling til I thought my head would split open. I dug my own claws into its back, spinning and smacking it into the wall. Then, for good measure, slammed him against the other wall. It slumped to the floor, still shrieking and flailing its arms in a hellacious tantrum.

I bent low to maintain my balance and wheeled about, keeping both imps in view. That would have been an excellent battle plan if there hadn't been someone else there. I remembered the other guy when a crowbar struck straight across my lower back.

I fell on my face, then rolled on the ground, gasping for air, but there was none to be found. Unable to breathe, I squinted up to see Blondie grinning down at me. I was too busy trying not to die to hear what he said, but the big bastard looked awfully smug. He allowed himself one more kick at me, catching me on the cheek and my teeth clicked together and stars went supernova in my brain. I was no longer in charge, which was what Shaggy was waiting for. Unable to stop him, I felt the change occur.

Tendons stretched to the breaking point. My expanding chest allowed room for oxygen into my lungs, and I felt the seams of my shirt part with a loud rip. Lifting my head, I howled to the ceiling. Blondie brushed past me, getting as far down the corridor as he could. The imps screamed in terror and backed away.

That was more like it. Shaggy let out another victory bellow for good measure.

Amongst all the furious screaming, I heard something that didn't belong and cocked my head to listen. From outside the building came the unmistakable blare of a car horn. *Who the hell is that?*

I allowed myself a moment of hope. Maybe Francine or Jasper had found reinforcements?

Of course, it wasn't a miracle. Or the cops. Blondie's ride was here. The big guy let out a sharp whistle and limped towards the fire door at the end of the hall, his two shadowy minions close behind. Just to vent his frustration, he launched a size-eleven kick at the door. It flew open amidst a storm of flashing red lights and blaring alarms.

The alarm was like a dagger in Shaggy's eardrums, and I dropped to one knee, covering my ears. It took a moment to adjust. I stood bent at the gut, clutching my head until the throbbing stopped. Then I chased after them down the hall. The bizarre trio was already out of the building and halfway across the parking lot, where a dirty white panel van idled, spewing exhaust into the night.

A male figure leaned out the window, gesturing them to hurry. "Raglan. Come on! Did you get it?"

It was clear from Blondie's empty hands how fast he was running, and the bad words he let out that the answer was no. He and the imps piled into the van, which took off before the door closed.

Half-transformed, bleeding and backlit, I'm sure the driver didn't recognize me, but I clocked him right away. It was the skinny nerd from the library. Ted.

I let out a full, frustrated werewolf scream as they fishtailed, then drove into the night.

CHAPTER 18

7 Days before the full moon. Waxing gibbous.

"Imps. Like, little demon imps?" Casper stared at me across the table, clutching his coffee cup, mostly to stop his hands from shaking. I nodded and took a sip of my own. After taking the time to settle down, he asked, "What did they look like?"

I closed my eyes, picturing their howling, hissing, nasty-ass faces. "Most of the time, like black fog. When they firmed up, they look like Satan boned a rabid chimp and had twins."

"Dude." Byron couldn't have said it better.

"Yeah, I know."

"Did they… you know, are you hurt?"

I considered lying for a moment, then figured screw it. I unbuttoned my flannel shirt a couple of holes, then bared a hairy shoulder. Casper flinched at the two ragged, deep, angry-looking scratches. I didn't show him the rest. He got the idea.

"Not as bad as it looks. I heal fast."

Okay, we're going there. Suck it up, Johnny.

"Look, I know I say I don't believe in all that stuff. But after all the crap I've seen… especially since Vegas. It's like if I keep pretending, I can just ignore all the weirdness in the world and it's business as usual." I looked at Casper, who licked his lips. *Shit, he knows what's coming, and he's enjoying it.*

"It's okay, bro. We're friends right? What do you need?"

Are we? Not like I have a choice.

What did I need? I needed to have a normal relationship with a normal woman without worrying about a calendar or drinking magic potions. I needed new floor mats for the Charger. I needed to live in a world that makes sense again. But mostly...

"I need your help." I thought Casper was going to jump into my lap with happiness. He started to say something, probably "Yippee." I held up a hand to shut him up so I could complete the thought. "No. Let me finish. Just because I will admit there are, I don't know, demons and curses and weird crap in the world doesn't mean I understand it. I can't fight what I know nothing about. It's gonna get me killed. Does that make sense?"

He leaned so close I was afraid he'd try to kiss me. "You need a partner."

"What? No. Not a partner. Definitely not a — I'm a lone wolf. Like, literally. No, I need a..." I looked for a word that would make him happy, but put limits on whatever our relationship was going to be. It took longer than either of us wanted. Finally, I spit out, "A trusted resource. Someone I can rely on for solid information. And advice."

"Like a mentor." I could tell the reporter liked that idea. He leaned back, pretending to play hardball and think about it instead of jumping into my lap. "What's in it for me?"

I'd given this a lot of thought, or at least more thought than I usually give anything. I had one thing he really wanted, which was the inside scoop on that damned video. It was the absolute last thing I wanted, but thought of an alternative that would satisfy him for now. "First kick at anything I uncover. You know, it's not like I'm going to see less weirdness as time goes on. I've already given you a head start on the Sons of Matthew Hopkins, right?"

The corners of his mouth twitched upwards. His first post on them had generated a lot of hits, discussion threads a mile long and leads on some other stories. "Listen, I'm not in denial anymore. I've got a ton of stories you might be interested in." *He'd love the*

Wendigo drum story. Americans love dealing with indigenous stories as long as they don't have to deal with the actual people. His readers would slurp it up.

I could almost see the barbed hook come out of his cheek as he grinned. "Cool. What do you want from me?"

I laid it on thick. "Bro, you're so much smarter about all this stuff than me. I might need... research. Information. Expertise. You're the man, right?"

I may have overdone it. His smile faded a little. "What else?"

Crap. "Drop the interview. It might cost me my job. And for sure, it's going to interfere with this Hopkins thing. A lot of people are depending on me, okay us, to solve this case."

He wanted to be part of a detective team so badly, I may as well let him feel wanted.

Casper waited a microsecond longer than expected. "Deal. Okay, what's the first thing, grasshopper?" Coming from me, that would be racist as hell. From him, it looked kind of childlike and endearing.

Ugh, this guy is going to be a flea on my fuzzy ass, but I need him.

CHAPTER 19

While Casper set out proving he would be a good (God help me) partner, I tried making sense of what little I knew about the Sons of Matthew Hopkins and their creepy father figure. What are you up to and why are you making my life miserable, you wiener-fingered freak?

Their work in Chicago was split between harassing Cromwell and generally disrupting the local paranormal scene. Oh, and calling me names. What were they up to elsewhere? As far as I knew, they'd been active, or at least present, in two other cities—Philly and Las Vegas. I had no contacts in Philadelphia, but I certainly had a Vegas connection. If I could summon the stones to call her.

Since returning from Las Vegas, there'd been the occasional text between Lucrezia Jensen and me. Sometimes flirty, but mostly not. We'd chatted briefly on my birthday. Okay, she chatted while I grunted like an idiot. It might have been uncomfortable anyway, but I was doing the drive of shame home from Francine's when Cree called, and I was afraid she'd know something was up. Not that it should matter if she knew. It's not like we had any kind of understanding or expectations. I still needed a long shower after we hung up to rinse the stank of unreasonable guilt off me.

As to Hopkins, we needed something to distract the cops after the Bowdens busted up the museum in Las Vegas. Cree was way smarter than me and remembered a creepy letter from the Sons of Matthew Hopkins. We used it to throw them under the bus and off our trail until we got the Paiute Egg back. She never mentioned it again, but that doesn't mean they hadn't been pestering her and Karmen's coven. If relics and witches were Hopkins and Son's focus, Karmen Mystère's Spiritual Curiosity Museum and Theatre should have been a prime target.

After a lot of debate with myself, I plunked into my battered, comfy recliner. I stared at my phone. A tightening knot in my stomach was half-and-half the anticipation of hearing her voice and dread at explaining why I didn't reach out earlier. *Come on, Lupul. If you can go nose to nose with a wendigo, you can call someone on the phone. You're not sixteen.*

With shaking thumbs, I fumbled out a quick text.

Me

Hey, you around?

I hit "send" and reached for the TV remote. The Blackhawks were a long way out of the playoffs, but there were still a few games left to wallow in misery. I'd barely gotten the chance to groan at the score when my phone buzzed in my lap. A video call. *Damn it.*

Cree's face stared up at me from the screen. I'd taken her profile picture out in the desert, just before she watched me change into Shaggy. Cree Jensen was the only human being besides Bill who'd witnessed my change and lived to tell the story. It felt like a big deal at the time. Now anybody with decent Wi-Fi knew my secret.

Taking a deep breath, I closed my eyes, plastered on a smile, and hit the green button.

"Hey, that was quick. Missed me that much?" *Ouch, you needy idiot.*

She flashed a crooked-toothed smile. "No. Oh, Jeez. I mean, I did, but... I just have a couple of minutes before I need to get back to rehearsal. Boudica's replacement isn't exactly working out." The second member of Karmen Mystère's magick show, Boudica, was a blonde Amazon Goddess and a deadly marksman with anything pointy. Not coincidentally, she possessed badass magick powers. Sadly, she was also a traitor. When she got booted from the coven, it marked the end of her stage career. Those weren't easy talents to replace.

"How's Karmen doing?" Our battle with Boudica and the Mothers, the coven's presiding spirits, had left the Mistress of Magick a broken woman, showing her true age for the first time. Her patented hot goth look took more than just makeup to maintain. Without significant help from the Realm Beyond, she was just another over the hill stage magician with droopy boobs and a grey streak in her hair. Last I saw her, she wasn't taking it well. In fact, she was shrieking like a banshee. I doubted she'd ever recover.

Cree hesitated before answering, her smile shrinking a little. "She's okay, but she's not the same person. It's not a lot of fun around here lately, but you know. The show must go on." She lifted her arm and bent her wrist in a "ta-da" pose and gave a super-cheesy grin. I grinned back.

She finally broke the silence. "To what do I owe the honor? It's been a minute." Her eyes were bright. Cree was glad to see me. "You need a refill on your meds, or is this a social call?" The knot in my gut tightened a bit.

"Actually, I still have all the..." Potion? Witch's brew? Shaggy-be-gone? I didn't even know what to call the chemical sludge she concocted that allowed me to silence my Lycan alter ego for a while and just be me. I hadn't used it since the night she and I made love at Caesar's. "I haven't used any of it. This is kind of a business call."

Only the slightest tic at the corner of her mouth betrayed disappointment. It was enough to make me feel like a dick. Cree kept a poker face. "Yeah. Of course. What's up?"

Keep it together, Lupul. You called for a reason. "The Sons of Matthew Hopkins. Have you heard from them?"

Cree's jade-green eyes rolled up to the ceiling as she tried to recall the name. "No. Wait, that's that bunch of creeps who sent us emails. The ones we sicced the cops on, right?"

"That's them. Did you ever hear from them again?"

She shook her head. "Nah. Most of the God-botherers scatter when the lights come on. Wait. We got one phone call. Like two months ago. A message on voicemail. The guy had this weird voice, like he'd been gargling with battery acid. The usual Don't-suffer-a-witch drivel. That's all."

I knew that voice. Raglan. "Nothing since?"

Her eyes scrunched together like they did when she was trying to solve a puzzle. "No, just that one message and that was it. Never heard from them again. Why do you ask? Have you heard from them?"

I had to tread carefully. It was hard to put anything over on her. "Something I'm working on here. They aren't being quite as well-behaved."

"Should we be worried?"

"Nah, this seems to be a Chicago problem. I think we have their undivided attention." I hoped to Whoever that was true. I didn't want her within a thousand miles of Hopkins and his creepy offspring.

She dropped the cheery, just-friends voice. "Should *you* be worried?"

About what? Someone who can control rats by remote control, thinks he's a 400-year-old Witchfinder, and has a bunch of creepy followers to do his bidding? What's to worry about? Just another day in Johnny Land.

I shrugged and smiled wider. "Nah. I got it under control. Just trying to figure out what I'm dealing with."

Cree gave me a look I didn't care for. Like she was studying me under a microscope and wasn't happy with what she saw. That was the problem with smart women. You couldn't BS them for long. Gramma, Francine, Cree. They all saw right through me.

After way too long, she nodded and let me off the hook. "Cool. Everything okay with you otherwise?"

Every molecule in my body wanted to spew the list of everything that was NOT okay. The video, Casper, his little paranormal menagerie. I ached to talk to her about all the weird things I could no longer ignore and have her tell me everything was going to be just fine.

"Yeah. It's all good." The silence that followed made me squirm in my chair. Finally, she took pity on me.

"Invitation stands. You could come out for a visit, ya know? Come before it gets too hot. You're too hairy to survive July."

I barked out a laugh. Cree's one of the few women who legitimately made me laugh.

She poured on the pressure. "Pooky misses you."

It was the first untrue thing she said. Pooky was her familiar, a sleek black house cat with a serious attitude problem towards me and Shaggy. The nasty little feline would have gladly scratched a hole in my chest and used it for a litter box.

Screw Cromwell, Casper, Francine, and Matthew Hopkins. I ached to just say "yes" and hop on the next plane. Instead, I shrugged. "Sounds like fun. Maybe when this is all over. Your birthday's in June, right?"

The smile dropped. "September, but I could say it's June if that helps." *Damn it, Johnny. Do you want her to give up on you? Are you trying to sabotage this? Poop or get off the pot, pal.*

"Might be fun. I'll call you when this thing is all over."

The disappointment was a bit more palpable this time. "Great. Yeah. Okay, I need to get back to rehearsal. Give my love to Bill."

"Oh sure, don't let me hold you up. Say hi to Karmen. Hey Cree?"

She looked into the camera, her bottom lip caught between her teeth. I croaked out, "It was really good to talk to you. Thanks."

She nodded, and the screen went back to her picture. She was gone.

I banged the back of my head against the recliner and threw my phone at the wall. I didn't know what this thing we had was, but I was pretty sure I screwed it up.

CHAPTER 20

1 day before the full moon. Waxing gibbous.

The breakfast special at the Golden Saddle was cheap, but not as cheap as Gramma's rubbery scrambled eggs and charred toast. Bill and I smirked across the kitchen table as the old woman plopped another spoonful of yellow latex on my plate.

"There, that should hold ya for a while. How are you ever going to buy a house if you spend all your money at that greasy spoon?"

Bill dropped his fork. "You know, I'm literally a financial planner, right?"

"Yeah, well. I make this food with love."

Meaghan's snarky voice chimed in, "maybe try salt next time." That earned her a smack across the back of her head. Bill and I bumped fists, and Gramma harrumphed her way back to the stove, muttering about us being ungrateful little bastards.

It was the first time we'd been together since the vandalism incident. Sure, we were playing nicely together, but there was an undercurrent of tension I couldn't shake. After my call with Cree and the attack at the Archives, it felt artificial and temporary.

My phone played "Evil Woman," by ELO. It was my ring tone for Francine Ball. I ignored Bill's eye roll and Meaghan's "ugh," noise and picked up.

"Hey what's—"

Francine's voice, hushed and sibilant, whispered, "You need to get over here. Someone's in there with Mr. Cromwell, and they're yelling. I think it's..." She interrupted by a man shouting something I couldn't make out, then the call dropped. There was something in Francine Ball's voice I'd never heard before. Confusion and terror. That worried me the most.

Before I could redial, a text came in.

Francine

Hopkins is here.

Chicago traffic doesn't care if you're in a hurry. I weaved between trucks, banged on the steering wheel, cursed constantly, and it still took thirty minutes to get to Cromwell's Gold Coast apartment. Assuming my employer would pay for the inevitable ticket, I parked in the closest loading zone and ran into the building, taking the stairs two at a time.

I yanked the door open and took three steps before freezing. There was the faintest whiff of nastiness in the air, like a hotel room someone smoked in the week before.

I waited to get yelled at for barging in like that, but the cavernous foyer was silent. *Where was the doorman?*

Shaggy snarled a warning between my ears before my eyes could register the scene. This wasn't good.

Jarhead Justin was facedown over his desk, unmoving. His enormous arms spanned the flat surface. I inched closer, my gut tightening in fear of what I'd find. I was about three feet from him when I heard it.

Snoring. Full out, wall shaking, fat-guy-in-a-cartoon, log sawing. The dumb bastard was asleep. I kicked at his chair, causing his left arm to slip off the desk, and he jerked awake. He had a paperclip plastered to his sweaty forehead. It slid off as he sat up. Justin looked around, confused, squinting and blinking.

"Dude, what the... Wait. What are you doing here?"

"You fell asleep, you moron."

"Bullshit. I've never fallen asleep on watch." He looked around, blinking. He was trying to convince himself more than me. It didn't work on either of us. "Fuck. I did."

"Yeah, you did. Nurse Ball said there was something going on upstairs. Now let me through."

"Uh, yeah. Okay." He buzzed me through the little swinging gate beside his desk. "You need me to come up with you?"

She hadn't responded to my texts and calls for the last thirty minutes. If Hopkins really had been upstairs, nothing good would come of it. If he still was, I'd need backup. Justin was a lunk but a second body and a good guy who'd watch my back.

"Yeah. Good idea." He opened the top desk drawer and reached for his sidearm. Shaking his head, he slammed it shut, opened the drawer below that and pulled out a much nastier-looking automatic pistol. He locked eyes with me, gritted his teeth and slid in the magazine, grinning as it clicked home. "if there's nothing there, we look like idiots. If there is, better safe than sorry."

If he was looking for an argument, he wouldn't find one. I was a step ahead of him into the elevator and we both muttered variations of "come on, come on," until the door pinged open at Cromwell's floor.

I banged on the door with no response.

Justin's voice boomed out. "Mister Cromwell? Miss Ball? Building Security. Are you alright in there?"

No answer.

My nerves were jangling. Shaggy felt it too, and I couldn't contain a low snarl.

Justin and I looked at each other. I took a step back to do a full-on cop movie kick to the door. The guard's forearm crossed my chest and pushed me backwards across the hall. With wounded pride, I whispered, "What the hell, dude?"

He held a finger to his lips to shush me, then pulled out his electronic key and swiped it over the pad. The lock clicked, and the door popped open a millimeter. There was no noise from inside, although my Lycan co-pilot was even more restless now. This was bad.

The jarhead and his tactical pistol led the way into the living room. A couple of lamps glowed, and of course, the blinds were all down, but otherwise the apartment was as empty and soulless as usual. The silence felt oppressive and wrong. Justin immediately clocked out the rooms on the left, but I knew there was no one there. If anyone was still hanging around, they'd be in the office. By around, I meant alive. My heart sank into my boots.

I couldn't remember the last time I'd pulled my Ruger and meant it. With shaking hands, I held it high and wrapped in two hands as I tiptoed toward the office. The heavy door was mostly closed. A halo of bright light shone around it. "Francine? Mister Cromwell? You okay in there? It's Johnny," I added, just in case they had never heard my voice before. Justin shook his head disapprovingly, and I shrugged. We both stepped closer, our bodies touching.

At the last minute, he barged in front of me and placed his foot at the base of the door. He gave it a quick kick. We had our weapons drawn as It banged open.

The room was empty.

The only sound to be heard, even with Shaggy's help, was the hum and beep of the dialysis machine, sitting unoccupied beside the unmade hospital bed. The IV tube dangled limply to the floor, an unsanitary move Francine would have never permitted.

Malcolm Cromwell's massive desk, the spotless symbol of his success, was knocked sideways, and the enormous monitor was face down on the desktop. I'd bumped into that desk enough to know it would take significant force to move that monstrosity. Someone had been in this room for sure.

I looked past the desk to the hidden safe room. Three giant scratches ran down the wall that hid the vault. They were jagged, beginning about a foot or two below the ceiling and reaching all the way to the floor. Not only had they torn through the wallpaper, but down to the sheetrock itself, leaving white powdery residue on the floor. Whatever did that reached eight feet up and had talons Shaggy would envy. *What the ever-loving hell has hands like that?* I reached out to touch the marks, but Shaggy growled a warning, so I pulled my hand back. *Duly noted, big guy.*

My nose burned with the slightest hint of rotten eggs, the same stench from the Archives. I took a couple of deep sniffs and turned to Justin. "You smell that?"

The big lunk took a couple of deep sniffs. "I don't smell anything." That didn't mean it was my imagination. The odor was just too faint to pick up without turbo-powered olfactory senses. *Why does this room smell like sulfur?*

I placed my ear to the wall, despite my misgivings, and listened. Maybe somebody'd taken shelter in there? The only sound was the quiet hum of the electrical system.

Justin, bless him, conducted a military style search of every nook and cranny, until I called him off. "They aren't here."

"Where'd they go, smartass? They didn't just fly out of here." I bit my lip and stayed silent as the thought occurred to him. "Unless they took them out while I was, uh, knocked out."

You mean sleeping, don't you, asshole? I wanted to scream at him, but an unsettling thought occurred to me. Even if he'd drifted off at his desk, there's no way he could sleep through two people being dragged past him. Especially when one of them was Francine Ball, who wouldn't have gone quietly. Christ only knows how much of a fight she must have put up. Whoever it was, drugged him or something. Either way, this was no time for laying blame, tempting though it was.

"Yeah. Okay, but who took them? And why?" I stole another glance at the claw marks. There was a "what" question to be answered as well, but first things first.

"Should I call the cops?" His shoulders slumped, and his eyes looked at me with confusion. It was a legit question for Justin to ask, although why was he asking me? Who made me the boss?

"Don't think so. The folks in this building pay for private security, and there's no need making you look bad or freaking them out if we don't have to. Why don't you poke around and see if anyone in the building has heard anything?"

Justin breathed easier. Some people need to be told what to do and are happy following orders. The big oaf may have been a badass, but wasn't officer material. That answered a few long-standing questions.

Like it or not, that left me in charge. Goodie.

Okay, Sherlock, what do you know for a fact?

Francine said Hopkins was there. Daddy Long-Fingers had to be behind this, but what did he want?

I already knew the witch finder wanted Cromwell to destroy his collection of psychic Happy Meal toys. Yet, there wasn't a lot of destruction in the room. There were plenty of smashable items in the penthouse that were left unscathed.

He's figured the book isn't at the Archives. My mind drifted to the scratch marks on the saferoom wall. Something in the hidden vault was the target. Something Cromwell obviously didn't give up. But why take him?

My leg tingled with an incoming phone call. I cursed under my breath.

I was about to find out.

CHAPTER 21

The video call was from Francine's phone, but it wasn't her face looming out at me. It was the blond, chiseled mug of the big guy from the Community Center and the Archives. Raglan. His mouth was a straight line from cheek to cheek, as if he'd never smiled a day in his life. The big guy's eyes were blue, but cold. Like dead stones set high in his face.

There was no time for introductions or social niceties. "Where is she?" I meant to say, "they." The big guy didn't notice or care.

When he spoke, it was the deepest voice I'd ever heard, a flat monotone. And raspy, like he'd been using broken glass and drain cleaner for mouthwash. The sound of it freaked me the hell out. "No. Listen to me, you abomina-abomination." He stumbled over the word, like he was unfamiliar with it, and squinted in frustration before regaining his cool. "Master Hopkins has use of you."

The creep had some stones on him, insulting me, then asking for help. I wanted to scream. More than that, I ached to reach through the phone and rip his trachea out, but that was both impossible and counterproductive. First things first. Get the people back, then kick this guy's pale behind.

I ran a hand through my hair, looked to the ceiling and counted to five, then looked back through the camera. Hoping to sound like I negotiated with kidnappers every day, I asked him, "Where are

Mister Cromwell and, uh, his nurse?" It probably wasn't a great idea to let him know I cared about Francine except as collateral damage. One less thing for them to use against us.

The corners of the big guy's mouth twitched in what was supposed to be a cocky smirk. "They are here, and safe. For now. The Master wants something in return for their safety."

"Your Master? What century is it where you live?" *Was this guy freaking serious?*

"The book. The Scottish book."

Before he could explain further, I heard Cromwell in the background. "I told you I don't have the damned thing." Anger usually strengthened his voice, but he sounded like crap now. "Lupul, don't give him anything. They can kiss my old, wrinkled ass."

Over the blond guy's shoulder, I saw a flash of white—Francine's uniform—dash towards the old man. At least she was with him, which was as much comfort as I could find at that moment.

My brain was going to give me five more minutes before I developed an aneurysm. "Let me talk to Hopkins."

"No."

"Wow, and I'm the dog? Okay, who's a good boy? You got a name, handsome?"

The big lug on the other end opened his mouth, but then said, "Not one that someone like you needs to know."

"Is Raglan your first or last name?" His lip curled into a snarl. That threw him off his game. Good.

Justin clomped across the living room and headed my way. I held up a finger to shush. He nodded and leaned against the doorjamb; his head tilted like a confused Rottweiler.

That distraction dealt with, I returned to the phone. "Let me speak to them. I need to know they're alright."

The camera image jiggled as Francine snatched the phone from him. "Johnny?"

"Jeez, Francine. Okay, where are you?"

Wherever she was, it was badly lit. She was clearly pissed, but at least her military training kept her on mission. "We don't have a lot of time. Mister Cromwell isn't doing great. Just get them what they need."

Shaggy chased his tail in the back of my head like he always did when someone I cared about was in trouble. He didn't like many people, but the ones he did, he liked a lot. Francine was in very select company, and there was no way he'd let me fail her.

A dissenting voice croaked from behind her. "Like hell. Don't you do it or you're fired. Both of you."

I would be out of a job if he was dead, too. "Where are you?"

Francine's expression changed, becoming stony, and looked straight through the camera. "You have everything you need to know." She gazed into the camera and nodded, as if that should mean something to me. It didn't. Panic built in my chest. It was hard to breathe.

Actually, lady, I'm not as smart as you think I am. Animal, vegetable, or mineral? At least give me a vowel or something.

Then the phone got ripped away from her. Raglan was back. "I'll reach out with further instructions." The screen went blank.

"What do we do now?" Justin asked through clenched teeth. He wanted to take action, but didn't know what to do. That made two of us.

"I don't know. She tried to tell me something, but I couldn't make sense of it."

"I know how you feel."

There was no time for his employee complaints. "They're supposed to call back with more details." I looked around the room.

Okay, Francine. What did I have already?

First, they'd kidnapped a sick old man and his nurse. I didn't know how long he could go without dialysis, but my understanding was not very damned long. Maybe twenty-four hours? The clock was ticking.

Hopkins had something big and nasty on his side. Besides the big guy with one name, that is. Raglan looked like he was enough of a handful. My eyes kept being drawn to the jagged claw marks on the wall. What kind of monster were we dealing with?

Not knowing what else to do, I snapped a picture of the scratches from a couple of angles. I held my hand up to it for comparison. These claws made Shaggy look like a nail-biter.

My temples pounded, and I felt the frustration build. Francine's faith in me was appreciated, but wildly misplaced. I didn't have squat. I held the phone to my face and let out a frustrated growl.

An icon on the phone caught my eye. My expression changed. It must have, because Justin noticed. "What? You thought of something?"

"Yeah. I have Fr—Nurse Ball's phone in my track phone app." *God bless Francine.* I dropped my ass into Cromwell's chair and laid the phone on the desk. One particularly rambunctious night, she'd left her phone at my apartment, buried in a pile of linens. In a moment of weakness, she asked me to help find it. I hadn't deleted the app. *Did she know that? Is that what she meant?*

"She let you do that? Wow, my girlfriend still won't let me..." The big lug's face dropped. "No. No effing way." His voice contained equal parts fear and amazement. "You and the boss... uh, Miss Ball? Seriously, dude?"

"Not relevant right now." *Talk about need-to-know information.* My cheeks flushed, and I did my best to ignore his awe-struck gaze, focusing on calling up her device. I hoped they hadn't turned the phone off after our call.

Up popped a map of Chicago. A bright red pin stuck in the map somewhere off to our north and west. Just a normal residential neighborhood next to a Forest Preserve. Is that where they were?

"I think they're up on the North Side. Kind of Skokie-ish. Right there." I stabbed the screen with my finger.

Justin's demeanor changed. The smile was gone, as was the disturbing image of me and Francine together. He was all Badass Soldier again. "So, are we going after them?"

I wanted to. Shaggy wanted to. Justin sure did. His default position was kick butt now, ask questions later. I looked down at the picture of the claw marks. Just charging in there was a really awful idea until I knew what made those. That hadn't stopped me before, but I needed to know what we were up against.

"No, we need to do some... what's the word?" I'd never served in the military. Any jargon I knew I picked up from playing Halo with Bill or watching old movies. "You know, looking around."

It took him a moment to figure out what I meant. "Recon?"

"Yeah, recon. You up for it?"

He pulled the magazine out of his tac pistol, checked it, then clicked it back into place with bad intentions. "Hell yeah."

"Whoa, big guy. We need to be smart about this."

That diminished his enthusiasm a little, but he nodded obediently.

I knew there was one person who would have a chance of identifying something nasty enough to make a scratching post out of a concrete wall. I texted the pictures to Casper with the question: "Any idea what could do this?" I hated drawing him deeper into the crazy, but I knew his little geek heart would explode with excitement. I hit "send," and looked up into Jarhead Justin's confused face.

"But seriously, brah. You and her?"

"Not now, Justin."

CHAPTER 22

Jarhead Justin and I sat up the block in the Charger, watching the location.

As kidnapper's evil-doer secret lairs went, it didn't look like much. There were a couple of minor differences between the mid-seventies suburban Tudor and its neighbors. There were vacant lots on either side and the blackout curtains in windows facing the street didn't add to the curb appeal. It backed into a conservation area, so they had no immediate neighbors. Pretty convenient if you're a four-hundred-year-old, slightly paranoid, bad guy.

Every ten minutes or so, another black-clad nerd would step off the bus in front or park up the street and go through the front door. Most of them were alone. Occasionally, they had company—usually a confused-looking nerdy dude in regular clothes. The Sons of Matthew Hopkins recruiting drive was in full bloom.

Since Francine's phone was there, I had to assume she and Cromwell were, too. There was no way to tell from here, though. Someone had to get closer. Maybe even inside.

Justin, bless his big lug-headed heart, offered to look around.

"Like that? Figure you'll blend right in?" I didn't want to hurt his feelings, but he wasn't dressed for undercover work. He was still in his cop-blue front-door security uniform. I dressed like always —

like a refugee from a Seattle garage band. I didn't look like part of the in-crowd, but at least blended into the neighborhood.

"Besides, you've got the better weapon. I need you for-" *what was the GI Joe word?* "-backup. If stuff goes sideways, I'll need you at my back."

That made him feel a little better. Lifting his military-issue binoculars to his eyes, he asked, "You're just going to go up to the front door and ask if they're in there?" When he said it like that, it didn't sound like such a good idea after all.

Plan B was to scout the place from behind. I knew from growing up in the burbs that what people saw from the street side of the house seldom told you what went on inside. Curb appeal and fresh paint revealed far less than the unkempt back yard behind the high fence. That's where they kept the scrap metal and dog poop. The window to the house's soul.

A better plan was to come through the forest preserve and check things out from there. I had a carry permit, but getting caught with the Ruger would undermine my "just walking in the woods," excuse. On the other hand, anyone who'd kidnap an old man and a nurse in broad daylight was unlikely to be persuaded to let them go through charm alone. I checked that the safety was on and tucked it into my belt holster.

Justin looked judge-y. "What?"

He sniffed. "Nothing," he said, putting his big ass automatic pistol on the console next to him.

"Size isn't everything." *Defensive much, Johnny?*

"That's definitely not what she said." His voice was flat, but the corner of his mouth twitched.

"Was that an actual dick joke? Look at you."

He shrugged it off while never taking his eyes off the action down the block. "Watch your six."

Five minutes later, I'd walked a wide loop and scoped out the back of the house from behind the biggest oak tree I could find.

Technically, I stared at the seven-foot brick wall, which wasn't at all helpful. I'd need some elevation to see anything beyond that.

With Shaggy's help, I sniffed and listened but heard or smelled nothing out of the ordinary. A doe temporarily distracted him about a hundred yards through the brush to the North, but with a little mental nudge, I got him back on track. *Francine, big guy. We're looking for Francine.*

My hand traced the cracked bark of the tree. Light circles in the trunk showed where someone had trimmed all the branches to a height of ten or twelve feet. This was public property and supposed to be left wild. Someone in the house wanted to make sure nobody climbed that tree and looked over that fence. Naturally, it increased the desire to get up there and take a look-see.

For most people, getting up to the lowest weight-bearing branch would be more than a little problematic. For a guy with Lycan strength and the ability to grow his fingernails into claws, it was a mere inconvenience. I didn't want to take my boots off and use my feet for grip. The alternative was to jump as high as I could and use my claws to gain the extra height. That meant a running start.

Backing up about ten steps, I took one last listen and sniff. Even the deer was gone. It was all clear. With a grunt, I let Shaggy have enough rein to change my hands into claws, but stopped there, biting my tongue and grimacing at the pain. Then I lowered my head, built up as much speed as I could, and leapt.

With arms extended, I was about a foot shy of the bottom branch. My nails dug into the thick bark of the trunk and my boots offered a little help as my feet scrambled against it. My dignity took a bit of a hit, but one hand reached up, then the other, and I was there. Gasping, I pulled myself onto the branch. That didn't use to be so much work. I made a note to add some cardio to my workout and stretching regimen.

You're not getting any younger, Lupul. The voice in my head could be a real asshole, but it wasn't wrong. There was no time to ponder my mortality, though. Malcolm Cromwell might very well be dying right then—if it wasn't already too late.

Any expectations about receiving immediate answers were dashed. From my roost, I saw a perfectly normal back yard; grass cut close, no furniture or grills. Backyard cookouts weren't part of the Sons' recruiting activities. They covered every window with thick, sad-looking blackout curtains. Nobody could see in, and I had no way of knowing how many people were in there, or who they were. That was no doubt intentional.

Under a wooden pergola sat about a dozen big cardboard grocery boxes, empty and stacked haphazardly. A whole pallet of bottled water sat next to it. Someone had stocked up. Was that because they had so many inhabitants, or were just planning to be there for a while? An unwelcome thought occurred to me. They could support a sizeable crowd in there.

Or withstand a siege.

For a moment, I toyed with going as far out on that branch as I could and jumping over the fence. With any luck, I'd stick a Marvel Hero three-point landing in the backyard. I remembered my luck and immediately ruled that out. Besides, Justin was still waiting for me, and I didn't want him getting proactive, which would happen if I took too long.

It would help to get inside, though. I needed to know what we were dealing with. I always did things alone. Now, everywhere I turned, someone else was involved. That bothered the hell out of me.

Shaggy picked up on the scuffling boots kicking through the undergrowth before I did. I stayed as still as possible, only my eyes scanning around frantically. I held my breath and did my best to look like a two-hundred-twenty-pound leaf. It took a moment to see the shadow. No, it wasn't a shadow, just someone really tall and dressed in black. With a shock of white hair.

Crap.

It was Raglan, striding my way. Shading his eyes, he looked up into the tree.

I said, "How's it going?" More to piss him off and stall than anything. Then gave an insincere smile and a little wave.

The "annoying him" thing worked, at least. He grunted and in that gravelly voice said, "The Master wants to see you."

"That's a coincidence. I want to see him. Give me a second." I closed my eyes and kept my hands hidden from view as they changed back into human form. I also bit back a scream because it hurt like a bastard. When the throbbing stopped, I gripped the branch, allowed myself to hang down, and did a decent impression of an Olympic gymnast dismount.

I was impressed with the maneuver. It was hard to tell what he thought because the big guy's stony face never changed. He nodded his head to the right and motioned for me to go ahead of him.

I thought about Justin being left alone in my car. Then I thought about the Charger left alone with Justin. Whatever was about to happen, I hoped it wouldn't take long.

CHAPTER 23

Raglan led me along the wall to a side gate hidden by shrubs. Without a word, he gestured me through. I gave him a sarcastic bow and passed into the yard. My smart-alecky attitude was intentional. I hoped it would irritate him enough to give something away. Or try something stupid. I could really use a chance to hit someone. With him being a couple of inches taller and leaner, it would be a decent scrap. Instead, his only response was a chest movement and grunt that may have been a quick chuckle or a hiccough. Hard to tell. His strong silent act was annoying but not as grating as that raspy voice, so sullen and mute would do for now.

I put a hand on the fence and stopped, looking back at him. "How did you know I was there?"

"He smelled your presence."

Oh, that explained everything.

We passed into a perfectly normal, boring suburban yard, hidden from the rest of the world. From down the block, Justin couldn't see in and know where I was. It was just as well. At worst, I'd be dead soon, spending eternity wondering what happened to my car. The best-case scenario was barely worth considering, given the odds. In a minute I'd know Francine and Cromwell were there, safe and they'd let us go in exchange for the Daemonolgie book. It was the infinite in-between possibilities that worried me.

Like a couple of kids home from school, we used the side door (complete with three deadbolts) to get into a mundane, Midwestern mudroom. From there I couldn't see into the house, but it was well lit and the babble of voices from the front room drew me. Then something stopped me short.

Blondie's hand on my shoulder kept me in place, but Shaggy damn near lost it after one good sniff. He growled a warning that shook my innards. My shoulder pressed against the wall, so it didn't knock me on my ass. Something horrible and nasty was in this house, and it was more than the original shag carpeting in the hallway.

The source of the problem wasn't my escort. There was nothing occult or other-worldly about Raglan other than the henchman/goon loyalty to his employer. I could deal with that. I'd succumbed to it myself over the past few months. After all, it was fealty to my employer that had me in the current mess.

Sure, I was worried about Cromwell, but Francine was my primary concern. I had to keep it together for her.

As soon as the basement door opened, a tsunami of supernatural funk rolled over us. Shaggy whimpered and growled as a thick oily rotten egg smell filled my nostrils. It was like a skunk's butthole with a touch of sulfur. Both hands clutched my gut. I bent over, fighting the urge to retch. The big guy just watched, bewildered.

"Seriously, dude? You don't smell that?" That almost got a response, but he said nothing. Whatever emitted that reek, it was on an olfactory wavelength the human nose couldn't detect. That was hard to believe, but it didn't seem to bother anyone else. There was serious bad juju at work in this house, and everyone was oblivious to it but me.

Still saying as little as possible, Raglan relieved me of my gun. That wasn't the fight I needed to have then, so I sucked it up. Breathing through clenched teeth, we descended a perfectly normal set of stairs to the basement. That led to a well-lit, spotless, tiled landing way with a corridor leading in two directions. To the left, a closed, ominously dark wood entrance had two oversized deadbolts.

In the other direction, the floor sloped several feet to a wooden door decorated with wrought iron straps and hinges. Orange-yellow light flickered around the frame. Through the funk, I smelled burnt string and beeswax. And skunk butt.

Nothing creepy about that at all. Move along.

"Are you going to stand there gawking, or will you come in?" I knew that voice. Fake English accent, loud baritone, with something a little shaky underneath. I was about to meet Matthew Hopkins face-to-face.

I wasn't sure how I felt about that.

It wouldn't do any good to let him know that, though. I literally gave my body a shake, then drew myself up as tall as I could. My escort did his silent "open the door and wave me through" act. As I walked past him, I noticed several long scratches on his neck, newly scabbed over and sore-looking. Whoever did that put up a hell of a fight, even if those nails weren't as nasty as the ones that scratched Cromwell's wall. I hadn't done it and wondered who did.

Cursing Malcolm Cromwell, I passed inside.

It was like stepping back in time. In contrast to the stale suburban motif of the rest of the house, this felt centuries old. Wall sconces held heavy candles that let off thick sooty smoke. The only nod to current health and safety standards was a large, noisy, smoke-catching duct system in the ceiling. It was the only twenty-first century feature in the room.

The walls were bare, stripped of any paintings or art, just plain white streaked with grey smoke stains. The wood beam ceiling looked much higher than a normal cellar. Whoever designed this had dug out and extended the usual floor plan. I doubted they had a city permit.

By an ornate fireplace sat a ginormous desk, easily rivalling Cromwell's in size but far fancier. It was hand-carved reddish hardwood, cherry maybe. I'm not an expert, but everything except the polished top was covered in hand-carved medieval symbols. I recognized Gargoyles and angels. There were also things I couldn't put a name to and didn't want to because they gave me the heebie-jeebies. The figures were perfectly rendered but felt...wrong.

Almost as big as the desk, and twice as fancy, was Hopkins' chair. Throne more like it. The back must have been six feet high, the arms a foot around, a thick red velvet cushion for a seat. I'm not sure it was ergonomically sound, but if the idea was to impress visitors, mission accomplished.

In that chair sat Matthew Hopkins. He wasn't dressed in the fancy suit I'd seen on the video. He was in more comfortable lounging garb. At least if you lived in the sixteenth century. Like the pictures in the library, he wore a black wool suit with a ruffly white shirt. Huge flowery cuffs nearly covered his hands, but they'd have to be huge fricking cuffs. He sat with those freakishly long fingers steepled in front of him. Hopkins spread his hands out towards me in welcome but didn't get up.

He enjoyed my stupefaction. When it was clear I would not start the conversation, he simply asked, "Did you bring the book?"

Oh right. This is all about that freaking book.

There was no choice but to BS my way through this. I stood as tall as I could. "No, sir. I told you I can't get in the vault without the code, and I'm not doing anything without knowing Mister Cromwell and his nurse are alive and well. I need proof of life."

"Such loyalty. They are alive, certainly. For now. As to well, that will depend on how quickly you give me what I seek."

"He's dying. Without that machine, he can't last long."

A rumbling chuckle came from down in Hopkins' chest. "One would think prayer might serve better than manmade machines, but this age lacks faith. More's the pity."

I didn't respond to his smug statement. "He's the only one with the combination. As you know, that's a hard room to get into. You tried, right?"

Hopkins unwrapped his hands and tapped an insanely long index finger on the desktop. It looked like his eyes got blacker for a split second, but maybe it was my imagination. After a second, he let a near-smile cross his lips. "Malcolm Cromwell is stronger than he looks. And he has compelling reasons for clinging to life. People who face what he does in the afterlife often do."

Whether he was the wall defacer or used someone else, he didn't give away the game. A shiver started at my tailbone, shot up and made my shoulders shake. *Focus, Johnny. One problem at a time.*

"What's so special about that book?"

The darkness oozed across his eyes. He paused, letting it pass before speaking again. "The book is a powerful weapon against the forces of darkness, and I require it to complete my task. There's much work still to be done. Beyond that, it's not for the likes of you to know, abomination."

I couldn't help myself. "The likes of me? Is that anything like 'you people?' I don't know how they did things in the before times, but you're not really supposed to say stuff like that anymore."

Hopkins knew I was stalling, trying to learn as much as I could. Despite my attempt to look cool and unbothered, the waves of putrid energy wafting off this guy made my eyes water and knees shake. The room became hellishly hot, and not just from the candles. It was hard to maintain my trademark smartass attitude when it took everything I had not to run puking and screaming from the room.

His palm slapped the tabletop, echoing through the room. That commanding voice dropped to a sibilant whisper. "I will speak as my conscience and my King command me. Now fetch me that book like a good lad."

Fetch. Again with the dog references. Shaggy growled, but I strangled the sound in my throat. Hopkins' nostrils flared but maintained outward calm. Crap. There was no sense starting something I couldn't finish. Moving too early would only get me, and probably a bunch of other people, dead.

I swallowed my pride. "Let me see them."

"They're safe. For now."

"He has the code to get into the safe room. I think I can get it from him. And I want your assurance you'll let him seek medical assistance soon as you have the book."

"You don't trust my word?" The idea amused the arrogant prick.

"Not even a little." A question occurred to me, and I had to ask, "By the way, how'd you do that thing with the rats? That was a seriously excellent trick."

He wasn't immune to flattery. Hopkins' shoulders relaxed, and he sat back with a smile. "Even the lowest vermin know when they're in the presence of greater power. A lesson you'd do well to learn."

"Some dogs take more training than others."

"I'll remember that." He turned to Raglan, who'd been lurking near the door. "Take him to them, then send him on his way. He has work to do."

The big guy stood, arms folded, and as close to the door as possible. Blondie nodded and waved me out.

Clearly, Raglan didn't want to be there either and was happy for an excuse to leave. That probably meant something, but I had no idea what it meant or how to use it.

The artificial light in the basement landing felt better than sunshine. At least I was back in the proper century. I rolled my shoulders and cricked my neck, shedding the weight of all that weirdness.

While I got my crap together, the big guy went about his business. He pulled out a keyring and sorted through it. The strikingly normal sound of keys jingling brought a familiar voice through the other door.

"You back for more, asshole? Let us go, and I'll take it easy on you."

Despite the sheer cluster-fuckness of the situation, I smiled. I had a pretty good idea who'd put those scratches on his neck.

I yelled through the door. "Making friends wherever you go, huh?"

"Johnny, is that you?" Her voice shook a little, and I could only imagine how hard she'd been working to hold it together.

Francine Ball was as relieved to hear my voice as I was hers. Thank God she was alive and kicking. Literally, from the looks of it.

Okay, now what smart guy?

CHAPTER 24

Snick-clunk. Snick-clunk. Snick-clunk.

The third lock popped open, and my escort reached for the handle. He put his head to the wooden door, took a deep breath and growled, "Stand back and don't do anything stupid."

The door opened, and I pushed past him into the semi-darkness. Faint light, obviously on a dimmer, revealed a sterile room with a white-tiled floor and two cots against the far wall. Francine stood at the foot of one bed, like an avenging angel. Her feet were apart in a fighting stance, arms crossed, eyes shooting daggers at the guy in black.

Malcolm Cromwell lay on the other cot, half buried under blankets. His watery eyes turned towards the door expectantly. Maybe I imagined the disappointment on his face when he saw who his rescuer was. The gargling groan he let out was all too real.

Francine and I locked eyes for a moment. I resisted the urge to run over and wrap her in my arms, but this was supposed to be about the old man. Plus, I didn't want them knowing we had any kind of personal connection. Better we were just two people working for the same old, rich, apparently doomed jerk. We both stood a little stiffer and straighter as I walked over to our boss.

We looked at each other briefly as I bent over the old man. "How is he?"

She glared at the guard. "Dying."

A faint voice from beside her rasped, "Like hell I am."

My heart ached to look at him. I didn't like the old bastard much, but he was my boss, and I had an obligation to do everything possible for him. "You can't die. You wouldn't be able to boss me around anymore."

He let out a single phlegm-laden laugh. "That's what you think."

I leaned close to Francine, hoping the big guy's hearing wasn't as good as mine. "How are you doing?"

She reached past me to pull the blanket higher over Cromwell. "Pissed right off. And worried about him. Fluid in his lungs, his wrists and ankles are swelling. Uremic poisoning." Her voice got louder so our guard could hear. "He needs to be in the hospital."

Jesus, he could really die here. Rage, confusion, helplessness all battled for control inside me.

"I need the entry code for the safe room. If that's where the book even is."

Francine nodded once. "It's there."

"Traitor," croaked the voice in the bed.

"Shush, you." Even Raglan raised an eyebrow at how she talked to Cromwell. He'd certainly never speak to his own boss that way. Of course, his Master was four hundred years old and capable of God-knows-what. Ours only seemed that way.

"You can't let him have that book." Fingers like chicken feet weakly gripped my arm. His wrist was swollen out of proportion to the rest of his emaciated arm.

I knelt lower, my back to Francine and Raglan. "What is he?"

Cromwell's eyes opened wide, his lips quivered, but all that came out was a wet cough that shook the entire cot and sucked the air from his body. Gobs of yuck flew through the air, landing on my cheek. I stayed calm and wiped my face on my sleeve. Three hacking spasms later, he lay panting, unable to say anything more.

Before he could give me the answer I desperately needed, Francine's iron grip latched onto my arm and pulled me close. "I have the code. Give them the fucking book so we can get him out of here."

I nodded and asked Blondie for a piece of paper and a pen. He resisted, thinking I could use it as a weapon, but I convinced him. "Do I look smart enough to remember 6 numbers?" That worked.

As he stepped out to get what we needed, I nodded at his broad, scratched neck. "Your work?"

Francine clicked her tongue, "Broke a fricking nail for nothing."

"I'll buy you a manicure when we get out of here."

She looked at me with watery eyes. "I'll hold you to it. But you have to paint my toenails. Again."

Our split second of humanity was interrupted by another spraying cough from our right. Pay *attention. You're working, Lupul.*

I took her hand in mine, looking at the broken fingernail. "How did it happen?"

"They showed up at the door. I don't know how they got past Justin…"

"He's outside, by the way. Worried sick."

She wasn't in a forgiving mood. "Anyway, Hopkins and the big mime show up and demand the book. Mister Cromwell refused. Next thing I know, we're getting sleepy."

"Sleepy? What do you mean?"

"I mean, one minute we're talking. Then Hopkins is waving those creepy fingers of his at us and we can't stay awake. Next thing I know, we woke up here."

"Same thing happened to Justin. He thought maybe this was all his fault, but… maybe not."

From across the room, a voice croaked, "He's not human."

That validated my gut feeling, but wasn't much to work on. "What is he?"

Cromwell beckoned me over.

Kneeling beside him, I patted his arm, trying to calm him. "I promise, sir. I'll get you out of here."

He dismissed my concern and swallowed enough air to speak. "Give the book to me. I'll deal with him."

The old codger was barely capable of inhaling and exhaling. *What's he going to do against whatever THAT is?* "What is he?"

"He's a—" Before he could tell me, a huge hand grabbed my shoulder.

Raglan said, "that's enough. Here's your pen."

I gave Cromwell a quick nod. That appeased him and he laid back on the cot, focused on something near the ceiling. The big guard thought about offering the pen and paper to Francine, but remembered pens could be pointy and gave them to me instead. "Let's go. You don't have much time."

I grunted, got the numbers from Francine, then repeated them to her just to double check. That earned me a hand squeeze that damn near snapped my fingers. It said everything she and I needed to say.

"I'll be back tonight, Sir." He nodded like he fully expected to be there when I got back. I wasn't as sure and swallowed a giant, mysterious lump lodged in my throat.

A rumbling bass voice muttered, "Clock's ticking, dog." He nearly flung me towards the door, and it took some work to stay on my feet. I wouldn't give him the satisfaction of falling, so I grabbed the banister and almost danced around the corner and up the stairs with him right on my heels. When we were nearly at the top, I heard Francine's voice.

"When this is over, I'm going to kick your ass, you big asshole." Then the door slammed shut.

I genuinely laughed. "Atta girl. I'll hold him for you." An enormous hand to my back pushed me through to the upstairs hallway and back to the twenty-first century.

Emerging from the basement, the burst of sunlight made my eyes squeeze shut. They opened when someone brushed against me. I opened them and found myself nose to nose with the skinny little dude from the library.

We gawked at each other for a moment. Eventually he squeaked out, "what are you doing here?"

Doing my best to sound calm, I shrugged. "Had a meeting with your boss."

His eyes flew open so wide the rest of his face nearly disappeared. "You met... the Master?"

"Yeah. Why?" Blondie was trying to hurry me out, but I braced my left boot against the baseboard and stood firm. "Just a second. I want my gun back."

"We didn't get properly introduced last time. I'm Johnny." I stuck my hand out and the skinny guy reflexively took it, offering a limp shake.

"Ted."

"Hey, Ted."

Our chat got interrupted. Raglan held out my Ruger with a warning visible in his icy blue eyes. He didn't have to worry. This close to the door, I wasn't likely to shoot my way out." It's okay, Ted'll walk me out of here, right?"

My new friend clearly wasn't enthusiastic about the idea. "Uh, yeah. I guess."

"Great." I grabbed his elbow and turned towards the living room. Screw Blondie. I was going out the front door so Justin could see me coming. With Ted at my heels, we strode through the living room. I counted five young guys, all in black, and a couple of civilians. All of them glared at me.

The closer the door was, the more Shaggy relaxed. The stench of sulfur and candle wax abated with each step. By the time I opened the front door and gulped in the fresh cool air, I believed we'd make it out of there in one piece.

Ted spoke over his shoulder. "I'll walk him to his car. Make sure he's really gone." Raglan must have agreed because my new friend led me down the front steps.

When we reached the sidewalk, Ted stopped and took a couple of deep breaths. He shivered and said, "You can't come back."

Didn't he know there were two kidnapping victims in the basement? "Don't have a choice. I need to bring Hop—your Master—something."

The color blanched from his face. He leaned in and said the last thing I expected to hear.

"Take me with you."

CHAPTER 25

My eyebrows were raised so high they almost flew off my face, and I gawked at Ted like he had three heads. "What are you talking about?"

The skinny nerd was snowman-pale and trembling. His voice was barely a whisper as he looked over his shoulder, then back at me. "Please. I have to—I can't—"

Before he could finish the sentence, his whole body spasmed once and stiffened. A noise more like the breath leaving his body than human speech escaped through his open mouth. Ted's eyes rolled up in his sweaty head. I had to grip his arm to keep him upright. The dude was having some kind of weird epileptic seizure.

"Whoa, Ted. Are you okay?" it was a stupid-ass question. If my nose could puke, it would have. The same foul funk I'd picked up in Hopkins' office hit me like a pickaxe. A shiver ran through Ted's body and his eyes changed color, from their normal blue to whatever hideous shade of black I'd seen in Hopkins' office. With a sudden jerk, he turned his face to mine and his teeth pulled back in a wicked, soul-freezing grin.

I let go and backed up, nearly going ass over breakfast down the stairs, but somehow staying upright.

A deep voice belched from between the poor sucker's clenched teeth and immobile face." You. Are. Wasting. Time. Dog." It was

Hopkins. And it wasn't. This voice was deeper, with an evil lisp. It felt like someone took a cheese grater up and down to the nerves in my spine.

In a shriek about two notes lower than a little girl's, I yelled, "What are you doing to him?"

What came out of Ted's face was supposed to be a chuckle. The body spasmed like a drunk marionette. "Making use of an otherwise useless vessel. Now bring. Me. My. Book."

Despite being deeply freaked out, it also pissed me off. Ted might be a weasel, but he didn't deserve whatever was happening to him. I acted on instinct and grabbed his thin arm and tugged, expecting him to come with me and make a break for it. Instead, the skinny nerd's arm flew up and backhanded me harder than I'd ever been hit before.

It sent me tumbling down the stairs. The way Ted's wrist instantly swelled and dangled from his arm; it was clear he'd fractured his hand on my face. You would never know from his stony expression.

"Save your master. Or this one. Choose."

From the bottom of the stairs, I looked up at whatever the hell Ted had become. My face stung, but I recovered some of my manhood. I bellowed at him, "What are you?"

His face turned stiffly to me and the voice within boomed, "I am the agent of vengeance and righteous wrath. Come to purge the world."

I believed him. Having no desire to be purged, I should have been making tracks. Problem was, he wasn't the only angry, vengeful thing there. Shaggy pounded on my temples to get out. Lycan energy rippled under my skin, and I wanted—needed—to shred whatever the thing was inside Ted. It would have been futile. Hopkins was manipulating the body by some nasty magical remote control. Tearing poor Ted to bits wouldn't solve the problem. Deep breaths sent Shaggy back into his hole, but only after a promise he'd get his turn.

"Lupul!" A voice from down the street filtered through the storm in my brain. Justin stood on the hood of the Charger, automatic pistol in his hands. Even from there, I could tell he had his warrior game face on and was looking for an excuse to kick ass.

I didn't know who he should shoot. There was too much potential collateral damage. Several other Sons of Hopkins and a couple of confused visitors stood on the stairs watching the freak show.

I considered several scenarios, but they all ended with someone dead—for sure Ted and probably me—and Francine and Cromwell still prisoner.

Over my shoulder, I yelled, "Be cool."

"What?"

"Stand down. I'm coming."

Justin lowered his weapon about two inches.

I returned focus to the thing on the stairs. The Ted-Hopkins mashup rumbled at me. "Bring me the book of King James. I may let you have this one as well." Then Ted's eyes rolled back and turned his normal color. His body crumpled, unconscious, to the ground.

Ted's head hit the stairs hard, and I lunged forward to help. So did a couple of his buddies on the porch. A familiar voice froze them where they stood. "Leave him."

Raglan left Ted lying there and went inside. The bystanders slowly joined him, although a couple of the normal folks thought twice about it. Eventually, I was alone on the sidewalk with Ted's unmoving body.

"You okay?" Justin yelled.

"Fine." I backed away from the house, afraid to turn my back. "And get the hell off my car."

The air was suddenly cool and clean again; the stench evaporated along with whatever had possessed Ted. I didn't know. I felt bad for the poor SOB, but he wasn't my primary concern. Francine and Cromwell needed me to get that book and get back while there was still time.

There was no negotiating, no room for clever bullshit. Just swap the book for two human beings.

When collecting debts for Meaghan's father, I occasionally had to deal with ugly negotiations that could have become hostage situations. They never did, because when it came down to it, people were inclined to stay alive and out of jail. Cool heads usually prevailed, and when they didn't, I was up to dealing with the situation. Humans were basically cowardly, self-protective, and didn't overthink things. That always made my job easier.

Ted's eyes stared at me accusingly. His colleagues just left him like so much garbage. It was his own fault. Not my problem. I didn't have time for this. I really didn't.

God damn it.

I let fly a string of curses a mile long and threw Ted's body over my shoulders in a fireman's carry. He was shockingly light and frail.

Trotting away from the Hopkins House, I shouted to Justin. "Start the fricking car."

CHAPTER 26

Adrenaline is a bitch. It makes your hands shake, tries to escape your body through the sweat glands, and sets your mouth into overdrive. It definitely doesn't help you order thoughts, keep your car on the road, or explain things in short sentences.

Eventually, though, Justin got the basic gist. "So, they're definitely in there?" I nodded while trying not to squeeze the steering wheel into powder.

"And we bring Hopkins the Demon-thingie book, then we get them back?" He couldn't stop looking over his shoulder at Ted slumped across the back seat.

"Theoretically. Yeah."

"So, why did you bring a dead body with you?"

"We don't know he's dead, dammit. I couldn't just leave him there." Justin reached back and placed two fingers on the body's throat, then turned back to me.

"Okay, first. He is. And yeah, you could. We don't have time for this."

He was right. I felt like an idiot, but felt compelled to defend myself. "I thought it was no man left behind."

"It's none of your *own men* left behind. The other guys can fucking rot where they fall."

I tilted the mirror down and studied the body with one eye while navigating traffic with the other. "He's really dead?" Justin nodded.

The skinny nerd was annoying as hell, but he didn't deserve this. As much as I'd wanted to deck him on at least two different occasions, nobody should have done to them what the Hopkins-thing did. I could have at least closed his eyes after throwing him in the back seat. His face was a terrible mask of fear. The lifeless eyes didn't help the overall effect.

I was wildly trying to come up with ideas. "Can we take him to a hospital, and just, I dunno? Leave him?"

Justin snorted. "You mean pull up in a black and orange Charger, in broad daylight, to a hospital with twenty-four-seven video surveillance, push him out and drive off? Yeah, that'll work."

When Jarhead Justin is the one making sense, you know you're at your breaking point. I shut my fat mouth and drove in silence. I seethed, hating a long list of people, including Justin, Ted, and Mister Cromwell. I reserved most of my loathing for myself.

Goddamit Lupul. Nice work as usual.

Justin squirmed in the silence. Finally, he asked, "Seriously, what were you thinking? Even if he was alive, what did you think was going to happen?"

"I don't know, okay? I thought maybe he'd know something about Hopkins we could use."

"What, like interrogate him?"

Justin nodded at the idea. "At least that I could have helped with. Sucks you can't question a corpse."

My opinion of Justin was improving. He and the rest of Francine's team helped me out in the past. Maybe I could use them again. "Uh, where did you take Koslov's body when, I, you know..." *When you all saved my ass by disposing of a dead werewolf that I turned in the first place?"*

"We took him to a lab the Boss Lady knew of. They wanted to know what kind of monster he... Oh crap. Sorry, dude."

I waved his apology away. I knew the basics: The Russian had been autopsied and broken down for parts as part of Cromwell's insane immortality scavenger hunt. It could have been me. Almost was. And once the video comes out, I'm sure everyone will want to know what kind of monster I am. I didn't take it personally.

The more people knew my secret, the more someone would try to figure out—literally—what I was made of. If Casper's readers loved "Alien Autopsy", imagine what kind of hell would break loose if they knew there'd been a Lycan on a table for real.

Casper. Crap.

I looked at my phone. There were seven messages, all from the Korean Jimmy Olsen. Maybe he found something useful about the book or Hopkins. Probably not, but it would take my mind off the corpse in the back seat and the lunkhead in the front.

Casper picked up on the first ring. "Bro. I was trying to reach you. "

"Been a little busy. Did you learn anything about the book? Or Hopkins?"

"Nothing that makes much sense. I was just talking to Zara about that and..." I heard something in the background. The dumbass had me on the speakerphone.

"Jeez, man. You got me on speaker? Take me off."

I didn't need any more people overhearing my conversations. *And who the hell's Zara?* I recalled she was part of Casper's paranormal posse. Muslim woman. She's the one that—

"Casper, is Zara there? Put me on speaker. Yeah, I know what I said, just...dude, come on."

I heard the reporter arguing with a female voice in the background.

"Zara? Are you there?"

"Yes. Why?"

"It's Johnny. Lupul. Listen, what you said your gift was. Can you really do that?"

"Mostly. Usually." Then she added suspiciously, "Why?"

Justin, bless his heart, was completely confused. I held up a finger to shoosh him. "I have someone I'd like you to talk with. Can you and Casper meet me at my place right away?"

She hesitated, then said, "I guess."

Casper chimed in. "It'll take us about half an hour. She'll, well we'll, be there."

"Great. Me too." I hung up before he could ask more questions. This wasn't the worst idea I'd had today, but was near the top of the list.

Justin had to ask, "Dude, what are you doing? We need to get the book and get Ball and Mr. Cromwell back. Mission critical. Remember?"

"This is mission critical. We might learn something important." I sped up. We needed to get back to my place before Zara and Casper arrived.

"Okay, but what are we doing at your place?"

I looked at him. "Okay, don't freak out. Promise?"

I took the corner to Wilson Street a little too fast for comfort and he gripped the door. "Dude. What are we doing?"

"We're going to interrogate a dead guy."

CHAPTER 27

Justin dumped Ted's body on my lumpy, thrift-store couch. "Like this?"

Like I knew what to do with him. "I guess so. I've never done this before." As an afterthought, I straightened Ted's legs so he at least looked comfortable.

A knock on the door at the top of the stairs startled the hell out of me. Crap. That could only be Bill, Gramma, or Meaghan. None of them were welcome right then. I shouted, "Not a good time. I'm busy."

The lock clicked, and the door opened anyway. Bill, then. It had to be important because usually he respected my privacy. He took three crutch-supported clunky steps down the stairs and said, "Dude, we need to talk about... Christ, is he dead?"

I lied, "No."

Justin didn't. "Uh, yeah. Who are you?" His hand inched closer to the gun in his belt.

Bill hesitated before answering in the coldest, flattest voice, "I'm his landlord. Who are you?"

I held both palms up in the universal sign for *everyone to chill the hell out.* "This is Justin. He works for Cromwell, too. We'll be out of here in less than an hour. Swear to God. We just need to do something first."

"Do what, an autopsy?" My friend wanted to scream at me but wasn't sure how the big Marine would respond. Instead, he sucked a long, slow breath through gritted teeth. "This is so not okay."

I moved to the bottom stairs and dropped my voice to a whisper. "Dude, I know this looks bad—"

He hissed back, "Ya think?"

"Yeah, I know. We'll talk about this soon as I can. You don't want to know what's going on any more than I want to tell you. Swear to God." I made my best puppy-dog eyes and telepathically sent a silent *please, please, pretty please with a cherry on top.*

"Oookay. But you, me, and Gramma need to talk. ASAP."

I dropped my head. This had been a long time coming. We all needed to talk about how messed up my life was getting and how continuing to live there impacted everyone else. In my defense, I was dealing with a dead body on my couch, a kidnapped boss, and a psychopath loose in the city. The timing wasn't ideal.

Bill bit his lower lip, gave Justin a cold side-eye, and nodded. My cheeks burned with the certainty I couldn't possibly foul things up worse. Being homeless seemed inevitable, but I could cope. Friendless was more terrifying. Bill hadn't taken one reluctant step up the stairs when there was a knock on the front door.

"Oh, come on," I said.

Justin had reverted to his usual shoot-first-as-questions-later self. He'd pulled his weapon and threw my door open in one deft move. His gun pointed straight into Casper's and Zara's blanched faces.

"Jeez, Justin. Be cool. These are the people I told you about." He grunted and lowered his weapon, took a step back, and waved them inside.

With the Korean reporter, the hijab-wearing woman, the ex-marine, Bill and me, there were more people in my apartment at one time than there had ever been. Fear, confusion, and exasperation were visible on everyone's face.

I turned to my best friend. "I'll explain everything, I promise. But you don't want to be here now."

He turned his back and crutch-thumped up the stairs. Without turning back to me, he yelled, "Unauthorized parties violate your lease." Then the door slammed shut.

Crap.

Casper was breathing and talking faster than he usually did. "Dude, what's going on? You said you needed Zara and me for something?"

"Oh, hell no." The woman stood beside my couch, looking down at Ted's body. Then she got an eyeful of Justin. "And who's this *abn al kalb*? Her back stiffened and hands clenched. I got the feeling this wasn't her first run-in with an armed American. Justin squinted back. He understood her just fine.

Justin always refused to tell me where he'd served, but I got a pretty good clue when he held his hands up, gun in hand, and said, *"Ana sadiq."*

Zara's dark eyes flashed with pure fury. "Friend, my ass." Then she turned her fury on Casper. "What have you dragged me into now?"

Clearly, I hadn't planned this well, but needed to regain control. "It's not Casper's fault. I asked for you, Zara. I need your help. Please. I wouldn't ask if it wasn't important."

She knitted her brows and scowled. Then she nodded her chin at Ted. "Who is he?"

"He's a witness. To a kidnapping. My boss and a, a friend. "

"Really?"

I moved away from the stairs. "Yeah. He knows all about the guy who did it. He can help us rescue my friends and stop a killer."

"What happened to him?" Her voice was calmer now. There was a chance she'd really do it.

Your guess is as good as mine. "I'm not sure. One minute he was possessed by—something. I don't know. Next minute he was like this. I need to know what we're dealing with. If Casper believes in you, then you're the real deal. Please."

Zara looked from me to the silent, sweating reporter and back. "I don't even know if I can do this. I only ever... talk... to people I know. Knew. I don't suppose he spoke Arabic."

"I doubt it. Sorry."

She averted her eyes and stared at the wall for an eternity and a half. Then she let out an exasperated breath. "Fine. Yeah, I'll try. But that one stays the hell away from me."

Justin acknowledged my nod and put his hands up. He then backed as far as he could until he was leaning against the kitchen sink. He stuck the gun in his belt, then raised his hands again. "Cool with me. I don't know what's happening, anyway."

Moving closer and staying as calm as I could, I asked, "What do you need, Zara? How can we help?" Not only did I not know the procedure in cases like this, I knew my Lycan-self often played havoc with anything paranormal. I'd messed up enough situations simply by being in the room and the stakes here were too high.

She never took her eyes off the corpse on my couch. After several slow, deep breaths, she shook her shoulders and shook out her arms and hands. "Everyone just keep back."

I gestured a shaking Casper to one dining room chair and gestured Justin to the other. Thinking I could be useful, I moved towards Zara, but she held her palm up. I mutely plunked down on the arm of my recliner.

The only sound was Gramma's tv filtering through the ceiling. Zara tugged at her purple hijab, then knelt beside the corpse. She stretched her arms and lowered her head in a prayer position and muttered in what I assumed to be Arabic.

From the corner of my eye, I spotted Casper raising his phone. "Don't even think about it," I growled. He whined a bit, then pouted and laid the phone face down on the table.

Zara bowed to the floor, then back to a kneeling position several times. At last, with shaking hands, she reached out and stroked Ted's forehead tenderly. I felt like I was intruding on an intimate moment. She spoke to him and caressed the body like he was a relative. Or a lover. I wondered if anyone ever touched him that way when he was alive.

Christ only knows how long it was before anything broke the silence. Her prayers grew louder, then she halted. In English, she asked, "What is your name?" With a tilt of her head, she listened to something nobody else in the room could hear. "Hello Ted, my name is Zara. Yes, that's right."

Suddenly, she grabbed his hand. "Don't be afraid. You're in *barzack*. The land in-between." Listening carefully, she muttered something soothing. "I will help you to Paradise, but we must ask you some questions first. Is that alright? It is very important."

She looked at me and raised an eyebrow. It was showtime.

Quietly as possible, I said, "Ask him why he was with Hopkins."

At the mention of the name, Zara gasped loudly and clutched her hands to her ears, like she was trying to stifle a scream. "No, Ted. Shhh. Shush. He can't touch you here. You're safe from him. Forever."

Ted must have been putting up an argument with her because there was a flurry of Arabic and English words that made no sense. Zara struggled and sweat broke out on her forehead. Her breath was ragged, fast, and shallow.

For my benefit she said, "His... master.... It's stupid...Is an *ifrit*. Ted calls him a demon."

My heart sank. I suspected as much, but confirmation didn't make me feel better. "Ask him why he wants the book."

Zara shook her head and shouted in Arabic. Then, "No. You have to talk through me, Ted. No. No, you can't..."

"Zara, are you alright?"

She couldn't answer. The woman's body spasmed like she was struck by lightning. Her mouth opened several times, and she clutched at her throat like she was choking. The terror in her eyes was horrible to behold. Tears streamed down her sweating cheeks as a familiar male voice screamed from within her and through her mouth.

"Luuupulll, help me."

"Ted?"

Zara's eyes were wide with panic. She pounded her fist on Ted's chest, hoping to cut off this unfamiliar voice. Unsure of what was happening, all I knew was this wasn't how it was supposed to go. Zara was powerless, as Ted claimed her body as his own vessel.

"Ted, let her go."

Zara/Ted shook her head. "I have to talk to you before it's too late. Listen to meeee."

I motioned with my hands for everyone to stay cool. As calmly as possible, I said, "Okay, but don't hurt her, Ted. I'm listening. What is it?"

Ted's voice was shaky but clear. "He is a demon. Straight from hell."

"But what does he want with the book? Why is he pretending to be Hopkins?"

The voice paused, then the words vomited out so quickly I could barely make any sense of them.

"Hopkins—the real Hopkins — defeated the demon using the book and bound him for four hundred years. Now he's finally free and seeks to rule. He pretended to be Hopkins because he needs a human form."

"If he's so powerful, why does he need the book?"

Zara's body shook. Sweat and tears streamed down her face. "The first book, the real book, contains the binding spell. If he destroys it, no one will ever be able to stop him again. You can't let him have it."

My brain hurt as I tried processing everything. "But why would a demon want to raise and bind other demons?"

"He's raising an army. Then he'll destroy the book so no one can stop him. He can't have that book. Don't let him have it."

"Okay, so..." A shriek cut me off. Zara's head convulsed side to side.

"No. I can't stay. Tell her to let me go. It's the only way I'll be free of him."

"Yeah, okay. But..."

"LET. ME. GO" Ted's frightened, furious spirit screamed. Zara twitched and writhed in agony. Her arms clutched at her stomach as she rocked back and forth. I had so many questions, but the woman's suffering was palpable, as was Ted's desire to be free.

Shaggy howled inside my head, picking up on the insane energy in the room. I growled and smacked my forehead over and over, trying to clear it. Zara was lying on her side, panting and gasping. There was so much more I needed to know, but at what price?

The voice added, like an afterthought, "He fears you because he can't control the thing inside you. Evil can't defend against evil." There was a soul-fracturing scream. "Tell the bitch to let me go."

I couldn't watch Zara's soul and body be violated any more. "Okay. Jesus Christ, Ted. Stop. Let her go. Let her go. Please, Ted. Zara, set him free."

There was a scream in Ted's male voice, which evolved into a female wail. Whether it was Zara claiming her power or Ted surrendering, her body spasmed one last time. Then Zara fell to her side and retched loudly. In seconds, I held her soaked, shaking body in my arms. I pressed her to my chest, rocking her, hoping the spasms would stop. *Jesus, Lupul, what have you done?*

Zara's body stiffened, then relaxed. Her eyes rolled into her head and she collapsed. After several agonizing seconds, she gasped twice.

"Are you okay?"

Instead of an answer, she squirmed out of my grasp and slapped me. Hard. "What the fuck was that? What did you do to me, you fucking freak?" Blows landed with each word. I knelt there and took it until her arms were tired.

"I didn't do anything. Zara, I swear."

Between giant, snotty sobs, she ranted at me. "It's not supposed to work that way. He fucking took me over. It was like being raped from the inside out. Can you imagine what that's like, you asshole?" I knew what it was like to cede control to something inside you. I could only imagine how violated she must have felt.

"I'm sorry, I didn't know. I didn't know this would happen." Tears ran down my own cheeks and I held my arms out to hug her, but she recoiled. The woman could never know how sorry I was. Not that it mattered. I'd screwed up someone else's life. Didn't even have a lot to show for it.

Zara turned her rate to Casper. She pulled her scarf tight around her head and scrambled to her feet. "You set me up, motherfucker. How could you do that to me?"

"I'm sorry. Zara. So sorry. What can I do?" Casper was pale and looked about to puke.

"Get me out of here and never talk to me again. You selfish, self-centered prick."

Zara took one last look at the three of us, then ran out the door.

Casper picked up his phone. "I guess I should help her. Still, that was the coolest—"

"Get out," I yelled at him. "Make sure she's okay. Tell her you're sorry. I never meant to, for any of this to happen to her."

When Casper was out the door, I collapsed in my recliner. I'd completely forgotten about Justin until he spoke. "Dude, that was intense."

"You think?" I paced and shook and cursed myself until his huge hand clamped down on my shoulder.

A million questions ping-ponged around my brain. *What did he do to her? What kind of demon was Hopkins then, and what did Ted mean, the first book?*

I paced circles around my apartment. "Oh shit. What have I done? How did I think I was smart enough to get everyone out of this? I've freaking killed them. All of them."

In a firm voice, Justin ordered, "Cut the crap. Focus on the mission. We need to get that book and get them back."

I nodded. "Yeah. Okay. You're right. Thanks."

"One more thing. I know what to do with the body."

CHAPTER 28

I held what remained of Ted under his arms, and Justin took his feet. We carried him out of my apartment to the driveway. The body was going into the trunk this time. One last indignity for someone who endured too many of them. I didn't kill him, so why did I feel so awful?

Could you make more of a mess, Lupul?

I slammed the trunk. "Now, where did you say we were taking him?"

Justin said nothing. He stood there and stared at me. Well, over my left shoulder.

Gramma's voice croaked, "I'm guessing it's not a hospital."

I didn't even face her, just dropped my chin to my chest. *I don't have time for this. The clock is ticking.* "It's not what you think. I didn't kill him."

Justin didn't know what to do. I motioned to the car. He was grateful to be out of the line of fire and scooted to the passenger side and shut the door. The marine knew better than to mess with a pissed off old woman. I didn't have a choice.

Shamefaced, I turned to Gramma. She clucked her tongue and, in a soft voice, said, "It's getting worse, isn't it? Don't look at me like that. The chaos, the darkness. The crazy. You're getting sucked under. Like I said, you would, if you weren't careful."

"I, I never meant to—"

"Jesus Murphy. I. Me. It's not all about you, idiot. You've got Bill, Meaghan, even me involved. Plus, that big hunk of cheesecake, whoever he is. Nice ass. Doesn't look much for brains though. Not to mention your, uh, cargo there. Not that I saw nothing."

"What am I supposed to do, Gramma?" I knew I was whining.

She shook her head. "I don't know, kid. But you can't go on like this. You're gonna get someone else killed. Yourself most likely. We all see it."

All of them. Bill, her, maybe Meaghan on a good day. Only three people on earth gave a rat's ass about me, and they were looking for the exits. Not that I blamed them.

"You know he's serious, right? You can't stay here forever. Not so much for himself, although I wish he had more sense than that. But I'm his family. He loves you, we all do. But if he has to make a choice..."

"Maybe he doesn't."

"He does. And I'm family. *Rat niamo.* Blood family. *B*lood means something."

Blood. There would be more blood on my hands if I didn't get out of here. Francine's or Cromwell's to start. "I wouldn't know," I snapped.

"No, you wouldn't. You have family but..."

"They never understood me."

Gramma put a wrinkled hand on my shoulder. I shrugged it off like a petulant child. She leveled her gaze. "Jim and Eileen? No, they never did. But you can't really blame them. They knew nothing about you. Or him, for that matter." She'd developed the habit of referring to Shaggy as another person. Like everyone did. It was a way not to blame me for the worst things that happened in my life. "Not that they didn't try. Hell, I know exactly what you're dealing with and I'm out of ideas. We've done all we can. Maybe you need to look to your own blood for answers."

The words erupted from my belly before I could stop them. "I don't have any. You and Bill. You're the only family I have."

"But we're not blood, kid. Much as we love you, you're *rakli.*"

It would hurt less if she'd shot me. After everything we'd been through, in the end, I was a non-gypsy. A *gorger.* "I don't—" My eyes were hot and blurry. A huge wad of something in my throat turned my voice to a bullfrog's croak.

The hand went back to my bicep and squeezed gently. "Yeah, you do. Not here. In the old country. Maybe the answers are there. With your own... people." At least she didn't say your own kind. I'm not sure I could have taken that.

My own people.

Cluj. Romania.

The same people who tossed me in an infectious AIDS ward to be sold off like a rescue poodle to a good home.

"I'll take my chances."

"Fine. But Bill won't. Not for much longer. I know I don't have much time left, but he's going to protect me til the end. We're all we have is each other."

I pulled my head out of my ass for a minute. "Wait. Are you, you know?"

She released my arm and swatted me. "Do I look like I'm dying? Not like it's going to happen tomorrow. But it's basic math, isn't it?"

My only response was a big, snotty sniff. Looking back to the car, Justin's eyes were reflected in the rearview mirror, pretending like he wasn't watching. "I've got to go. If I don't, people... more people...are going to die."

Gramma nodded and rubbed my sleeve affectionately. Her hands were crepey and two big liver spots adorned her wrist. I'd never noticed them before. *Christ, has she gotten that old in the last ten minutes?* "Yeah, do what you've gotta. But this has to end, kid."

I stared down at her. My eyes welled up and my brain and mouth wouldn't form coherent words. "I..." was the best I could do.

"Yeah, me too. Now get the hell out of here. He's not going to stay fresh forever."

She turned, almost lost her balance, then marched up the building's front stairs and went inside without looking back.

I slammed my palms on the Charger's trunk. "Fuck." Justin found something out of his window fascinating enough to avoid meeting my eyes.

The Charger roared to life. I revved the engine three times just to blow off steam, then threw it in reverse and bounced into the street.

We were two stop signs away from home when I finally spoke to him. "Okay, what do we do with Ted?"

CHAPTER 29

"It's the Hummer over there."

Justin drove a giant desert-camo war beast with a "Semper Fi" sticker in the back window. Of course he did. My *muy macho* Charger looked like a Mini-Cooper next to the damned thing.

It was nearly dark in the alley back of Cromwell's fancy lakefront apartment building. I stepped out and scanned for prying eyes. When I was sure no one was watching, I popped the trunk.

Without hesitating, Justin scooped Ted's body in his arms and transferred it to the back of his vehicle. Something fell to the ground, and I snatched it up. It was Ted's wallet. The last thing we needed was to leave evidence lying around.

It was a little late to worry about his privacy or respecting boundaries, so I flipped it open. The expired Ohio driver's license was in the name of Theodore Hermann Wallich. Age twenty-five. *Theodore Herman. Damn, even his parents hated him. The poor bastard never really had a chance, did he?*

Justin motioned for the wallet. I slapped it into his palm. "Where are you taking him?"

"Miss Ball has a guy."

I knew she did. The same guy who did the werewolf autopsy on Kozlov. Or ran the blood tests on me without permission. A chill ran up my spine like an icy xylophone. Even after all we'd been through together, Francine Ball scared me more than I wanted to admit. I'd deal with that later. After we got her and Cromwell back.

Justin handed me a key fob. "For the building." Then the big jarhead fished in his pocket for car keys and bounced them in his palm. "Okay, let's do this."

Strangely, I didn't want him to go. We didn't like each other much, but being alone for the rest of this madness bothered me more than having the big lunkhead around.

"Yeah, okay." We nodded, all manly-like, to each other. Then he climbed into the Hummer and fired it up. I watched him pull down the alley until the red lights disappeared into traffic. A stiff wind blew my coat open, and I pulled the flannel tighter around myself.

The afternoon sun was getting lower. It had already been, what, three hours? The knot in my stomach pulled even tighter than I imagined possible.

Five long minutes later, I stood in my boss's cavernous empty penthouse. The first thing I did was flip on every light I could find. They weren't necessary, what with my Lycan-assisted eyes, but it made me feel slightly better. The reek in Cromwell's office had almost dissipated, and Shaggy was pretty much quiet, so I was alone. All alone. Again.

The three jagged claw marks on the wall reminded me of what waited for me.

Cromwell's panic room sat behind the mahogany wall panel to the left of his desk. I reached under the desktop to push the button. With a hiss of air, the panel popped open. Shaggy gave a wary moan as I opened the door and he got a vibe of what lay inside. Powerful psychic objects and small spaces were two of his least favorite things, and we were walking right into both.

Easy, big guy, we're just getting the book and getting out of here. I promise.

Fumbling through the code on the keypad, LED lights that were way too bright for the space zapped to life. I blinked stupidly until my eyes adjusted properly. Shelves ran along three of the walls. One was stocked floor to ceiling with everything you'd want to eat or drink while locked in a bunker waiting for rescue. Ignoring the French champagne, I grabbed a room-temperature bottle of sparkling water, twisted the cap off, and chugged half of it in one go. Being scared spitless was thirsty work.

The other shelves were nearly bare. We'd sent a load of relics to the Archives only last week. The only things remaining were some old boxes of business records, and maybe a dozen ornate boxes and chests of varying styles. Most were the wrong size or shape to hold a book, even a big one. All but the two identical cases on the middle rack, right-hand wall.

I moved towards them, but Shaggy stopped me short. This close to the moon, he might be overly sensitive, but I doubted it. He could sniff enough danger to raise his hackles, which told me we were in the right spot. The book chests were identical in every way. They had lids of dark, dry leather with an enormous cross embossed in something—probably gold. The carrying cases for these stupid books cost more than I made.

Each had brass hinges, recently oiled and polished from the smell of them. A thick hasp and pin kept the chests shut. If there had been actual locks or keys, they weren't anywhere around. *Has Cromwell been going through them lately?* As obsessed about his pending mortality as he was, and knowing Hopkins was after the books, I wouldn't put it past him. And he seemed confident he knew what to do if he could only get his hands on the book.

The boxes were unlocked. I flipped them both open and ran a shaking finger over the tooled leather, examining them both. Gold leaf around the edges and jewels I didn't recognize were set in each of the four corners. No wonder Hopkins wanted his creepy hands on the damned thing. He could sell both books for millions.

Correction. Cromwell wanted the *right* book. That meant Hopkins wanted the contents, not the fancy cover. Expensive as it was, one of these purely decorative. Useless.

But which one was which?

The boss admitted one of them was fake, or at least not as valuable as the other. I flipped pages, hoping the answer was obvious, but couldn't see a damn bit of difference between the two. I didn't read Latin, and the old-time print may as well have been hieroglyphics for all the good it did me.

It was when I flipped through the second book that Shaggy offered his opinion. The deeper I got into the book on my right, the more he resisted. It wouldn't stand up in court, but was enough evidence for me. That was the real Daemonologie.

A buzzing in my pocket caught me by surprise and damn near sent me through the roof. Pulling my phone out, I prayed it was Justin.

My unanswered prayer streak was unbroken. It was Casper.

I could only handle one problem at a time. My phone went back into my pocket. His timing sucked. I needed brainpower, not conversation. Ordinarily, I'd have called on Bill's accountant brain to help me puzzle things out, but he was in no mood to help, and I didn't want him dragged into this, anyway. That was yet another thing to deal with.

If I lived through tonight, I'd have a hell of a to-do list.

Stepping back into the office calmed Shaggy enough to gain control of my brain for all the good that would do me. Breathing easier, I dropped my butt into Cromwell's chair.

Doodling often helped me gather my thoughts, so I grabbed a pen and a notepad. The three-hundred-dollar Mont Blanc floated over the page while I made three columns: what I knew, what I guessed, and what I had no damned idea about. One column was way longer than the others.

What did I really know?

Fact number one: I was up against a real honest-to-God demon. Hopkins was no joke, and what was one hairy idiot against something that nasty?

Next on the list, he had Francine and Mr. Cromwell. That should have been number one, but to be fair, a demon was a pretty big deal.

Francine was tough, but the old man needed to get to a hospital. He needed a doctor and a dialysis machine. First, we had to get him out of that basement.

Finally, there was the matter of having two nearly identical books. I had a pretty good idea which was the original, but it was still a guess. Ted said there was some spell in the original book that could control the demon. Cromwell said he knew how to use it. That was the good news. It meant getting the book to the old man instead of Hopkins. That wouldn't go over well with the long-fingered freak.

What if I could get the original book to Cromwell and the fake to Hopkins? When Hopkins found out I gave him a fake? The demon would gut me with one fingernail. Not a great option. The more I thought about it, the dumber it sounded. But if Cromwell could use the binding spell quickly enough, I'd only have to keep the Witchfinder busy until the spell was cast.

It would be easier if someone could deliver the Daemonolgie to Cromwell while I distracted Hopkins. Bill wouldn't be much help with his bum leg. I didn't know where Justin was or when he'd be back. *Who's dumb enough to waltz into a nest of demons with me?*

My phone buzzed again with the answer to the question. This time I answered.

"Casper! Bro, I was just thinking about you."

CHAPTER 30

Casper had never been in a real penthouse before. He stood with his mouth open, gaping around at the desk, the shelves, and the open panic room ahead of us. Impressed though he was, the guy was considerably less excited than a few moments ago. He'd gotten there as fast as his Uber could manage. After hearing my brilliant plan, he wished he hadn't. I didn't blame him a bit. It was my idea, and I thought it was idiotic. Suicidal, in fact.

"I still can't get hold of Zara. She's really freaked out."

"I know, and I feel awful. But there was no other way. Don't you want to help rescue people instead of just writing about it? You gotta break eggs for omelets, right? You can make it up to her."

I hated myself more than he knew. There was no forgiving—let alone atoning—for what I'd done to her.

"Okay. Let's say I do it. You want me to what, now?"

"You get the actual book to Cromwell while I take the fake to the... to Hopkins. Soon as he has the book, he lets us all go..." I laid out the scheme, speaking calmly and slowly, so it didn't sound like the ravings of a madman. "Easy peasy, right?"

"And he's going to just hand them over when he gets the book?"

"He gave his word." The words stuck in my throat.

"The word of an ancient soul-sucking demon lord?"

Casper was only half-listening. He shifted his weight to one foot, making it easier to peer inside the safe room. His curiosity battled with his good sense. I needed to make sure his good sense lost out.

"Want to see them?"

"An original Daemonologie? Dude, are you kidding?" My cheeks burned at the greedy look in his eye, but I wasn't above exploiting it for a good cause.

"Over here. See?"

I maneuvered him in front of the book chests. With shaking hands, he reached out, then stopped, hovering over the books. "Which one is the original?"

"This one I think." I pointed to the book on the right.

"You think? You don't know?"

"Pretty sure. It would be easier if I could read them. You don't read Latin, do you?"

"Latin? Dude, I can't even read cursive." He studied the books and scrunched his eyes. "What's the difference?"

"Apparently, there're spells in the first one that got deleted from the newer version. You heard Ted. Whatever the real Hopkins did to bind the demon, it's in one book and not in the other. So's the ability to release them from that binding. Maybe the real Hopkins and King James felt it should stay a secret. Other than that, I don't know." Casper didn't know how much power Shaggy had in my decision making these days. It was best to let him think I was large and in charge. "Call it a hunch."

"And when you show up with me, how are you going to explain that? 'Hi, this is my friend the blogger. Mind if he tags along?'"

Details. Details. Casper couldn't hear the clock ticking like I could. I left The Sons of Matthew Hopkins' clubhouse over three hours ago. Cromwell might be dead already, which would ruin our only chance to use the book against Hopkins.

My boy was right about one thing. I didn't need a reporter. I needed a doctor, but you go with what you got. And as for Francine, if we didn't get her out of there, it was only a matter of time before she tried something desperate that could get them both—hell, all of us, killed.

I took a step back and stared at the wall. The hazy outer edges of an idea coalesced in my overworked mind. I had a beginning and an outcome in mind. The middle part where the details lived was still foggy. We needed a medical professional. What we had was Casper Pak.

"Casper, Could you pretend to be a doctor?"

"Huh? Yeah, but who'd believe it?"

Raglan had already proven he was a racist asshole. A chubby Asian might look exactly like a doctor to him. And Hopkins. There weren't a lot of Koreans in Restoration England. He might buy it, at least long enough to get Cromwell the book. I sized up my partner. Fortunately, His khakis and polo ensemble looked like he might have just come off the golf course. That worked. Another piece of my half-assed plan snapped into place.

I got an incoming text from Francine's phone.

Francine

Where are you? Time's running out.

I didn't know if she'd sent it or not, but it didn't matter. If we were going to save them, there was no time to come up with Plan B.

"This is the only way, man."

As my dark side expected, Casper's curiosity won out. "Won't I need, like, I don't know, a stethoscope or something?"

He had a point. If only we had a medical kit like they used to have in old movies when people made house calls. I didn't even know if they still made them. I'd only ever seen one of them in my life, and that was Francine's.

Francine's bag. Holy crap.

I grabbed his sleeve. "Come with me." We hurried out of the panic room, through the office and down a corridor to the little spare bedroom/office Francine used. There, on the shelf where I'd seen it last, was her black leather medical bag. I grabbed it, slammed it down on the desk, and popped the latch.

While I cackled like a maniac, Casper suspiciously asked, "What are you doing?"

"Being brilliant. Look, a full medical kit." I showed him a stethoscope, blood pressure cuff and a couple of stainless-steel things I couldn't name. There were also two long red scarves Francine had used on me when she stopped by my place once. I stuffed those in my pocket and kept digging around. Ignoring Casper's nonstop questions, I kept foraging. The bottom of the bag had a plastic pad that sat on top of the bag's real bottom.

Perfect.

Once Casper stopped sputtering, I laid out my plan. We'd slip the original Daemonologie into the bottom of the bag and put the pad over it. As long as nobody dug around in there, we should be able to get Francine some help keeping Cromwell alive while getting the book into the old man's hands.

"That's a big if," Casper said. He wasn't wrong, but there was no time for logic or common sense.

"They'll be so busy looking at the book I'm carrying to worry about it." I said with more confidence than the plan deserved.

Casper's face relaxed a tad. He was falling for it. A little more encouragement might be in order. "And think of the story it will make."

"The exclusive, right?"

"Who else is gonna write it, me? This is all yours, buddy."

His face lit up at that word. Damn me. "Fuck yeah, let's do this."

I felt horrible about manipulating him like that, but options were scarce. I looked down at my phone. There was no more time to worry about it.

"Let's do it." He held his hand up for a high five. I hesitated before obliging.

I grabbed my phone and texted back.

Me

On my way.

CHAPTER 31

Night of the full moon.

The nearly full moon wasn't up yet, but I felt Shaggy swim through my veins like a shark looking for something to chomp on. My hands wouldn't stop shaking, so I gripped the steering wheel harder.

Casper and I sat in the Charger a block down the street from Hopkins' creepy house. Since the most useless words in the English language are, "Johnny has an idea," I needed to make sure we had a contingency plan. "Look, this is going to work, but if something goes sideways—"

Casper was in no mood for hypotheticals. "Dude, you said this was foolproof."

"No. I said I was almost positive. But look, if something blows up, the most important thing you can do is get Mr. Cromwell and Nurse Ball out of there. And you, of course. Just get the three of you out of there."

"What about you?"

If it's gone that wrong, I'm demon chow and won't have to worry about anything else. All I can hope is he takes so long to eat me that there's time for them to get away. "I'll be fine. Don't worry about me."

That didn't provide the reassurance Casper needed. None of this was going to work if I couldn't keep him focused on the mission at hand. I was freaking out enough for the both of us.

"Okay, tell me again. Who are you?"

"Doctor Pak. Kidney specialist. Necrologist."

I slammed my palm on the steering wheel and in a voice that was part jangled nerves and part werewolf snapped at him. "Nephrologist, dammit. Come on, man, you gotta get this right."

His voice shook. "Jesus. Alright, nephrologist. I bring the bag in and give it to the nurse and pretend to check out Mister Cromwell. What about the guard?"

"I'll take Raglan with me. He'll want to watch me give the book to Hopkins. He's not missing the chance to see me crawl. You just get Francine what she needs and stay safe."

Casper let out a slow breath and stared out the windshield. "Safe? In a house with a giant, monster demon? Check." Well, put that way, it sounded stupid, but his curiosity and desire to help me overrode his good sense. And I was letting him do it.

Not for the first time, I thought about how much I sucked as a person.

I slapped the steering wheel one last time. "Let's do this." We stepped out of the car and into the chilly dusk. I held the second decoy book under one arm. Shaking like a leaf, Casper put one foot in front of the other, clutching the black medical bag to his chest.

My hearing was so amped up I couldn't help but hear Casper's heart pounded like it wanted to make a getaway through his ribs.

Why do you always put people who trust you in danger, Lupul? When are you going to get someone you care about killed?

There was no time left for self-flagellation. From the bottom of the stairs, I looked at the house. It was dark and quiet, which increased the creep factor. At least they'd gotten rid of the wannabes, so there was less chance of witnesses or collateral damage.

Before our feet hit the first step, the front door flew open. Raglan glared down at us; arms folded across his chest. Behind him stood another, younger guy dressed all in black. Ted's replacement, no doubt.

That sandpaper voice rasped, "Who's this?"

From the corner of my mouth, I whispered to Casper. "Keep going."

I talked and walked up the steps. "He's a doctor. For the old man. Don't worry, I have your book." I waved the second book around like it was nothing. "Who's your little friend? I'm Johnny Lupul. You are...?"

The new Ted was dumbfounded that I'd spoken to him, but croaked out, "Don. Donald." Then Raglan cut him off.

"He's not coming in," he said, nodding his chin at Casper.

Before I could come up with some brilliant answer, I heard a voice next to me, like Casper's only way more confident.

"Look, I don't know who you are, and I don't care. I'm Casper Pak. Doctor Casper Pak, to you. I'm a nephrologist from Northwestern and I'm here to make sure he's not trading the book for a dead man. Let me in so I can keep the old bastard alive and stay the hell out of my way."

Raglan looked more surprised than I did. He hesitated just long enough to make my bladder flex, then looked at me. "You have the book?"

I held it up but made it clear I wasn't handing it over yet. The big henchman hesitated just long enough for my butt to clench, then nodded and waved us in.

As we passed through the door, I whispered, "Jesus, where'd that come from?"

Casper said, "My cousin's a doctor. Huge douchebag. My mother thinks the sun shines out his ass." Then he grinned and yelled at the slow-moving Raglan's back, "Let's go. We don't have all day."

"Don't get cocky, kid." The Han Solo reference warmed his nerd's heart.

With each step, Shaggy's agitation increased. Breathing deeply, I kept him more-or-less calm. *Hold on. I'm going to need you soon, big guy.*

When we arrived at the bottom of the stairs, Raglan held up his hand and nodded to Donald. The younger man knocked tentatively, unlocked the door and said, "Stand back. We're coming in." Then he pushed it open and stood aside. Raglan stomped inside first, then me. It took a very dirty look to convince Casper to follow. He steeled himself and stepped inside, white-knuckling the medical bag. His breathing was short and rapid, almost hyperventilating.

Francine stood against the back wall, defiance blazing out of her eyes, but it was clear she was exhausted. Completely drained. Her dark hair hung limp and damp, and she had bags under her eyes that could carry groceries. Next to her on the cot, a frail body wheezed and moaned. The room smelled like urine and rot. My heart sank. We were probably too late. I stood there, useless.

As usual, Francine recovered first. "Who's he?"

I needed to exert some control over the situation if we had any chance of pulling it off. I drew on my massive reservoir of bullshit and bravado. I locked eyes with the nurse to make sure she was paying attention. "That's Doctor Pak. He's brought his medical kit. Thought you might need some help. Everything you need is in there." My eyes darted to the kit and back to her face, hoping she was following along. She recognized her own bag and gave an imperceptible nod.

"Ooookay. Over here, Doctor." She motioned to the patient. Clearly, she only had the faintest idea of what I was trying to do, but had enough faith in me to play along. That was one of us. I put my hand on Casper's back and propelled him forward.

Raglan's huge hand grabbed the fake doctor's shoulder and jerked him to a stop. "Wait a minute. Give me the bag."

Crap.

Casper swallowed hard and handed it over while offering me a silent apology. Raglan immediately popped the bag's latch and opened it roughly.

If he finds the real book, we're screwed. What are you gonna do now, genius? Think Goddammit.

It wasn't so much thinking as reacting. I took the fake book and slapped it into Donald's belly, knocking the wind from him. "Hold on to this. If anything happens to it, it's your ass." Then I grabbed for the medical bag, snatching it from a startled Raglan.

"We don't have time for this. It's a freaking doctor's bag, see?" I shoved one hand into the bag, pressing against the fake bottom and turned it upside down, hoping my grip would hold. All Francine's equipment clattered to the tile floor. She let out a yell at seeing all her precious gear treated so badly, but nobody paid attention to her.

The book was heavier than I thought, and my grip almost slipped on the pad, but I held on until the last item fell out. Then I flipped the whole thing upside right, to the relief of cramping fingers. "Happy?" I asked as I flashed him the inside of the bag. When he nodded, I tossed it in the corner near Francine's feet.

Cromwell let out a cough, followed by a moan. He turned his head and saw the book in the flunky's hands. He beckoned me over and I leaned over him. My nose filled with awful, deathly smells. His chapped lips moved slightly. Barely audible, he whispered, "Dumbass."

Loud enough for everyone to hear, I told him, "You just take care of yourself, sir. I'm going to get you out of here soon as I can." Then I leaned in and whispered, "that's the second book."

The old man's eyes scrunched shut and shook his head weakly. "No."

No doubt we were thoroughly screwed. He was in no shape to survive the next hour, let alone summon binding spells from a dusty old book. Still, if Casper and Francine could help him rally while I stalled for time, there was a minute chance they'd get out of there alive. I felt a slight flicker of hope I could accomplish that much. It was enough.

That faint spark of optimism was quickly drowned when Raglan turned to Donald. "You stay here with them while we take the book to the Master."

Young Donald's face turned ashy gray, but Raglan had trained him well. Obediently, he gulped and nodded. I reached over and wrestled the book out of his hands. "Gimme that. And don't let anything happen to them or it's your ass." My reward was a loud gulp of fear. Small victories.

Francine was already on her hands and knees, scrambling through the contents of her precious kit. She looked up at me, then over at Casper. "Doctor, can you give me a hand here, please?" Casper looked around quickly before remembering he was the physician in question.

"Yes, nurse."

Now to get Raglan out of there and hope Francine could handle it from here. "Your boss is waiting for this. Let's do what we need to do so I can get them home."

Raglan chuckled like he knew something I didn't. "Let's do that." He held his hand out for the book.

"Not a freaking chance. I'm giving it to him personally. A deal's a deal."

A voice echoed down the corridor. "Bring it, Dog."

I yelled back, "Don't get your lace panties in a bunch. We're coming."

Donald and Raglan both gaped, shocked at my attitude. Screw it. There wasn't much time left, and I was going to enjoy being a smartass for as long as possible. I made an exaggerated bow to Raglan and motioned him forward.

"Shall we?"

"Johnny." Francine's voice stopped me. I looked over at her with a fake smile. "Don't do anything stupid," she said.

My only answer was a hysterical laugh. Then I left the room with Raglan on my tail.

CHAPTER 32

It was a short walk to where Hopkins sat waiting for his prize, but halfway there my feet refused to move. Part of my hesitation was a blend of self-preservation and common sense. When the murderous animal inside you wants nothing to do with something like Hopkins, it's probably not a good idea to push the matter. Fear was only part of the problem, though.

My entire life was crashing down around me. The secret I'd carried my whole life was no secret, and what would life be like when everyone knew what I was? My best friend was about to evict me, leaving me homeless—again. Gramma had all but given up on me. I'd probably blown any chance of a future with the one person who accepted me as I was. Francine and Cromwell were still in danger, and who knew if the old man was going to make it even if they escaped? He was certainly in no condition to hold the book, let alone read it and bind a mega-demon. Oh yeah, and I was stalling for time with a centuries-old hell-spawn, armed with a trick any second grader could see through.

What rooted me to the floor wasn't so much the fear of dying—been there and had a drawer full of t-shirts. It was something I had trouble naming because I'd never felt it before. The best description was coal black despair. Fake bravado, willingness to fight, even putting one foot in front of the other relied on the one thing I no longer had.

Hope.

Somewhere in my brain, I recognized I wasn't just likely to die in a spectacularly ugly manner. That was always part of being a Lycan, along with the super hearing, fur coat and the seven-inch nails. Werewolves seldom died of old age. It was what it was.

The awful truth was, I didn't care all that much. I was done. Doesn't mean I was in a hurry.

"Hey." Raglan growled.

I looked up from my shoes and shifted the book securely under my arm. "Yeah. Whatever." Over Shaggy's protests, I followed him to the door.

The Master was expecting us, so the blond henchman put a hand on the knob, turned it, then returned my sarcastic, exaggerated bow.

I brushed past him with a snarky, "Thank you, Jeeves." The giant glared at me, put his hand on my back and shoved. Rude. I stutter-stepped to a spot across the desk from Hopkins. Raglan crossed his arms and leaned on the doorjamb, clearly planning to enjoy the festivities.

Raglan was more surprised than I when Hopkins focused his dark gaze on me and drummed those freakish fingers on the desktop. Without looking at his flunky, he growled, "Leave us."

"But Master, I—"

His reward for talking back to his boss was a glare that could freeze vodka. I shivered at the intensity and malevolence of the demon stare, glad it wasn't aimed at me. My turn would come soon enough. Raglan nodded his head and then told me with as much menace as he could, "I'll be right outside." The "don't do anything stupid," was implied. Then he backed out and gently closed the door, leaving me face to face once more with an honest-to-God, centuries-old, motherscratching, demon. The difference between this and the last time I faced Hopkins was I knew exactly what he was now. That made it a thousand times worse.

With Blondie gone, I had Hopkins' undivided attention. Avoiding his coal-black eyes for the moment, I looked to the ceiling and focused, trying to drown out Shaggy's complaining and the knocking of my knees. I tuned my ears outside the door, trying to get any clue what was happening and how Casper and Francine were doing. I heard nothing but Raglan pacing back and forth.

Hopkins had learned patience in the last five hundred or so years and relished my discomfort. He leaned forward and licked his lips with the thin tip of his tongue. The corners of his mouth turned up just a little too far, his grin turning into something far too sinister for his human disguise. Those long fingers slowly drummed on the desktop as he sat there waiting.

Best you can do now is stall for time, smart guy.

I stared back. Hopkins found my attitude amusing for a while. After who knows how long, he simply tapped the table with a pointy fingernail.

"The book."

"Not until Fran—Mister Cromwell and everyone are free. Unharmed." I laid the book on the desk and leaned forward, pinning it to the table with my weight.

That snakelike tongue flashed out again. "You know I could simply take it."

"Maybe. Okay, probably. But I'd put up a hell of a fight which I'd lose, but who needs the aggravation? I probably taste horrible. Plus, my fingernails can be awfully destructive when I'm irritated. Something might happen to the book. Am I right? It would be a lot easier to just keep your promises and get us all out of your hair."

Hopkins weighed the decision for a moment, then turned to the door. "Come."

The door flew open before the word was finished. Raglan didn't even pretend he wasn't waiting with his ear pressed against it. "Master?"

Hopkins looked from his flunky to me and back. "Let them go."

The henchman allowed a second of irritation to cross his face before he bowed his head sharply. "My Lord?" Then he turned his attention to me. "What about him?"

Since Cromwell wasn't in any condition to use the original Daemonologie and its binding spell, all I could do was serve as the decoy until they got away. "Don't worry, big guy. I'm not going anywhere until everyone is gone and safe. Then your, uh, master, here gets the book. After that, whatever happens, happens."

Shaggy hated the smug bastard and I let a growl escape just to see the look on the guy's face. Looking down at my feet, I cursed the fact I'd worn boots with thick laces. There was never a plan to fight my way out of this. If I needed to allow my inner Lycan loose, it would hurt my feet like a bitch. Next time I might switch to those slide-on sneakers they advertise for old people.

If there was a next time.

Raglan flexed his hands into fists and then relaxed them. He bowed to his master, discreetly gave me the finger, and left the room.

The tapping of fingernails on the desktop pulled my attention back to the real threat in the room. "Now. The book."

There was no way I would give it up until I knew the others were safe. Idle chit chat was never my strong suit, but it was my best option until the building was clear. "Just curious. What's the big deal about this book? I mean, you've obviously escaped whatever the real Hopkins did to you, so you're powerful as hell. Pardon the expression."

Hopkins' eyes lightened slightly. From deep in his chest came a deep sound, like a stuttering cement mixer. The evil son of a gun was chuckling.

"Someone like you can't imagine the possibilities. This book contains the only spell that can bind me, even temporarily. More important, it allows me to release my brethren, bound around the world. Once they've joined me, I will destroy that infernal tome forever."

"But there are other copies, right? The British Museum—"

"A poor copy. The original book was destroyed by a fire two centuries ago. But the fools won't admit they are charlatans, so there it sits in the open as thousands of people walk by it each day, not knowing or caring it is a sham."

My heart sank a little. "And the one in the Vatican?"

This time, an actual laugh filled the room as he threw his oversized-head back. "Bah. Those ignorant priests are no threat to me. What passes for the church no longer has faith in its own God. Do you think they would believe in other forces besides their own greed and voracious appetites? No, I will eventually get my hands on that copy too, but for now, the only threat would be from someone who could bind me again. And that is no longer a possibility, is it?"

I'm not much of a poker player, so I don't know if something in my face gave me away, but the laughter died in his throat. The darkness once again took over his eyes. "Unless you have brought me the wrong book."

I gulped and said nothing. Hopkins' voice dropped to a rumble like thunder a long way off. "That would be a very, very foolish thing to do."

"Well, to be fair, sir, I'm not all that smart."

The sulfur smell in the room got thicker, coating my nose and throat, even my tongue and I gagged, tasting bile in my throat. It was like the air shimmered around him. Waves of heat and something I couldn't name but felt infinitely evil washed over me. My head pounded as I backed away, only to find the wall behind my back. Shaggy let out a growl that I didn't even try to stop. This was no time for subtlety.

The sound of something gouging into the wood drew my eyes. The demon's freakishly long fingers were undergoing a terrifying change. Any semblance to human fingers were gone. Instead of pink, soft flesh and bone, his digits were black, skeletal claws. Each sported five-inch eagle's talons for fingernails that left long trenches of raw wood in their wake.

I let out a quick, "oh crap," dropped to my knees and untied my work boots. Shaggy had to come out and play for however long the fight lasted.

From that low on the floor, what happened next looked more awful than it must have been. Hopkins leapt to his feet and rose to full height. The perfect clothes had been a disguise from the waist up for when he was sitting. Where the jacket ended, a monster began.

One of those hellish claws reached to his collar and ripped the clothes off his upper body with one swipe. The demon's face melted, revealing charcoal grey, wart-laden skin. The thing's mouth opened like its jaw hinged behind his ears. A gaping hole took up half his face and contained triangular, needle-sharp teeth. Worse, below the waist were hairy goat-like legs with hooves the size of my head. My brain couldn't process the horror.

That wasn't the only change underway. I hopped on one leg, trying to wrestle my pants off as Shaggy assumed control of my body. I fell butt-first to the floor. Then I heard the tearing of cloth and felt constricting around my arms and legs before my pants and shirt exploded into rags.

The Hopkins demon bellowed, "Insolent cur. You thought you could play me for a fool?"

Since there was no way to speak, I let Shaggy bellow back as I circled the room, desperate to put as much room between me and the hell-spawned thing as possible. If I couldn't win this fight, I'd at least drag it out until the others got away.

The brilliant strategy of keeping the desk between us died within seconds. With a roar, Hopkins grabbed the ancient heavy piece with one hand and threw it against the wall, where it splintered against the stone. There was nothing between me and a seriously pissed off demon.

He was twice my size, but I was quicker. Shaggy sensed the attack before my human brain did and leapt halfway across the room as one of those claws snatched at empty air. I landed in a crouch, howling in temporary triumph.

Shaggy wanted to run. I really wanted to make a break for it, but there was no way to know if Casper and the others were safely away. Running was the smart thing to do, but not an option. I squatted and snarled, looking for my opportunity to attack.

Hopkins' eyes changed from black to the deep red of hot coals. A gut-melting scream shook the walls. Not to mention the depths of my soul. Shaggy hesitated a moment before my jaws opened and leaped at the monster's throat.

I've no idea how close we came because the back of a claw struck us from the side. It sent our body end-over-end into the wall. All I heard over the ringing in my head was a hateful laugh.

"Did you really think you could fight me, pathetic dog?" One of those enormous claws put a vise grip on my calf and whipped me across the room. My body sailed across the space, smashed into the wall above the fireplace, and slid to the hearth. The room spun and hot cinders singed my fur.

Shaggy snarled. The monstrosity took a step forward, opening and closing its hands to prepare for ripping me apart. I closed my eyes, awaiting those razor-sharp claws. I never expected my last thoughts to be, "fuck it."

With eyes shut, I awaited the end, but it was a long time coming. I opened my eyes to see the Hopkins-thing shaking its head in confusion. Waves of energy filled the room again, but felt different this time. The vibrations weren't coming from him. They appeared to move towards him. But from where?

Not about to waste the opportunity, I refilled my lungs and tested my limbs. To my surprise, I was sore, but the only thing really wounded was Shaggy's pride. I got to my feet, waiting for our next chance to strike.

Befuddled as I was, it was nothing compared to what Hopkins was going through. He bellowed and shook his ugly head, then swiped his claws at something unseen. Attempts to move his feet were useless. It was as if they were cemented to the floor.

The demon searched around the room for the source of its problems but saw only me. He yelled, sending saliva flying everywhere. "What are you doing to me?"

Even if Shaggy wasn't in control, I couldn't have given him an appropriate answer, so I just snarled in response.

The room spun wildly, so it was hard to orient the source of the energy. Somewhere behind me — the door, maybe—my ears detected a voice speaking in a foreign language. Hopkins heard it too, and emitted an unfamiliar noise; a low, terrified whine. The son of a bitch was worried. The voice drew nearer, and Hopkins shrank into himself a bit. His giant claws covered his ears, then his eyes. The demon was in full-blown panic.

Behind me, the door flew open. Through blurry eyes, I saw Casper standing there, holding a gun in shaky hands. Beside him was a figure holding Cromwell's book. The person's head was down while they read from it in what I recognized as Latin. Only it wasn't the old man reading.

It was badass Francine Ball.

CHAPTER 33

"Liga te et tene…" Francine's voice trembled, but her eyes blazed with fiery determination. Read slowly and used her finger to trace the lines. She kept her head down, doing her best to stay focused on the book and not on the horror in front of her. I kept my attention on the demon and moved between them as a shield.

Those glowing red eyes flamed up again, and Hopkins stopped his shrieking. He stood completely still, focusing on Francine. Behind me, her voice faltered. Casper shouted, "No. Keep reading."

I'd seen Hopkins do his remote control thing, and knew it was trying to gain dominance over the woman, just like he had with Ted. If he did, what little chance we had to beat him would be gone. We needed to break his concentration.

One hairy distraction coming up. *Come on, big guy, let's do it.*

Freed of any reasonable mental control, Shaggy howled and charged the demon. The hideous beast was so focused on its battle with Francine that it didn't acknowledge the attack until the last minute. At the last second, it threw one of those enormous arms up just as my teeth sank into it.

If the hellish sulfurous reek wasn't awful enough, the taste of its black, motor-oil thick blood was worse. Even as Shaggy's fangs sunk deep into the flesh, my stomach roiled. It was all I could do to hang on as Hopkins screamed and flailed wildly, jerking my body around.

Inevitably, between the horrific taste and being flung around like a rag doll, my teeth lost their grip. I somersaulted across the room, landing in a furry, snarling heap.

With Shaggy in full control, my human brain had only the foggiest notion of what was going on in the room. A maddening cacophony filled the air. Francine's voice, the demon's high-pitched keening, and someone—Casper no doubt—yelling, "What the fuck?" Painful noises assaulted my hearing in a horrible, indecipherable noise-storm so loud I thought my skull might split open.

To my Lycan-assisted eyes, the monster seemed to shrink. Still too damned big, but less imposing than he'd been a moment ago. Whatever Francine was doing, I hoped she'd keep it up. Preparing for another head-first charge, I squatted and gathered my strength.

Whether it was overconfidence or just blind fury, I misjudged the next attack and paid for it. Hopkins might be less powerful than before, but those claws hadn't dulled at all. He swiped wildly at me as I flew into the wall. Three white-hot lines of fire raked across my ribs and Shaggy screamed.

The nauseating stench of blood, sulfur, and fear filled my nose. Lightning bolts of pain shot up and down my body. The skin of my torso felt like it was dipped in acid. I lay panting for a moment, reveling in the blessed relief of the air filling my lungs.

Casper shouted...something. I looked to see the demon straining to attack Francine in a desperate attempt to silence her. He managed three or four steps closer to her, putting me behind him.

No. Goddam. Way.

I don't know how I got to my feet, but summoned enough strength to stagger within arm's reach of Hopkins. I fell, more than jumped, forward. My claws sank into the demon's shoulders, then I yanked with all my strength. That stopped the monster's forward motion, and I leaped onto his back. Knowing how much it would suck, my fangs sunk into the demon's throat. The reward of its screams compensated for the sickening sensation that flooded my senses.

The spell was working. I sensed the power leaving Hopkins' body, weakening him with each heartbeat. Francine's voice was weaker now, too. She stuttered and stumbled through the spell. My Lycan brain made no sense out of the sound, but it didn't have to. The demon was breathing its last, but not fast enough for me.

My brain didn't really grasp what Shaggy did next, but it was out of my control, anyway. Sinking both claws into the bloody rent in the demon's throat, the talons sunk as deep as they could go. Then, with the last drop of strength, I pulled my arms apart. With a sickening sound, the monster's throat tore open. Its horrendous head fell backwards, hanging by a thin sheet of bloody muscle, and its body crumpled to the ground. I collapsed on top of him.

As Hopkins spasmed and died, I rolled off him, panting and whining. The room was spinning too fast and my Lycan body twitched, then retched. Slowly the fog lifted, and my Johnny brain regained control. A woman's voice drew closer, still speaking in Latin.

"Nomen patris et filii et spiritus sancti." The book fell to the ground beside my body. Bleary-eyed, I watched as she spat at Hopkins and added, "you ugly motherfucker." Then she sank to her knees beside me, shaking and sweating.

I begged more than commanded Shaggy to grant me control. My head and eyes cleared, but being in my own body made the deep scratches across my ribcage burn worse than ever. I was completely naked except for the sad, ruined shreds of my boxer shorts.

"That was freaking awesome." Casper shouted from the doorway, where he maintained a cautious distance. He was the only one of us with the good sense to step forward, pull the book—the real one—out of a growing pool of demon blood, and retreat to the door again.

Cool hands touched my cheek, and I looked up into Francine Ball's wide, watery, freaking beautiful eyes. It took all my strength to lift my own gory hand to her face. "You okay?"

She sobbed. "Fuck no. But we're still here."

Nice as that moment was, something wasn't quite right. I looked around until my mind registered what was missing. I asked, "Cromwell?"

"He's not doing great. He's still in bed." She was using her flat, professional voice. He must have been in terrible condition.

That made sense. Something didn't, though. "Wait. You read Latin?"

Francine managed a weak smile. "I'm older than you, remember? I went to Catholic School when they still taught it. I don't know what it meant, but I could pronounce the words."

Imagining her as a schoolgirl at the mercy of nuns was more bizarre than reading a spell and destroying a demon. "Seriously? You went to Catholic School?"

She managed a proper smile this time. "Where do you think I got that uniform I wore?"

"You are something else, lady." I put my head on the floor, ignoring the fact I was in a pool of black, tainted blood and demon meat.

"She's a freaking ass kicker is what she is." Casper piped in. "Dude, she choked out that Donald guy with a stethoscope."

That accounted for them getting out of the room, but left another question. "What... Raglan. The big guy. What happened to him?"

Francine shifted to squat beside me with her back to the wall. "You left a couple of vials of sedatives and my hypodermics in my bag. He's out cold." Then she added, "I would've preferred you'd left my Glock in there, but I get it."

I reached for her hand and lay there, just breathing and staring at the ceiling as my body recovered. Every muscle throbbed and my ribs were caked in blood. "Crap. I'm gonna need a nurse."

"Let me get my bag." Francine slowly, shakily rose to her feet.

"I hate to be that guy," Casper said, an apology in his tone, "but you're not done yet."

"Huh?"

"According to Magda, the only way to really kill a demon, if you haven't bound him to an object, is to burn its heart."

Francine sniffed. "Really? It looks plenty dead to me."

My head dropped to the floor in resignation. "He's the expert on this stuff. I'll do it."

Casper looked like the next ten Christmases came early when I called him the expert. He shifted the book to under his other arm. "Can I help?"

I waved him off and rolled my exhausted carcass onto my hands and knees. When I had enough energy, I crawled over to the monster's corpse. This was going to suck.

It took a moment, but I brought Shaggy back, just enough to change my right hand. The sinews popped and groaned. I may have cried a little as my fingers grew murderous nails. Then my claw took aim at Hopkin's rib cage. It took a couple of hefty blows to break through the ribcage. A little more effort and my hand found its way into his chest, clutched a rock-hard object and pulled hard. In my Lycan fist was a demon's jet black, malformed heart.

With what strength I had left, I tossed it into the fireplace. The coals sizzled, and the room filled with the stench of wood smoke and rotten eggs. "Grab some of this broken furniture. We need to make sure it burns up."

Francine gagged, then nodded and pulled on the old desk. A carved leg came off in her hands and she threw it onto the coals. Multicolored flames leapt up.

I was a little pissy that Casper wasn't helping with the effort. "Bro, you going to help or what?"

Except the doorway was empty. I looked at Francine, then around the room. "Where'd he go?"

She wiped her hands on her stained nurse's uniform. "Maybe she went to check on Cromwell?"

That made sense. We added a couple more chunks of wood to the fireplace-slash-crematorium. Then, holding each other up, we made our way down the hall to what had been their cell.

We heard Cromwell's ragged, irregular breathing from the doorway. I could make out the slight form of his body under the blanket. Poor Donald the newbie lay on the floor, Francine's stethoscope still wrapped around his neck. Casper hadn't exaggerated. The woman was lethal.

"Casper?"

He wasn't there. My blood ran even colder when I realized something else was missing. "Where did you knock out Raglan?"

Francine said, "right there."

The blond giant was gone, along with Casper Pak and the blood-soaked original Daemonologie.

I punched the wall behind me. "Oh, gimme a break!"

CHAPTER 34

I was naked, dizzy, and bleeding. Francine didn't have time for me to get my bearings. She shouldered me out of the way and ran to her patient. Kneeling over him, she ran an appraising hand over his forehead, then used her thumb to pry open his watery, bloodshot eyes.

"Fuck, fuck, fuck," the nurse cursed as she dug around in the pile of spilled medical gear. Francine hung the stethoscope around her neck as she ripped open a blood pressure cuff and wrapped it around Cromwell's frail, skeletal arm.

The old man tried shrugging her off, but she put a firm hand on his chest and ended the fight by pushing him back onto the cot. Through gritted teeth, she hissed, "Keep still, Goddamit."

As Francine fussed over him, Cromwell turned his head towards me. His chapped lips opened and closed silently, lines of spit connecting them. Finally, he crooked his finger at me. I drew near, staying carefully out of the nurse's way as I bent over him. "Yes, sir?"

Francine wiped a sleeve across her arm and let out a sniff. She didn't think I saw it, and I let it go. Cromwell was trying to speak, despite the monumental effort required. My Lycan senses were a blessing and a curse. On the downside, his breath smelled like a buzzard's butthole and had the unmistakable blend of halitosis and imminent death. On the other hand, I could make out his words, despite his weakness. Under the rasp and rattle of his breathing, he asked, "Book?"

"I don't know, sir. I think the big guy—Raglan—took it." *Along with Casper.*

"Stop him." Those two words almost spent what remained of his life force.

"I'll do my best. Sir. You just get better." My hand patted his chest instead of doing anything helpful.

His hand grasped my upper arm tighter than I thought was possible. "You can do it. Have to."

Francine's patience ran out. "Screw the book. We need to get him to the hospital. Stat."

Cromwell shook his head ever so slightly and let out a, "Bah." Then he waved me closer.

My face apologized to her as I leaned in again. The pale eyes that always gave me the willies were focused on the ceiling. The old man's throat made several aborted attempts at speech before he managed, "Fa...mily. Find them." Then he pointed his finger at me and dropped his hand.

Family? I didn't have one. His family then. Did he have kids? Was he worried about heirs? I had a big enough job to do without the ramblings of a dying man.

Francine got my attention by smacking me across the back of my head. "Hey, snap out of it. We need to get him to a hospital, and you need to get that fricking book."

Put that way, she made it sound so simple. I did not know where Raglan had gone, what he'd done with Casper, or what he planned to do with the book. I was naked except for a few scraps of bloody boxer shorts, and my clothes were in rags scattered all over the room and covered in demon guts.

Nurse Ball's commanding, matter-of-fact voice cut through the fog. "Come on, Kid. Get on it."

I looked back down the hall, then at her. "What about...that?" Someone would come back eventually and find their boss in pieces. Then all hell would surely break loose.

The fleeting moment of empathy I witnessed a moment ago had passed. Her eyes were cold steel now. "I'll call an ambulance, and my guys will take care of it. Get out of here." Her guys. A harmless euphemism for the cleanup crew I'd seen sanitize the warehouse after Kozlov died. Body disposal, evidence destruction. She commanded a one-stop felony mitigation unit.

My head was clearing. What was my next move? I wasn't exactly dressed for sleuthing and thought about going back for my boots. I realized Shaggy was going to be far more use in finding Raglan than Johnny. Good foot ware would not help on this hunt.

Taking the stairs two at a time, I sniffed wildly. Sure enough, the air contained the sweaty, frightened presence of the blond goon. My nose also tracked Casper's unique scent of perspiration, kimchi, hard candy and something else. *Was that urine?* I wouldn't blame anyone who peed a little after seeing what he'd seen. Something else occurred to me. I realized if he was that frightened, he wasn't with Raglan voluntarily. That was a relief. It also increased Shaggy's protective instincts.

At the top of the stairs, I was blessed with the scent of fresh air. A cool, clean night breeze wafted through the open door. They'd gone out the back towards the forest preserve. Two steps later, I looked out into the backyard and the open gate that led to the woods.

Raglan had the book, a terrified hostage, and at least one gun. I had bare feet and a murderous Lycan inside me, looking for payback. That made the odds about even. I stepped onto the back stairs, looked up at the moon, and let Shaggy take over.

My brain flooded with images of Raglan and Hopkins. I pictured a frightened Casper. And so much blood. Raglan's stench filled my brain. Shaggy howled like an entire pack of bloodhounds. I was going to find Raglan and kill him.

Oh yeah. And get the book back. And Casper. This long night wasn't anywhere near over.

CHAPTER 35

The full moon hung just over the treetops, filling half the sky. Shaggy felt its pull and my whole body thrummed with high-voltage energy. I sniffed wildly while my jaws dripped with saliva at the idea of a hunt. The prey had taken off through the gate and into the forest preserve beyond. Raglan had the advantages until now, but he was heading onto my turf and picking a fight he wouldn't win. He'd hurt me and mine. My whole body throbbed with the desire to rend his flesh, to drink his blood. It was time for him to pay.

As Johnny, I should have been horrified at such thoughts, but I was done. The universe had abused me enough. Every muscle screamed in agony. My friends were deserting me, innocent people under my protection were hurt. There was no after. It was only now. The hunt.

I bounded off on all fours, covering yards with each leap. Muddy tracks showed me the direction. My other senses told me I was gaining on them.

"What the—help!" Casper's voice carried on the breeze, along with the sound of something striking flesh, and then my friend was silent. My heart pounded faster, pumping more blood to my raging wolf's heart. Saliva flew from my jaws. Claws left furrows in the muddy undergrowth and dead leaves.

Just ahead to my right, I heard a bass voice growl. "Stupid chink son of a bitch." Casper lay on the ground, clutching his knees to his belly in a quivering fetal position. Raglan stood over him, pistol pointed down.

He knew I was coming. After delivering a vicious kick to Casper's body, Raglan stepped back with the Daemonologie under one arm and pointed the gun my way. He must have known small caliber bullets wouldn't kill me, but it'd hurt just the same. Instead of firing, he yelled, "I'll kill him."

I pulled up, growling and snapping, with just enough Johnny in control to stop my attack. Casper looked towards me, first with relief at the possibility of rescue. Then his expression changed to one of shock. His nervous system had long passed rationality. He was just hoping I wouldn't eat him. I recognized the horror that filled him when he—or anyone—understood what I really was. This wasn't some grainy video. It was the real deal. Casper put his hands over the back of his head and buried his face in the undergrowth. It was the small prey's attempt to avoid being devoured.

Raglan stood in the moonlit clearing, smiling. We were at a standstill, and he knew it. Worse, he was enjoying himself. "Stay. Who's a good boy?"

Between the moon and his smug superiority, Shaggy went wild. Screw Casper, the book, everything I wanted Raglan's neck between my jaws, to feel it snap and bleed. With a growl, I leaped forward. His smile grew even wider. Some sane part of my brain knew that wasn't right. It didn't matter. He needed to die. Shaggy was happy to oblige.

I was two bounds away when he reached into his pocket and threw a handful of dust at my face. The powder acted before my brain processed what it was. Flames exploded in my skull, and I dropped to the ground, blind and retching.

Wolfsbane. The son of a bitch carried wolfsbane.

Aconitum napellus is the most effective natural anti-werewolf chemical there is. Gramma used it in her Lycan repellant. Cree used it in some of her potions, although not as an offensive weapon. Raglan was using a super concentrated dust, the strongest I'd ever felt. The bastard knew what he was doing. He wielded it like a hammer.

I lay in a heap, panting and whining. My nose and mouth were stuffed with mud. Some part of me realized the less Shaggy was in charge, the less that vile stuff could hurt me. With a grimace, I changed back to myself, naked and in hellish pain, but at least I could breathe and see again.

Rolling onto my stomach, then onto my hands and knees, I looked up at him. I was truly up the creek, but at least I could save Casper. It was agony to speak yet, but I managed, "Let him go."

Raglan's top lip curled. "He's no use to me. I'll just take the book and go. But first, I want to see you crawl a bit more like the abomination you are."

Every second brought a little more clarity and a return to my senses. I was exhausted. Bone-tired. Of everything. "Sure. Fine. Whatever."

Raglan's face looked like I'd given him a pony for his birthday. "I should thank you for killing the Master. Now, I'm free and I have the book."

Maybe if I kept him talking, I'd regain enough strength to be useful. It always worked in the movies. But those guys like Bond or Jack Ryan had the shit kicked out of them and come back for more. They didn't roll around naked in slime and puke. They were also cracking wise, with memorable lines. The best my mouth could manage was, "What... why?"

"With the Master gone, I'm free from him. But now I have the power. With this book, I can control and bind all the powers of hell."

Casper's voice jumped in. "Dude, that's messed up. Johnny, are you okay, man?"

This wasn't a great time for him to get involved. Casper was better off in a fetal position and out of the way. He shouldn't draw

Raglan's attention, so I said something stupid to make it all about me. "That's crazy. You can't control that kind of power. No one can."

That got him somewhere in his feels. He snapped at me, "Just because an animal like you can't control itself doesn't mean I can't. I was his apprentice. Now I'm in charge."

Stall, Johnny. Strength built up in my muscles and Shaggy was almost ready for round two. *A few minutes more.*

I thought about poor Ted, and all the little minions the Hopkins-thing had gathered. "What about the Sons of Matthew Hopkins? What happens to them?"

Raglan shrugged. "Those sheep? They're still useful. Spreading the word, helping eliminate pests and vermin like you and the pathetic hags you live with." He paused, and the smug look returned in spades. "Maybe we'll go national. I hear there's a half-assed coven in Las Vegas could use a lesson in humility."

At the thought of anything happening to Cree or Karmen, I let out a Shaggy growl. "If you touch them—"

His voice grew louder. "What? What are you going to do? You can't stop me, you pathetic animal."

My eyes burned. Shaggy was trying to burst through them from the inside. Raglan sneered again. "Oh, you want a fight? Fine. You've already met two of my servants. Remember them?"

The wannabe demon master extended his arms in front of him, palms down. He began muttering something in Latin. Casper and I watched as his whole body shook. Raglan gritted his teeth and ended the incantation with an animal grunt. About six inches below each down-turned hand, black spots hung in the air like little clouds. The formations slowly grew and extended downwards until they touched the ground. The clouds became more and more solid until they took their true form.

Between Raglan and I crouched two familiar figures. In a whisper, Casper said, "You've got to be shitting me."

That summed it up nicely. They were the imps from the archives.

The larger of the two let out a shriek and that chittering laugh-growl sound was like a spike to the brain. The other bared its teeth and pounded its fists on the ground. Out of the corner of my eye, I watched approvingly as Casper scrambled and kicked his way out of the war zone.

My body tensed and everything went dark. The imps screamed again, this time louder and more fearful as my werewolf form emerged, snarled, and snapped its jaws at them.

The two demons shrieked and attacked. Raglan's voice shouted something, Casper answered back, but I was past hearing or caring.

Johnny had left the building. It was Shaggy's show now.

CHAPTER 36

When Shaggy runs the show, I remember only snatches of what happens. My vision is literally a red blur, a kaleidoscope of blood and lightning. My body feels everything, though. Shaggy went in swinging, and he caught the closest imp and sent the ugly sucker flying face-first into an oak tree. That left the other free to jump on my back. His spiral fingernails dug into my shoulders, deep into the muscle. Shaggy screamed and smashed it into the ground with a satisfying crunch of body on body. The imp let out a high-pitched shriek.

I flipped over and pulled my arm back to eviscerate it with my claws. That's when the second one latched onto my free arm, teeth first. The mini-demon clamped down hard. Shaggy flailed wildly, snapping and swinging. Some part of me worried about what kind of hellish infection that mouth might carry.

One thing is for sure, these two understood the notion of teamwork. One drew attention and even risked damage for the other one to get their shots in. Shaggy's thick pelt offered some protection, but not enough. Blood matted my fur, and each heartbeat pulsed more of it out of my veins. If this was a war of attrition, it wouldn't last long.

In the dark, I got glimpses of Casper on his knees in the muck, whimpering and unable to avert his eyes from the horror. His pupils were dilated and his gaze unfocused. He would be in full shock any minute. If he was lucky, he'd blank most of this out.

Sound filtered through better than vision did. Raglan laughed maniacally, cheering the mini-demons on. Banshee screams, howls, and the blond giant's mockery filled the part of my brain not focused on survival.

Fighting both monsters at once was a losing proposition. They were pack hunters, like hyenas or jackals. Or actual wolves. The longer the battle dragged on, the weaker I'd become and the bloodier their victory. I needed an advantage. Higher ground.

Shaggy sensed a momentary lull in the battle while both imps took a moment to recover. That was all I needed to retreat a few steps until my back felt the rough bark of an old oak. Looking up, I saw the lower branches were within reach, but too thin to hold my weight for long. The ones above them, though...

Crouching low and faking an oncoming attack, I could confuse the ugly bastards for a second. They waited, trying to figure out what suicidally stupid thing was about to happen. Then, with an effort, I focused on those higher, thicker branches and the sanctuary they might provide. Shaggy responded.

I turned and sprang with all my might. My back claws dug into the bark, kicking up til reaching the lower branches. A herculean pull of my arms, and my feet scrambling to gain purchase a little higher. I monkey-barred past the first and second limbs to the thicker, stronger branches above it.

Shaggy found us a secure place to crouch, then issued a challenging growl to the creatures below. The imps bellowed in outrage, probably the demon version of "No Fair," then began climbing up after him.

With the advantage of height, Shaggy held them to a stalemate. The trunk was thick, but not big enough for both of them to climb together. For a moment, I thought we could relax. Then something hard hit me in the head.

The smaller imp stood under the tree lobbing rocks and sticks at me while its partner scaled the trunk. Ignoring the pain, I swiped a claw down and knocked him to the ground again, but paid the price by taking a clump of mud to the tip of my snout. Stars burst in front of my eyes. A lucky swing knocked the closest imp to the ground, but this couldn't go on forever.

My best efforts didn't deter him. The imp started climbing again. Between the bruising projectiles and blood loss from bites and scratches, I could already feel my grip on the branch weakening.

A noise in the distance drew my attention. Raglan had the book open, muttering another spell. He was calling in reinforcements. For all the good it would do, Shaggy bellowed a challenge. It was met by mocking laughter from the imps at the bottom of the tree, who leapt around waiting for more help from the netherworld.

Stuck up a tree and alone, there was nothing I could do to stop him. What if he called up another one of these things? Or something even worse? He looked up from the book long enough to offer a mocking sneer. "Think you can win, dog? No way."

He dropped his head back to the book and chanted. This time, he stopped. I looked to see what happened and looked up, confusion written on his chiseled face. Raglan's eyes widened and a clump of mud smacked him in the mouth.

"Leave him alone, you… you… asshole." Casper stood on wobbly legs. Apparently, he'd drawn inspiration from the imps and weakly tossed mud pie after mud pie at Raglan. Most of them missed or fell short, but his efforts sufficed to interrupt the spell casting. It was so ludicrous even Shaggy let out a harrumph.

Raglan didn't share the amusement. He roared and charged poor Casper, grabbing him by the shirt and lifting him off his feet. "What are you doing?"

Casper's voice quavered, but said, "Leave my friend alone." Realizing what he'd done, he added, "please?"

The blond was in no mood to be polite. He growled and head-butted Casper right between the eyes. Blood exploded from his nose.

Casper let out a squeal that was drowned out by Shaggy's howl of protest. The aspiring demon master curled his lip and pulled one fist back to deliver a brutal punch to the semi-conscious reporter.

From up in the tree, I saw it before Raglan did. A red laser dot moved up his body, stopping right between those frigid blue eyes.

Raglan didn't have time to do more than gasp, "What the..." before gunshots rang through the forest, sending birds and animals skittering everywhere.

The first shot caught the big man in the chest. Before he hit the ground, the second blew the top of his skull off. His lifeless body sailed backwards and landed on its back in a pile of leaves. Casper crumpled to the ground.

From the darkest part of the forest, a figure moved forward, an automatic rifle swinging back and forth in case of more trouble. Jarhead Justin chimed out, "We clear?"

In Shaggy form, I couldn't respond properly, but he got his answer. The two imps roared and whooped, shaking their fists, then forgot all about me and charged towards the marine. Justin's eyes widened, but his highly trained instincts took over. One round caught each of them in their chests, dropping them immediately.

If Shaggy moved now, I'd take a bullet, sure as hell. Fortunately, Justin didn't know I was in the tree. After one more visual sweep of the area, he dropped to one knee beside Casper. "Dude, you okay?"

Casper was too stunned to talk, but nodded. "Huh? I'm okay. I think."

Justin was still in full rescue mission mode. "Anything else out here? Where's Lupul?"

While they were distracted, I lay across the length of my roost, willing Shaggy to withdraw. I didn't want to draw any attention while the jarhead was in a shooting mood, but the transformation pain was too intense. Fur, fangs and claws receded in a wave of so much soul-killing pain I had no choice but to groan like a barn door, roll over and fall out of the tree. I face-planted in a naked, bloody heap on the forest floor.

Crashing like that knocked the wind out of me. I rolled over and stared face up into the night sky, gasping like a bass in a boat. Justin's colossal form blocked out the moon as he stood over me, cradling his weapon. "Dude, you okay?"

My last words before passing out were, "Just freaking ducky."

CHAPTER 37

The sky was turning lighter. Shaggy disappeared along with the moon, leaving me naked, shivering, and immobile. Talking was pure torture, but I had to ask, "Where'd you come from?"

"She called. Alpha Team took her and Cromwell to the hospital, the rest are cleaning up the scene. She said to find you two."

That checked out. Francine's cleanup crew was frighteningly efficient. "How is he?"

Justin's shrug spoke volumes. Cromwell didn't look in shape to make the trip, let alone survive a Chicago ER. My first thought was *Great. Now I'm out of a job.* My second was, *what a dick you are, Lupul.*

Something moved behind me and I wheeled around with a feral growl, ready to go full Lycan on whatever it was.

"Jesus, dude. Chill. I just thought you might need this." Casper draped his mud-splattered, slightly pee-smelling jacket over my shoulders.

"Thanks." Casper had his second wind and appeared to have resisted going into full shock. I could only imagine what the next few nights would be like. Then again, did anyone who saw little baby ghosts have nightmares? "You okay?"

Casper's muddy, bloody face beamed. "That was so epic. Dude, I fought a demon." He'd thrown mud bombs at a glorified flunky, but let him have his moment.

"Yeah, you did." I let him hug me, awkward as it was for everyone.

"This is adorable. Anyone going to tell me what those things are?" Justin stood about a yard off, studying the dead imps.

Casper couldn't wait to illuminate him. "They're demons. Well, Imps. Mini-demons. The guy you... shot summoned them."

"These are mini-demons? What do the big ones look like?"

I rolled to my knees and coughed to get the mud and yuck out of my mouth. "You didn't see the one in the house?"

Justin shook his head. "No, headed straight out here to find you. It was bigger?"

Casper laughed. "Dude, it was the Mack Daddy of demons. Seven feet tall, cloven hooves, the whole thing."

Justin looked down at me, his eyes wide. "You killed that thing? Goddamn."

I hand-walked up a tree trunk to get to my feet. "Your boss did most of the hard work. I just finished it."

"I told you she scares me."

"Yeah, me too. Is she okay?"

I shouldn't have been surprised. When the team arrived, Nurse Ball became Major Ball once again. She directed the rescue team, got everyone organized on the cleanup, hustled Cromwell into an ambulance, and didn't chip a nail doing it. Justin gave me the rundown. Even naked and freezing as I was, I felt a little better.

At least until Casper said, "Seriously?"

We followed his horrified gaze to where the two imps should have lain. There were two chimp-sized indentations on the forest floor, but no bodies.

Justin asked, "Do I want to know where they are?"

The answer struck him in the chest as Imp one attacked from the side, knocking him to the ground. The other screamed and came at me, murderous spiral claws leading the way. I sidestepped just long enough to catch a breath but had enough time to change into Shaggy before he was on me.

Miniature or not, they were demons. There was only one way to make sure they stayed dead. I didn't really have the strength to change one more time tonight, but it's not like there were a lot of choices.

Every joint, ligament and tendon screamed with the pain of the metamorphosis, but it distracted me from the scratch the little demon put on my arm. Reincarnating must have tuckered the thing out because if he'd been at full strength, there was no way I could do what I did.

Grabbing its wrist, I flung him hard against the tree. With one claw, I pinned it by the neck to the ragged bark. The other claw, nails extended, ripped into its chest. There was a high-pitched shriek before I pulled its heart out and dropped it on the ground.

Justin was on his back in the muck. The second imp squatted on his chest, trying to disembowel him through the Kevlar. Casper wailed on it with a fallen branch and swore loudly in Korean. Shaggy grabbed it by the neck and ran his claws across its furry throat. Thick black blood spewed everywhere as it toppled to its side.

Snarling and licking demon blood off my lips, I repeated the heart-removal. Shaggy looked around for someone to attack and spotted Casper. I talked him out of eating my friend. The effort to control the monster within, mixed with changing way too fast, was too much. I hit the ground, puked once, and passed out.

When my brain sputtered to life, I was looking at the ground while bouncing up and down. Justin had me in a fireman carry and was heading back towards Hopkins' house. I was weak enough not to be humiliated. I phased in and out of consciousness. Aware of my nudity, I tried squirming out of his grip. Justin held me tighter.

"Dude, stop moving. Your junk is rubbing against my back."

As we neared the gate, I let him know there was a change of clothes in the Charger's trunk.

He never stopped carrying me to safety. "Roger that."

Casper trudged beside him with something wrapped in the remnants of his jacket. He displayed them triumphantly. "Can't forget, we need to burn these. I mean, they're demons, right? if we don't want them coming back again..."

Blessedly. I blacked out again and came to as Justin passed through the gate into the backyard. Through the fog of everything that happened, one item seemed most important.

"Hey, Just... you think they could save my boots? They were new."

CHAPTER 38

Dawn. Day after the full moon

By the time we got to the hospital, I'd splashed enough of the gore from me that nobody would think I was a walk-in to the ER. I wore clean jeans, my best AC/DC t-shirt, and work-out sneakers. The boots were still AWOL, and I mourned them.

She was waiting outside the entrance. Francine had her arms wrapped tight across her chest and was pacing back and forth on the pavement. Hearing our footsteps, she looked up. The indestructible Major Nurse Francine Ball looked like hell. Her hair was all over the place and her normally pale skin was now cadaver white. The lines around her eyes formed deep crevasses, and her brown eyes looked sunk in lava.

I noticed she gave herself a little shake, slapped a neutral expression on her face, and strode towards us, all business. She waved a "just a second" finger at me, grabbed Justin by the arm, and pulled him out of earshot to debrief him.

My Shaggy-hearing wasn't at full strength. Nothing was. I could barely stand from exhaustion. I caught enough to know that everything was under control. Control being relative when you have three heartless demons, a dead piece of shit for a human lying in the woods, and a houseful of blood and guts. *Just another day at work for this bunch.*

Some part of me knew this—all of this—was unsustainable, but I had to suck it up. With everything I was facing, there was still work to be done this morning.

We embraced briefly. At the same time, we said,"You okay?"

I gave her another squeeze, then took a step back. "Yeah, I'm good. How is he?"

Francine took a deep breath. "Dying. Probably wouldn't have survived the kidnapping anyway, but beginning that spell was too much for him. Tough old bastard's too mean to let go. He's already shooed the Grim Reaper away twice."

My hand brushed some stray strands of hair from her face. "No big surprise. He has a hell of a nurse."

Francine snorted, then patted her hand on my chest and stepped out of my reach. "He wants to see you."

"Me? Why me?"

"Why does Mister Cromwell do anything? He just does. Go, you don't have much time."

Halfway to the door, I stopped. "You're not coming with me?"

"You go. I need a minute." Then she turned her back and walked towards the sidewalk and away from the building. And me.

A few minutes and three wrong turns later, I stood at the door to Cromwell's suite. It was only semi-lit and empty. The old man was in a standard surgical bed, nowhere near as nice as the one he had at home. If he was aware of his surroundings, he'd be ticked right off. Machines buzzed and hummed in the silent, lonely room.

Unsure of the protocol, or even why I was there, I hesitated in the doorway before taking several slow steps towards the bed. I'd seen all kinds of violent death. Natural old age and illness were more terrifying.

He looked like one of those shrunken apple dolls Gramma made for Halloween when we were kids. His entire body seemed smaller, frailer. Those ancient chicken-wing arms had bruises from all the needles and IVs and probes. Those raptor eyes were closed, which was a blessing. They freaked me out whenever he looked at me. They were likely more awful now.

I doubted it would do any good, but I said, "You wanted to see me, sir?"

The silence lasted an eternity. I gave it one last chance. "Sir?"

Cromwell's chapped lips parted. Then, if I didn't have better hearing than most, I'd have missed it. "Lup...Lupul?"

"Yeah. Yes, sir."

Malcolm Cromwell semi-turned his head to me and made the herculean effort to open his eyes halfway. His mouth twitched a little. "You made it." There was no way to tell if he was happy to see me, surprised, or having a spasm.

"The book?" The damned thing had nearly killed him, and he still wanted to know about it. I wanted to scream at him, to shake him. I didn't.

"We have them. Both of them, actually. The real one and—you know."

He crooked his finger and beckoned me closer. "Burn them." *Oh sure, now.*

"Yes sir. With pleasure."

He lay back, closing his eyes and summoning strength from somewhere. "Ice." Unsure what that meant, I followed his vague finger wave to the bedside table. Grabbing the bowl of ice cubes on the bureau, I offered one to his lips. The tip of his tongue licked at the cube. I passed it back and forth over the flaky skin. Cromwell gave a sigh of relief.

He paused again, then said, "She's going to need you."

"Sir?"

"Nurse... will need you." Okay, he knew about me and Francine. Mortifying but irrelevant under the circumstances.

"Okay. Sure. You rest, sir."

Francine spoke from the doorway. "He said something similar to me a few minutes ago."

"Jesus, how long have you been there?"

She managed a smile. "Long enough. Nice job with the ice cubes. You have a future in nursing."

"Well, it looks like I'm going to be unemployed, so I'll look into it."

"That makes two of us. Do me a favor and watch out for anyone coming in."

That seemed odd, but we switched places. I stood guard as Francine knelt over Cromwell's body, stroking what remained of his hair.

He struggled to speak, but looked at her. His expression softened. "Time."

Francine bit her lip. Slowly, she reached into her pocket and pulled out a syringe. Practiced fingers pulled the cap off and tapped the plastic vial three times.

I stepped forward. "What the hell are you doing?"

Cromwell whispered, "Her job."

I couldn't move as Francine gently took his arm. Without even looking, she probed for a functional vein. She didn't bother swabbing the arm, but infection would not be a problem from now on.

Her voice shook. "This is going to sting a little, sir. Deep breath."

As always, Cromwell obeyed. He closed his eyes and relaxed. "Bastard beat me this time."

I asked, "Who did, sir?"

"Death. The fucker." Then his body spasmed ever so slightly and sank into his bed.

The shrill beep of an alarm went off, scaring the bejeezus out of me. Francine moved like a cat, dropping the used syringe into the Sharps bin on the wall, then stepped back just as two nurses burst through the door.

"He's crashed." One of them shouted.

"He's gone," Nurse Ball said, wiping her eyes with a tissue. "Come on. Let them do their job." She grabbed my fingertips and gently pulled me into the corridor.

Francine waited until the door closed before pulling me close and burying her head in my chest. She let out a sob and wept into my chest. All I could do was rub her back and hold her heaving body. I gently rocked her, unsure what else to do.

Doctors and nurses dashed past us in a useless attempt at saving Cromwell's life. One woman took a moment to put her arm on both our shoulders. "I'm so sorry for your loss."

Francine squeezed me again, then stepped back and wiped her eyes. She looked up at the ceiling and said softly, "Goddam him." I didn't have to ask who. She was the loyal caregiver to the very end.

Even when it damn near killed her.

CHAPTER 39

Three days after the full moon. Waning gibbous.

I had two full days to sleep and recover before Cromwell's memorial. Bill, being the good friend he was, agreed to come with me for moral support. Gramma accused him of being a drama queen, which made him laugh. That was progress of a sort.

He even loaned me a tie, since it had been years since I wore one. I squirmed in a suit that used to fit properly, in shoes I'd only worn twice. We hid out near the back of the small, nearly empty chapel. Francine took charge of the arrangements, so sat up front.

Being the closest thing Malcolm Cromwell had to a widow, she ran the show with her usual efficiency. We had a few minutes together when I arrived, then I got the hell out of her way.

The few people attending were mostly old white people. They appeared to be business associates of Cromwell's or flunkies they'd deputized to go in their place. Francine explained Cromwell had been surprisingly generous to several non-profits over the years. That explained the smattering of middle-aged women, mostly women of color, who took time to offer condolences.

There was no family at all. If I was supposed to look for them, it wouldn't be easy.

I was just steeling myself to endure a short but generic homily from a priest who had never met the dearly departed when the chapel door opened behind me. Someone arrived fashionably late. A figure strode down and sat in the aisle directly across from us. Someone I never thought I'd see again.

A tall, dapper African-American man smiled at me from across the aisle. He saluted us with his ebony lion-headed walking stick. His teeth flashed when he said, "Mister Mostoy. Mister Lupul."

Bill reached across the aisle to shake his hand. "Mister Collins."

The last time I saw Lemuel Collins was in a Las Vegas Hospital fighting the psychic remnants of an alien object and stage four cancer. He looked great. I leaned over to speak to him just as the priest began talking. The old man shooshed me back to my place and faced forward.

The good thing about being a funeral pastor for hire is that when you don't actually know the deceased, you don't have to prepare funny anecdotes or embarrassing, very specific prayers for his soul. The brief service comprised Psalm 23, a short bio ripped from the newspaper, condolences, and veiled spiritual warnings for the rest of us. Amen.

As soon as the service was over, everyone filed out like their hair was on fire. Some slipped next door where the Ladies Auxiliary provided way too many sandwiches and sodas. I slipped across to Lem's pew. I almost hugged the old man before remembering his strict "no touching" rule. Instead, I offered an over-enthusiastic fist bump.

He smiled. "Good to see you, young man. How are you?"

"I'm good. Well, except, you know." it was probably poor form to be so glad to see someone you forgot the occasion. "What are you doing here?"

"Malcolm and I have known each other a long time. Only seemed right to pay my respects and say a proper goodbye."

"But... should you be traveling? How are you feeling?"

"Oh, I'm finer'n frog hair." That was his standard phrase when avoiding questions about his health. "Doctors say I'm in remission. Fancy word for stay of execution, but I'll take it. Good to see you, m'boy. You look well."

I looked better than I had, for sure. After twenty straight hours of sleep and some Shaggy-strength, most of the bruises and scratches healed pretty well. I still ached when I walked, but getting back to my stretching routine would help.

His smile faded away, and he nodded to the front of the room. "How's Miss Francine doing?"

"About as well as can be expected, given her only patient just died. She's shaken. And unemployed, but then we both are."

Mister Collins gave me an odd look. "You sure about that? Huh. Oh, Lucrezia sends her condolences. Asked me to report how you were doing."

"Finer'n frog hair." That got a chuckle from him. "I'm good. What's up with her?"

He shrugged. "Ask her yourself." Lemuel studied my face, waiting for a response he would not get. With a harrumph he added, "She's good. The show is going well. She's babysitting Miz Karmen more than she should. And doing her homework. The girl's got some oomph to her magick."

We chatted a little more, then he slapped his knees. "Well, I have to get going."

"You're leaving already? You don't have time to grab a drink or a bite or anything? Francine would love to see you."

"Nah. Docs won't let me eat or drink anything fun, anyway. Flying home tonight. The shop won't run itself, you know." He ran the most unique pawn brokerage in Las Vegas, which was saying something. It was his pride and joy, no matter that he made way more money working side-hustles for rich eccentrics like Cromwell. "Come out and see an old man some time."

Las Vegas seemed like a hundred years ago. "I may just do that. Travel safe."

With an exasperated sigh, he said, "Safely. It's an adverb. You still need to work on your professional vocabulary. Nice tie, though." Then he stood up, white-knuckling the lion's head of his cane. Once in the aisle, he turned to Bill.

He waved the tip of his stick at my friend's metal crutches. "Good to see you too, Bill. You know, you might think about trading those in for a proper walking stick. Much more stylish." Bill had no responses, so the old man added, "Take care of yourself. And him. Try at least."

"Yes sir. I'll try. Can't promise anything, though."

With that, Lemuel Collins walked away, dignity personified.

Fifteen minutes later, Bill and I sat in a tavern staring at our beer. It wasn't his kind of place, but that's what friends do.

"Thanks for coming. I really appreciate it."

"No problem." He sipped his beer, working his way up to the conversation we'd been avoiding. "Look, about the other day—"

I stopped him. I'd been rehearsing this all morning. "No, you're right. I have no right to put all of you in danger like that. I don't mean to, but it's like I'm cursed or something."

"Something? Dude, you're a fucking werewolf. Yeah, you're cursed. But you're still my friend. You can stay if you want to."

Now it was my turn to take a big swig of my beer and set it on the table. "About that. I don't think you'll have to worry about my hanging around. I'm going to take off for a bit."

He looked surprised. "Where? What are you going to do?"

"I'm out of a job. I have a little money saved up, thanks to my brilliant financial advisor. I'm about to be evicted, also thanks to my brilliant financial advisor. Maybe I'll go back to construction for a bit."

"Building Waffle Shacks? No way."

"Maybe you can keep me on the lease while I'm gone. That way, I'll have a place to crash when I'm in town, but not enough to get into trouble."

Bill's face lit up at the thought of keeping the income while salving his conscience. "That'd work. Gramma would like that."

I pushed my luck. "Maybe let Meghan stay there while I'm gone? She needs to get out of that sober house situation, and she's at your place most of the time already, hanging with the old broad."

"Ugh, buzzkill. She's around enough already. Okay, I'll talk to her. Gramma will like that too."

I took another sip. "You know what else would make her happy?"

"What?"

"Tell her. Enough already. She already knows. Just say the words."

"I know she knows. I'm not stupid. It's just hard."

"Bet she makes it easier than you think. After busting your balls, of course."

Bill laughed. "They will definitely be busted. But yeah. It's time."

We toasted with our beers. "I can see how you fooled her all these years. You drink beer like a straight guy."

He said, "Asshole," exactly like a best friend should.

My phone buzzed with a text from Francine. "I have to go into the office tomorrow."

"How come?"

It was a mystery to me, too. "Probably just need to do some paperwork. I likely have some severance coming or whatever."

"Put some in the savings account. Construction doesn't pay like being a security consultant."

"Yes, dad. Let's drink up and get out of here."

CHAPTER 40

Francine was specific about what time she wanted me at Cromwell's apartment, but still wouldn't give me a reason. Justin at the front door wasn't much help.

"Dude. Gun." Justin held his hand out.

"Seriously? You're worried about me going up there? Are you afraid I'm going to shoot her?"

He smirked and pointed to the top drawer. "It's for your protection. I have a feeling you're going to want to use it on yourself when she's done with you, but rules are rules."

As always, I complied. "What do you know that I don't?"

"Oh, so many things. Have a good one," he said with a smirk. I guess that meant we were back to our old frenemies relationship. That was fine, just a little weird for someone who'd seen my junk.

In the elevator, my stomach did a loop-de-loop. It wasn't Shaggy's doing. After the full moon and a couple of good days' sleep, he was pretty chill. No, this was just good old-fashioned nerves. I stepped off onto the penthouse floor for what I believed to be the last time. To my surprise, I was a little nostalgic.

After being buzzed in, I entered Cromwell's apartment. For the first time, the drapes were open and the blinds up. I took a good look around in the daylight. The penthouse had always been sterile and unlived in, but now there was an air of sadness to boot. Bill made me watch enough real estate shows to know that wouldn't be good for resale value.

"In here." Francine's voice came from Cromwell's office. I stepped inside and looked around. All the medical equipment and the bed were gone, leaving one corner of the enormous space lifeless and empty. Hopkins' claw marks were still clear on the wall in front of the panic room. At least the sulfur stench was gone. Someone replaced it with the smell of medical grade cleaning products and something else. I inhaled and realized it was Francine's perfume. The good stuff she seldom wore.

"Nice of you to dress up." Because I didn't know what we were meeting about, I'd worn my usual jeans, a Pink Floyd shirt and a new green and black flannel just to switch things up. Truth be told, I looked better than usual. Nurse Ball, on the other hand, was dressed like I'd never seen her.

All the times we'd seen each other at work, she wore her starched Nurse Ball outfit, albeit with scandalous underthings. Off duty, she was a casual jeans and sweater kind of gal. Today she wore a tweed business suit, obviously expensive, and dangly earrings that may have been real gems. Her raven- black hair hung relaxed and styled to her shoulders. She looked beautiful. And a little intimidating.

"Hi. Ummm, you look, I don't know, amazing."

It was the first time I heard her laugh in days. "Don't sound so surprised." She pretended to inspect me up and down. "You look okay yourself. You smell better, at least. Have a seat."

"Wow, have I been called into the principal's office?" This was getting interesting, since "called into the principal's office" was one of our more successful role plays. I complied.

"What's up?"

She tapped a pile of papers on the desk in front of her. "Did you know I'm the executor of Mister Cromwell's will?" She clicked the expensive pen in her fist. "Yeah, came as a surprise to me too, but the old man had no family and didn't much like anyone else."

"Sounds like a paperwork nightmare to me. So, what's all this?"

Francine had done her nails up in what I think was called a French Manicure. Nurses don't get much chance to do things like that when they're cleaning bedpans and shoving catheters up people's hoohoos.

She pulled out a thick folder and pushed it across the desk at me. "This is everything Cromwell had on you. Everything that isn't encrypted on a disk somewhere, anyway."

The file was maybe eight inches thick. From the looks of that folder, he knew more about me than I did. "Have you read it?"

"Some of it. You're not as fascinating as you think you are." Her eyes sparkled when she said it, so I didn't take offense. Francine leaned forward and looked into my eyes. "Johnny, he really thinks the answers you're looking for are out there; your family, your medical history, all about your, uh, condition."

Pretending I wasn't fascinated, I thumbed open the folder. The top page was a screen capture of the Nevada fight video. So he knew. I fought the urge to dive right in. I had to pretend to pay attention since she clearly wasn't finished.

"He really thought you should go to Romania and dig around. So do I, if that matters."

"Trying to get rid of me?" I meant it as a joke. She didn't laugh.

"I think you'd feel a lot better about yourself if you got the answers. Plus..." She paused and looked up to gather her thoughts before adding, "It might not be a bad idea to lie low for a while. People are asking a lot of questions about what happened out there. What's left of the Sons of Matthew Hopkins are demanding a police investigation. Plus, your profile is probably going to be pretty high for a while." She tapped a shiny fingernail on the screenshot.

"Crap. Well, I was thinking of going on the road for a bit. Maybe hook up with my old construction crew."

"Come on, kid. Don't get all dramatic. You can do better than that." She took a plain white envelope from the top drawer and pushed it across the table. "You were in Mister Cromwell's will. He left you a token of his appreciation."

She leaned back in that big chair, looking awfully pleased with herself. I sat looking at it like I was unfamiliar with paper. "Open it."

I finally opened the envelope and stared at a certified check. I'd never seen one before. It looked like a regular check except for the number printed on it. "This has to be a typo."

"Really? They're usually pretty good about this stuff. Let me see." I handed her the check. Francine took a cursory look and threw it back at me. "Nope. Pay to the order of John Lupul. Four hundred and fifty thousand dollars. That's correct."

"That's a token? What am I supposed to do with this much money? I mean, it's a hell of a severance package."

"What can I say? He liked you."

Who knew?

"Are you going to say anything?"

I didn't know what my response should be. I settled for being a smartass. "I feel like we should celebrate or something. What do you think? We always talked about making it on his desk some time." It had been her idea, mostly. Pillow talk about having sex in the old man's office made her a little crazy. I reached for her fingers and gave her a dirty eyebrow-wiggle.

Her smile disappeared. "Yeah, about that." She withdrew her hand and wiped it on her skirt, then pursed her red lips before continuing. "You're not the only one who was in his will."

I was a bit confused by her reaction, but if she wanted to keep it all business today, it was her show. "I would imagine so. What'd you get, a million dollars? Did he leave you this apartment?"

"A bit more, and yes. The big news is, it seems I'm the new head of the Cromwell Foundation. This is my office now."

I sat straight up. She didn't look like someone who'd just inherited a butt-ton of money. "The Cromwell Foundation? What's that?"

"In his will, Mister Cromwell insisted that his entire collection of arcana and other crazy shit be broken up. Either sold or repatriated to its country of origin. Unless it's too dangerous. Then I—we, I suppose—get to decide how to dispose of it."

I was stunned. So was she, I think, but Francine was trying to maintain her ice-queen façade. Just to break the silence, I asked, "What's the deal? Do I say congratulations? Offer condolences?"

"No, it's good. I think. It certainly pays better than nursing."

I stood up and leaned across the desk lecherously. "Then we should really celebrate."

She held her hand up like a traffic cop. "Whoa big boy. It's tempting, but it wouldn't be appropriate."

There was a word I'd never heard her use. Trying not to show either disappointment or my boner, I asked, "Why not?"

"Because technically, kiddo, I'm your boss now. Chain of command. That kind of thing could get you kicked out of the military. Most hospitals too."

"But I'm not..."

"You are if you want to be. Nobody's been fired. The foundation needs someone to handle the relocation and security. We'll give you a bit of a raise and a two-year contract."

I sat back down, my mind reeling. "But his collection's done. What's there to do?"

Francine leaned back in her chair, looking very officious. "Same thing you've been doing, only in reverse. Some of this creepy crap needs to go home and let them worry about it. Some of it we'll have to figure out what to do with. The rest just needs to be buried so deep it's never found again."

"Justin and the team are still going to be around, I gather."

"They have their uses."

I tried being flirty again. "So do I."

"Kid, it's been great. But there's twenty years between us. You know, whatever this is, it's not going anywhere. Maybe we just keep it professional from now on, huh?"

There was the kid thing again. I was an adult, dammit. An adult who could add getting dumped to my worst week ever. At least I had a job if I wanted it. "Is that what you want?"

"Not really. You're a pretty good time when you lighten up. It's just time. Feel free to continue sneaking peeks when you think I'm not looking, though." This time, she gave me a wink. "Makes an old lady feel good."

What could I say to that? "Yeah. Okay. Whatever you want."

"Jeez, you could have put up more of a fight." Her tone grew gentler as she went on. "Johnny, you're a good guy. It's time you found someone right for you. She's out there somewhere."

Francine's words buzzed around my head like a cloud of gnats. My brain wasn't a highly tuned machine to start with. This was all a lot to process. Finally, she slapped the desktop, bringing me back to earth. "Are you in or out?"

I wasn't sure. A job would be good. A raise was better. The truth was, I was too exhausted to make serious life decisions. "Can I think about it? When do you need to know?"

If she was disappointed, she hid it well. "Take some time to recover and clear your head. Go sit on a beach somewhere. How's three weeks?"

I thought about everything going on in my life. A smart man would just cut and run. Then I envisioned Raglan with the book. I flashed on Kozlov, and what the Anubis Disk would do in the wrong hands. I could stop that.

I remembered the look on the Oneida woman's face when she handed me their sacred drum to pay a rich old white man. I could do some good, assuming it didn't kill me.

"Yeah. Three weeks is good."

CHAPTER 41

"Four hundred and fifty thousand?" Bill bounced up and down in his chair. "Dude, that's great. You could buy a place now. Get some equity going. Maybe get a new ride."

I sipped my tea and looked over to Gramma at the sink. "I don't think I'm ready for that level of being a grownup yet. And why do you hate the Charger so much? But do you think you could hold my spot here for a while?"

"How long?"

"Three weeks to start. I'm going to take a bit of a road trip and I'll need a place to come back to. If I take the job, I'll be gone a lot. Probably can't get us into too much trouble."

Gramma poured more tea into my cup and placed her hand on my shoulder. "This is good, kid. I'm proud of you. Where are you going to go?"

"I don't know. Lots of places I haven't been. California, maybe. I need some fresh air and some pool time."

Gramma laughed. "Pool time? You'll probably clog the filter, you hairy bastard. They'll kick you out of the hotel."

I pretended her words stung. "Guess I'll have to keep on moving then." Gramma Mostoy was like my scarecrow from the Wizard of Oz. I might miss her most of all.

Bill grinned. "Are you going to, I dunno, maybe go through Las Vegas on your way out?"

I shrugged, which meant yes. Assuming I was welcome.

Gramma sat down with a groan, picked up her teacup, and took a sip. The three of us stayed like that, sipping tea and comfortably not saying anything at all for a couple of minutes. Warm spring sunshine streamed through the window.

Finally, the old bird asked the big question. "When are you leaving?"

I'd given it a lot of thought. It would take a couple of days to get myself organized. One day to Wisconsin and back to return the Wendigo drum to the Oneida Nation. There was also something else I needed to do. One more big promise to keep.

I hadn't seen Casper since everything went down with Raglan and Hopkins, and wasn't sure what kind of shape he'd be in. It surprised me to find that Horatio had a real honest-to-God office space in the heart of Boy's Town on Halstead, above a vegan bakery. Vegan bakery. Shaggy shuddered at the idea. Maybe it was time to take a break from Chicago after all.

He buzzed me up. The office was small, with just a couple of desks pushed under the window side by side. In the corner was a setup for shooting video. I barely had time to take it all in when he wrapped me in a bearhug.

"Bro, we're finally doing it. This is gonna be great."

I patted his back. "Yeah. Of course. Said I would, right?"

We weren't alone. Magda occupied one desk. In a rocking chair near the window, Zara glared at me. Neither said anything.

I hadn't expected witnesses. I honestly thought it would be just me and Casper. "What are you guys doing here?"

Casper continued fidgeting with the set, moving the stool over a few inches. As he fussed, he said, "Dude, Magda helps with the video and stuff. That way, I can just focus on the interview, you know?"

Zara tugged at the loose part of her hijab but wouldn't look at me. "I want to hear what you have to say. Besides, Casper told us what you did. For him."

The reporter wheeled around. "It was epic. We killed what, three demons? And this guy is so frigging badass."

Magda spoke quietly, "you really killed three demons?"

"And almost got Casper killed," Zara sniped.

Casper leapt to my defense. "No, it was cool. I wouldn't have missed it."

Zara wasn't having it. "Bullshit. You've had nightmares ever since."

That shut him up for the moment. He turned to me. "Well, yeah. Doesn't mean I'd have missed it though. Just trying to make sense so I can write about it. You should see the comments on the Sons of Matthew Hopkins piece. Totally viral. Like Grumpy Cat numbers."

I pretended I knew what that meant. "That's great. Are we doing this, or what?"

Casper ran back to the stool and gave it a pat. "Absolutely. So, you sit here. We'll get you all mic'ed up." Magda came over to the camera and fiddled with it, not saying anything. Casper prattled on.

Glad as I was to see Casper so happy, and that Zara was relatively okay, I wanted to get on with it. "How do we do this?"

"Just like we said. I'll ask you about the video, give you a chance to tell your story."

Oh yay. Just what I always wanted. "And you're sure they won't see my face?"

"No. Dude, we're going to pixelate your face and alter your voice a bit. No names. It'll be good. And thanks for doing this."

I gave him a weak grin. "That's what friends do, right?"

It was almost sad how that made him so happy. Casper beamed and said, "Yeah. Absolutely. This is great. Magda, are we set?"

She nodded silently and circled her finger in the air. Showtime.

Casper had a lot of papers in his hand for a supposedly brief interview. I immediately regretted agreeing to this nightmare, but I owed him at least that much.

He shook himself, ran a hand through his hair, and fidgeted in his seat as Magda counted down with her fingers. Three... two... one.

"Hey Horatio subscribers. Today, we have a major exclusive for you. As promised, I'm talking today to someone very special. You all saw the video a couple of months ago from Nevada. Well, with us in the Chicago Horatio studios is the werewolf from that fight vid. We're protecting his face for everyone's protection. Dude, it is so good to talk to you."

"Good to be here," I lied.

"Are you really a werewolf?"

Here we go. "Actually, we prefer the term Lycan. There's less baggage with that word."

That went on for another half hour. Yes, the phases of the moon affect the change. Yes, I change form. No, I don't fear silver bullets any more than I worry about getting shot in general. I answered his questions as best I could without giving away too much. Casper honored his word and kept my private life separate.

When it was over, he stuck his hand out, then laughed and hugged me again, burying his round face in my chest. "Thanks, Johnny."

I finally broke away. "John. Call me John."

"Huh? Since when?"

"I'm trying it on for size." Johnnys don't get checks for half a million dollars.

Zara spoke up, "Adulting, huh?"

"Something like that, yeah."

Casper looked at me with genuine concern. "You sure you're okay?"

Out the window, Chicago went about its business, not giving a rat's ass about me and my problems.

"Yeah, man. I will be."

THE END

OBLIGATORY AUTHOR STUFF

Let's get the necessary stuff out of the way: if you enjoyed this book, please tell someone. Leave a review, tweet, or just share it with a friend. Everything helps. Even anonymous stars make a tremendous difference (and if you read this on Kindle, it's actually more work to avoid it than it is to rate a book.)

Thanks to the team at Black Rose Writing. Reagan, Dave, Christopher, and the rest who helped me give birth to this odd baby. I literally couldn't have done it without them.

And, of course, I have to thank the Duchess, Her Serene Highness, and all my patient, loving friends and family.

Now some stuff you might not know.

I always intended the Werewolf PI to be a trilogy. Unlike the Lucca Le Pou stories, which simply ended after Acre's Orphans, leaving my poor orphan Lucca stuck in a castle in Tyre for eternity. I knew from the beginning there'd be a beginning, middle and end to the Johnny Lycan stories. I also knew I couldn't pull it off by self-publishing, which is where Black Rose comes in. In the words of Clint Eastwood, "A man's got to know his limits."

Cliché as it sounds, Johnny Lycan came from a vivid dream. A werewolf detective was fighting a Russian gangster. And it was funny. That's all I had, but it was the starting point.

As book three loomed, I had another dream (stick with me.) I dreamed I was a TV producer and was rebooting the old series, The Night Stalker. Oh, and I needed the Korean-American actor Randall Park to star in it. (Admit it, you'd totally watch that.) That's where Casper Pak and the Horatio Team came from. Now you know.

If you're asking what's next, I can't tell you. I have a non-novel project in mind, and the day job is demanding as hell. I'll continue to pump out short stories. There may be a return to historical fiction. The Foreign Legion has always fascinated me. Maybe it's back to the desert. Or Casper's team might warrant more attention. Anything's possible.

Some of those decisions will depend on you. I love hearing from Readers.

Join me on my Facebook page (Wayne Turmel Author)

Twitter @Wturmel

Keep up with the latest at WayneTurmel.com.

I know you have a lot of choices when you choose to spend time and money reading. I appreciate your excellent taste and/or poor judgment. Thank you.

Don't let the weasels get you down.

WWT
Las Vegas, 2023

OTHER NOVELS
BY WAYNE TURMEL

The Count of the Sahara (2015)

In 1926 "Count" Byron de Prorok was the most famous archaeologist in the world, splashed across headlines and beloved by audiences. By the end of that year, his career, his reputation and his life lay in ruins. From the scorching Saharan desert to the frigid American Midwest, this tale is based on the real life of one of the 1920s most colorful characters.

Acre's Bastard: Part 1 of the Lucca Le Peu Stories (2017)

The Holy Land-1187. Lucca the Louse is a ten-year-old orphan running the streets of Acre—the wickedest city in the world. When a horrific attack forces him to flee his orphanage, he finds himself thrust into a world of leper knights, Saracen spies, and holy war. Can one lone boy save the Kingdom of Jerusalem from defeat at the Horns of Hattin?

Acre's Orphans: Part 2 of the Lucca Le Peu Stories (2019)

Lucca narrowly survives the worst disaster ever to befall the Crusader army, but he's not safe. His beloved city of Acre is about to fall to the Saracens. With the help of a determined Druze girl, a leprous nun, and a Hospitaler knight with a tragic secret, Lucca must get a message to the last Crusader holdout at Tyre. Can he and his friends fetch help before it's too late?

Johnny Lycan and the Anubis Disk (2020)

Johnny Lupul is riding high. He's got a PI license, a concealed carry permit, his first big payday and a monster of a secret. After rescuing a bookie's daughter from Russian mobsters, the newly minted PI catches the attention of a rich, mysterious client. At first, it's easy money. After all, magic isn't real and those "occult" objects have to be fake. But while chasing an Egyptian relic, an obsessed enemy from his past emerges. Johnny learns that the world is much stranger—and more dangerous—than he ever suspected.

Johnny Lycan and the Vegas Berserker (2022)

The world's favorite werewolf P.I. is off to Las Vegas. What could go wrong?

Life's good for Johnny Lupul. He has a steady gig and a growing reputation as a guy who gets things done. He's even learning to keep his Lycan side under control—mostly.

But when he's sent to Sin City on a simple retrieval job, things go sideways. He bumps up against a coven of unconventional witches, a psychic pawnbroker, and a mysterious enemy with a secret darker and more violent than his own.

ABOUT THE AUTHOR

Wayne Turmel is a former standup comedian, car salesman and corporate drone who writes to save what's left of his sanity. Originally from Canada, he writes and lives in Las Vegas with his bride, The Duchess. This is his sixth novel.

www.wayneturmel.com

NOTE FROM WAYNE TURMEL

Word-of-mouth is crucial for any author to succeed. If you enjoyed *Johnny Lycan & The Last Witchfinder*, please leave a review online—anywhere you are able. Even if it's just a sentence or two. It would make all the difference and would be very much appreciated.

Thanks!
Wayne Turmel

If you enjoyed *Johnny Lycan & the Vegas Berserker*, make
sure not to miss the first book in the series:

Johnny Lycan & the Anubis Disk

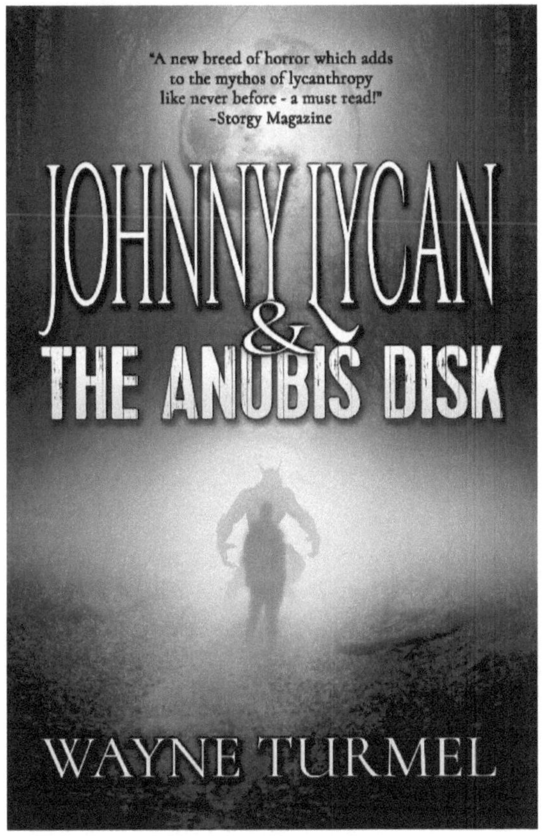

"A new breed of horror which adds to the mythos of lycanthropy
like never before - a must read!"
–Storgy Magazine

We hope you enjoyed reading this title from:

www.blackrosewriting.com

Subscribe to our mailing list – *The Rosevine* – and receive **FREE** books, daily
deals, and stay current with news about upcoming
releases and our hottest authors.
Scan the QR code below to sign up.

Already a subscriber? Please accept a sincere thank you for being a fan of
Black Rose Writing authors.

View other Black Rose Writing titles at
www.blackrosewriting.com/books and use promo code
PRINT to receive a **20% discount** when purchasing.